STRANGE TALES

in Fiction and Fact

RICHARD HOWARD

PUBLISHING

Front cover picture: "Soldier", acrylic on board, by Dorthe Rosefalk.
Private collection, Copenhagen.
Reproduced by kind permission of the artist.
The artist can be contacted by e-mail at vild_rose@yahoo.dk and more of her work can be seen at the following website address:
http://tegnebordet.dk/index.php?vis=brugergalleri.php&id=7883&visning

Note for Librarians: A cataloguing record for this book is available from Library and Archives Canada at www.collectionscanada.ca/amicus/index-e.html
ISBN 1-4120-9339-2

Printed in Victoria, BC, Canada. Printed on paper with minimum 30% recycled fibre. Trafford's print shop runs on "green energy" from solar, wind and other environmentally-friendly power sources.

TRAFFORD
PUBLISHING

Offices in Canada, USA, Ireland and UK

Book sales for North America and international:
Trafford Publishing, 6E–2333 Government St.,
Victoria, BC V8T 4P4 CANADA
phone 250 383 6864 (toll-free 1 888 232 4444)
fax 250 383 6804; email to orders@trafford.com
Book sales in Europe:
Trafford Publishing (UK) Limited, 9 Park End Street, 2nd Floor
Oxford, UK OX1 1HH UNITED KINGDOM
phone +44 (0)1865 722 113 (local rate 0845 230 9601)
facsimile +44 (0)1865 722 868; info.uk@trafford.com
Order online at:
trafford.com/06-1093

10 9 8 7 6 5 4

DEDICATION

To my beloved wife
HELEN
for all your love,
kindness, friendship
and understanding

★ ★ ★

CONTENTS

ACKNOWLEDGEMENTS

I'd like to express my gratitude to the following people for the many and varied ways in which they have contributed to the realisation of "Strange Tales – in Fiction and Fact". This has been an on-going process over many years. Some I have lost touch with, which in no way diminishes the influence they had. Some have since left this life. Some have had the patience to read various drafts of my stories and have offered invaluable criticisms. Some have given me the inspiration for new work. Some have provided me with the situations and opportunities that have led to some of my most interesting experiences. Others, knowingly or not, have encouraged me in bringing this venture to fruition.

My sincere thanks are due to the following, who appear here in alphabetical order:
Clive Barndon, Julian Boulding, Helen Carroll, Nicholas Clarry, Charles Elsworth, Jon Flint, Coral Guest, Peter Hilton-Rowe, Alan Hovhaness, Peter Kauth, Sue Kauth, Tom Lewis, Bernard Palmer, Alfred Reynolds, Dorthe Rosefalk, David Toltek, Peter Underwood, Kevin Waite and Howard Wright.

Also to my maternal grandparents, Emily Frances Goatly and Sidney Arthur Goatly.

★ ★ ★

INTRODUCTION

Since childhood I have been interested in ghost stories, whether factual or fictional, and I've always been drawn to that borderland separating this world from the world I believe we have come from and where I believe we return. The ghost seems able to bridge these two worlds of existence, travelling at will, or so we presume, from one to the other and returning here for any number of reasons. A ghost can inhabit our world unrestricted by its laws and can be a messenger between this and its own world. The notion of life continuing beyond earthly death seems to me utterly natural and when we look about us at everything in nature we see that there is nothing that ceases to exist – all things change form, are recycled and continue. So why should we be the exception? Just because we might not understand how, doesn't mean it cannot be. While our five senses throw light on our surroundings in five different ways, equally we are confined by them. When people speak of a sixth sense they refer to a completely different kind of perception. So what of the seventh sense, or eighth, or ninth, ad infinitum? In an infinite universe with infinite variations of form and design there is no reason why there should not be an infinite number of potentially available senses, the nature of which we cannot begin to imagine because we are confined to the five – or six – that we have in this life and in this world. Equally there is no reason why there should not be an infinite number of worlds, be they material planets or ethereal planes of existence, in which we might continue beyond our present lives.

Things do not cease to exist simply because we cannot see or hear them. Light and sound "disappear" at each end of the tiny scale of our perception but we know they still exist and we can measure them. Before we could measure them we would have said they didn't exist. So why shouldn't we reasonably suppose that any number of phenomena, which we cannot perceive with our limited senses, *could* exist? Is it not naive to think that the wonders of the universe only begin to exist at the moment we find a means of perceiving them? Many scientists agree that everything in the universe vibrates on its own frequency. Who is to say that there are not countless other universes of existence, like radio wavebands, a little further along the dial on other frequencies of vibration? And how long might we expect this dial to be in an infinite universe? The idea of a "ghost" appearing from "nowhere" or walking straight through solid objects is perfectly reasonable, especially when we also consider that the objects we think of as solid, as science again will testify, actually contain more space than matter. These objects are held together by energy and it is energy that animates each one of us. Equally, someone who seems perfectly "solid" and "normal" could be a "ghost". We don't necessarily know whether the person we just passed in the street, brushing our sleeve as they went by, is "real" or not. Just because we have not yet discovered how to travel from one frequency of vibration to another doesn't mean that it cannot be done or that the inhabitants of another world or universe cannot do so. Many people believe that we can raise or lower our vibration of existence through the practice of various mental and spiritual exercises. But surely to do this we must first entertain the possibility of a spiritual level of being. Ghosts, elemental forces, nature spirits, angels and messengers all connect us with other worlds of existence and make us aware that there is so much more than we know. They awaken something inside us so that we can rise above the mundane and exercise our dormant and undeveloped senses.

It seems to me that we stand between two infinities. We look outside ourselves at the night sky with its trillions of stars and we feel our infinitesimal size in the scheme of things. We can also look inside ourselves to find another infinity of options and possibilities. We are contained by one infinity while we in turn contain another. The notion of infinity is itself disputed but I think it is impossible to imagine "finiteness". If the universe ends, then what contains it? And what is the extent of this container? And in what is the container enclosed? And what is beyond that? There must be something, even if it is empty space. And empty space isn't nothing. There is no such thing as nothing. It is impossible to imagine a finite end to anything. It is always possible to double or halve the value of any number. One doubled is two. One halved is a half. Any number can be doubled or halved, ad infinitum – to its nth trillion or its nth decimal point. At no point will that number cease to exist. Worlds exist within worlds and whether we think of another world as a macrocosm or a microcosm depends on where we are standing in this infinite chain of existence. From this vantage point anything is possible. As above, so below. We are giants and dwarfs, supreme and humbled. We are the point at which opposites meet, both inner and outer, and we have the power to reconcile them. And when opposites are reconciled, they cease to exist and all becomes one.

Mankind wants to be able to explain everything to give him the appearance of being in control. But this is an illusion. In this fragile, ephemeral world we are not in control, which explains why many people are unnerved by ideas that remind them of our mortality and how little we really know. We constantly delude ourselves that we understand our universe and cling desperately to established ways of thinking to prove our point. But as other commentators have pointed out, within fifty years science has usually changed its position on most subjects. If only we can overcome such obstacles as professional pride and vested interests, we might perhaps make more room for speculation and imagination alongside rationality – and above all, cultivate an ability to at least keep an open mind.

Perhaps everything in these twelve stories is possible.

THE TEMPLE OF LIOR

The last banner fell. A shriek pierced the air and the will to live drained from the remnants of a shattered army with the blood that ran from the conqueror's sword. Varazin spurred his horse which reared in triumph and thundered to the crest of the hill. Cries, sharpened with anguish and heavy with fear, echoed over the plains as gathering dusk fell like a shroud on the people of Lior. Varazin's horse reared again, lifting high the conquering giant who stabbed the air with his sword and proclaimed himself ruler of the fabled land.

Out of the clamour of battle, Varazin's Commander rode. The screams of the vanquished gradually dwindled as shouts of victory overwhelmed them.

"Lior is ours, my Lord," shouted the Commander.

Varazin looked at him, eyes bright with authority, and laughed maliciously.

"Mine!" he bellowed to the Commander whose rash enthusiasm was firmly rebuked.

Varazin's Aide came swiftly to his side, shouting urgently as he spurred his horse.

"All resistance is crushed. Every detachment is moving forward. Our losses are few. The last message from the west flank is that they have begun to take prisoners."

Varazin grunted approval and signalled for him to draw closer. Flanked by his Aide and his Commander, he pointed to a great forest below, stretching away to mountain slopes beyond. The wind rippled across the valley and the treetops swirled like a vast green ocean tinged with gold that grew darker as they watched.

"The land of Lior yields up its riches to Varazin. Here, at the edge of the plains, I shall raise a city. It will be the greatest, the strongest, the most extravagant, the most awesome city in the world. It will be the seat of all power, the source of strength to my allies and of fear to any who dare oppose me. We shall fill that valley with the corpses of slaves who will give the last of their strength and consider it an honour to have been spared for service on the monument to my supreme power. And there, my friends," Varazin continued in confidential tones as he pointed beyond the forest to the nearest mountains, "there lie the treasures that will enable me to rule unchallenged. The Temple of Lior awaits my coming."

"But Varazin!" interrupted the Aide, "The Temple of Lior is held sacred by all. The myths that surround it are the most potent in our history."

"And so?" asked Varazin, glancing at the Aide who continued hesitantly.

"None has dared to desecrate the temple. For centuries it has been undisturbed... shunned... respected. Surely even you, a greater warrior than any known, would not risk everything by entering the temple?"

Varazin smiled an uncommon smile and placed his hand on the shoulder of his Aide.

"Since childhood I have known you and always you have been a faithful friend. I know you speak from deep concern. But am I mighty or am I not? You yourself know, as will all, that none before me has accomplished such dominion. Am I to tremble before a myth?"

The Aide drew breath to reply but Varazin stopped him and beckoned his Commander to move closer.

"I trust very few," he continued. "You both have served me well and that is why you shall benefit from this new venture. The city I speak of will also be the richest city in the world and you will be its governors. The temple is our source of wealth. It must be entered."

The Commander looked doubtful and ventured a further caution.

"It is said that an ancient hermetic cult abandoned the temple in the face of ruthless persecution and that the priests invoked its protection in the form of phantoms that no violator could withstand."

"I know what is said," answered Varazin with contempt. "Phantoms! Phantoms of the mind! Priests are priests. What they do, they do in order to remain what they are. Who they serve, they serve the better to serve themselves. Never be afraid of priests. That they're clever is proven by your fear, but it's the only way they have of surviving. Cleverness is no match for skill and might. By such might do I now rule more than half our continent. Soon my banners shall fly from coast to coast. You are standing, my friends, at the centre of the world. With each new triumph, we grow stronger – I your master, and you the most loyal of my faithful servants. Many peoples have surrendered themselves rather than face my armies in battle, for they have recognised that my rule is ordained. When I claim the riches of the sacred temple – the most fabulous riches in the legends of our age – then all who doubt will know at last that I am Varazin, the supreme Lord."

Darkness enfolded the three figures silhouetted against a crescent moon that hung above the hilltop with ominous stillness and leant an air of prophecy to the words there spoken. Varazin drew attention to the night. The sounds of battle had become distant and occasional. Subdued cries drifted across the plain as the agonies of an age expired forever. The wind from the mountains swept more steadily across the valley and the treetops rustled. He looked at his Aide and then at his Commander and wondered what they were thinking. He wondered what eyes gazed up at them from the forest. And he wondered, too, if the walls of the temple could sense the presence of he who did not stand in awe, could sense the imminence of their violation.

Commanding officers, standard bearers, messengers, cavalry, drummers, infantry, war machines, kitchen wagons, prisoners and the rear guard were organised and ready to advance shortly after dawn. Battle drums sounded across the valley as Varazin's army snaked slowly along the outskirts of the forest. Losses had been counted. Prisoners were herded together in chains with occasional arbitrary executions to ensure fear and submission. Weapons and spoils were loaded into carts, allied casualties tended, and scouting parties despatched to seek out enemy supplies, strongholds and hideouts. Deserters were mutilated and left to die slowly. Those remaining inhabitants who hadn't fled were rounded up and killed or spared for slavery, depending upon their age and usefulness. A few resisted with swords against hopeless odds and provoked the certain death they had chosen in preference to prolonged life in misery and pain.

Varazin's household retinue had been summoned from its nearby hidden quarters as soon as the battle was won. All the favourites from his extensive accumulation of women were customarily kept close by to serve the conqueror and exude the adoration he required at the close of a triumphal day. By dusk the formidable cortege had gained with difficulty the further side of the valley and was encamped at the edge of the forest.

Varazin's tent was pitched at a greater distance from the others. His liking for luxury was indulged in every form imaginable. Sumptuous draperies lined the sides of the extensive shelter that bore his emblem on its sloping canopy. The ground was strewn with richly embroidered mats and cushions and the skins of many and varied beasts of prey. Jewelled lanterns gave a sparkling glow to the many coloured silks employed in upholstery and decoration, to delicately carved woods of every hue from which were wrought the most elegant chairs and couches, and to shining precious metals, embossed, moulded and tempered into the finest utensils, knives and vessels that any had seen or felt privileged to use. Fragrances mingled and wafted continuously within the precincts. Musk, cinnamon, sandalwood and roses intertwined with the scented warmth of tanned leather, the burning oil of lanterns, and the sensuous aromas of those of Varazin's women last present.

Throughout the night and the following day, Varazin issued orders, despatched messengers and discussed plans with those he decided to trust. In his private quarters, where entered only those he summoned, he glanced up as he sat musing and toying with the hair of a girl who lay restless and in pain at his side. Hesitating by the door were his Aide and Commander.

"Enter," Varazin called, noting their quizzical glances towards the girl.

"You summoned us?" asked the Commander.

"Yes. Sit. It is important that our expedition to the temple be known by only a few. There are certain men I am willing to trust. Some others who normally would be reliable are likely to fall prey to superstition and, in failing to dissuade me, cause panic and possible rebellion," Varazin announced.

The Aide glanced at the girl whose face contorted as she turned suddenly on her side and drew her knees up to her chest. Distractedly, Varazin ran his hand through her hair.

"I asked you to bring certain officers with you," he continued. "Where are they?"

"None of them could be found, Varazin," explained the Aide a little nervously.

"None?" asked Varazin, a stern expression spreading across his face.

"We searched through the entire camp. No one has seen them," said the Commander.

Varazin eyed them until neither could conceal his discomfort.

"Good," he said quietly as he let fall his pretended irritation. "You see? No one knows where they are. Not even you. They are, in fact, locating the temple at this very moment. That is the kind of secrecy we need." He looked at the girl who had become subdued and ominously still. "It is unfortunate that she won't see another night. The son she bore was dead and she has lost much blood. You need not worry about her presence," he said dismissively. "As soon as the temple is..." He stopped in mid-sentence and listened intently like a gigantic animal scenting out unfamiliar territory.

An officer entered the tent and his eyes met Varazin's. The look told all. Varazin signalled for him to speak.

"It lies within easy reach, my Lord," said the officer. "It is sheltered on the lower mountain slopes but solid as the rock itself."

"It will not defeat me," assured Varazin.

"We took a prisoner, my Lord. I thought first to kill him, but as he was found so near the site of the temple, it seemed possible he might be of use in some way."

"Near the temple?" interrupted Varazin indignantly as though the prisoner had been discovered in his own luxurious tent.

"Yes, my Lord. He seems to be a hermit who lives on the mountain."

"He might well be of use," Varazin said. "We'll question him. Bring him in."

The officer went to the door and called out to his guards. A moment later an old man was thrust into their presence. He was tall and lean with white hair and beard. His plain garment, which reached his sandaled feet, had been recently torn where previously it showed evidence of having been meticulously repaired and kept clean. He looked at Varazin. His blue eyes were clear and unblinking.

"Come here," Varazin ordered.

The old man approached with an even step.

"That's far enough. What is your name?"

"My name is Tyrus, Varazin," the man said calmly.

Varazin's surprise at hearing his own name spoken by the man was evident to all.

"You know who I am?" Varazin asked.

"Who doesn't?" replied Tyrus. "Are you not the mighty conqueror whose name is known in all lands?"

"Indeed. Then show respect to your conqueror," barked Varazin, pointing to the ground. "Kneel!"

Tyrus smiled.

"You are conqueror of Lior. Are you conqueror of Tyrus?" he asked.

"I punish insolence as many know to their cost," shouted Varazin. "On your knees!"

The girl at Varazin's side moaned and clutched her stomach. Tyrus looked at her. The officer approached him from behind and cracked the back of his sword against the backs of the old man's legs. Instantly Tyrus fell to his knees and Varazin smirked.

Unconcerned at what had happened, Tyrus looked at Varazin and rose to his feet. Three paces brought him to the side of the writhing girl. Varazin, taken aback by the old man's boldness, commanded him to retreat. Tyrus ignored him and touched the girl. The officer strode forward as Varazin, the Aide and the Commander all leapt to their feet. A moment later the girl stopped clutching, her hands fell limply away and she sighed with relief as Tyrus placed his hand gently on her stomach and stood motionless. As the officer was about to wrench him off, Varazin stayed him and they all looked on in silence. Still with his hand on her stomach, Tyrus took hold of her limp fingers and waited. As the moments passed, the girl began to breathe more deeply. Suddenly, she turned her head, opened her eyes and looked into the old man's face. He smiled at her and she seemed confused. Then she recognised Varazin standing close by and smiled at him.

"She is well," announced Tyrus as he let go of her hand and stepped away.

The officer retreated and stood between Tyrus and the door. The Aide and Commander resumed their seats and Varazin eyed the old man suspiciously. A moment later the girl was arranging her hair and sitting up beside Varazin's chair, pulling at his tunic

and urging him to sit. He turned on the girl, dismissing her
angrily, glared at Tyrus and sat heavily down.

"What sorcery is this?" he asked.

"Since when have you been afraid of sorcery, Varazin?" said
Tyrus.

"What were you doing near the temple?" demanded
Varazin.

"Passing by," replied Tyrus.

"From where, to where?"

"You ask impossible questions. I live in solitude on the slopes
of the mountain. I wander about, I see things, I hear things. This
way I live at peace. I had come from nowhere in particular and
was going nowhere in particular. I was simply there," replied
Tyrus.

"Why were you there?"

"Why is anyone anywhere? Why am I here?"

"Because my officers brought you here. Why were you
there?"

"My footsteps took me there. There's no other reason,"
answered the old man.

"What are you, Tyrus? A priest?" suggested Varazin.

"A priest of what? I live alone, so I am called a hermit," he
explained as if to a child.

"What do you know about the temple?" Varazin asked impatiently.

"It is ancient."

"And?" shouted Varazin.

"It is made of stone," added Tyrus, unruffled.

Varazin stood, drew himself up to his full gigantic height
and stepped closer to the prisoner.

"You know exactly what I mean," he breathed angrily. "What
do you know about its contents?"

"You mean the legendary treasure?" asked Tyrus.

"Yes."

"How can I know? Can an old man like me pass through

stone? The temple has been sealed for many hundreds of years. It is said that none who desecrates it will survive," he added pointedly.

Varazin smiled.

"You talk like a priest," he said. "Hermetic religions seal up their treasure and await revival. Hermit priest guards mountain temple. You answer with questions and evasions and think to frighten us with your cleverness and sorcery. No, Tyrus, I'm not afraid of sorcery. It is a tiresome inconvenience, not unlike yourself."

"If you enter the temple you will be destroyed," said Tyrus with unexpected gravity.

Varazin looked sharply at the old man's solemn face.

"How could you know that when you know so little?" he asked. "Are you hoping to frighten us?"

"No, Varazin. I speak the truth."

"You simply confirm my suspicions. You'll not keep me out with clever stories of phantoms. Priests are useful to keep the masses in their place with such tales, or to keep them happy while protecting their own interests. But I don't need them. You're insolent, arrogant and as cunning as any priest. Yet I have a use for you. You'll bring joy to my soldiers this very day. They've had no entertainment lately and I can't afford to let you live. You can be their guiding light. You'll burn at the stake tonight."

The officer shouted instructions. Guards rushed in and seized Tyrus who gazed piteously at Varazin.

"Now how are you going to destroy me, Tyrus?" Varazin asked with hate in his eyes.

"It isn't my intention. I don't have to. You'll do it yourself," the old man replied.

Varazin dismissed the guards and Tyrus was dragged away.

A pyre had been built on open ground away from the forest. Tyrus had been chained all day and many had come fruitlessly to mock and bait him. His imperviousness to their efforts earned him even greater scorn and by nightfall excitement was rife among the soldiers. Amid cheering crowds he was brought out and conducted around the pyre. Then his chains were removed and the soldiers tried to tempt him to escape and provide them with the pleasure of trapping him. Bursts of laughter swept through the crowd as someone tripped him with a spear and stabbed at the earth all around him. But his lack of response galled the impatient onlookers and soon they were chanting for his execution.

Amid further cheers and mounting excitement, two soldiers leapt onto the piles of logs and faggots. Two more below hoisted the prisoner's arms over his head while the other two grabbed them and pulled him onto the pyre. Another cheer greeted their efforts as they dragged him to the stake and re-fastened the chains with his hands behind him. Enthusiasm almost ran riot as even before the soldiers were off the pyre, flames were rising between the logs. In response to a challenge, two more soldiers from the crowd leapt among the flames, racing with each other to reach Tyrus. The first one there grabbed the victim's robe, ripped it from his body and tossed it into the air.

Screams filled the night as a girl ran hysterically through the crowd, threw herself on her knees before Varazin and begged him to stop the execution. Varazin pushed her away but she clung frantically to his belt, tearing her nails across his arm as she pleaded. The pain suddenly registered on the disinterested conqueror and he kicked her into the crowd of soldiers who clutched at her and tried to pin her down as soon as she fell amongst them. Wildly she thrashed with her arms and legs to free herself. Panic-stricken, she shouted, stumbled and ran between the cheering crowd and the crackling flames. A moment later a gust of wind swept over them, the flames leapt into the air, sparks funnelled upwards and she looked with horror on the blistering running flesh and the blackened splitting hands which had so gently banished her pain and restored her to health.

Varazin laughed and leant across to his Commander.

"The way is clear. We leave before daybreak."

When the sun rose, only the trusted few who were left

behind could allay suspicions and fend off the importunate who sought to know the whereabouts of certain of their comrades and to understand the cause of Varazin's inaccessibility. That he was preoccupied in his tent with planning and preparations was doubted by none.

The small but well-equipped company moved easily around the outskirts of the forest, picked its way along hillside paths and eventually began the gradual ascent towards low mountain slopes. Varazin rode with his Aide and two officers at the head while the Commander followed with thirty hand-picked soldiers and a single wagon containing tents, ropes, food supplies and equipment for hewing stone. They rounded a rocky edifice and confronted vast mountains lying directly ahead with whitened peaks shimmering in haloes of cloud. One of the officers pointed to the mouth of a gorge on their right and the party veered onto a path that led towards looming surfaces of unrelenting rock. Varazin noticed that the path was fairly well defined. He thought it odd in such a remote place but reconciled the fact with the eminence of the legends concerning the temple.

The fabled shrine rose before them. Sequestered in the shadows of the gorge, its sheer façade was carved with symbols that none had fathomed since before the first scribes had committed to parchment the names and deeds of their peers. The symbols were clearly etched, preserved by the sheltering gorge, and filled every available space from the ground to the furthest point of a central geometric figure, imposingly mounted high above what seemed like an entrance. In carving the symbols, no allowance had been made for the narrow crack that suggested the outline of the door and each character overlapped where necessary as though the rock were an uninterrupted expanse. This feature served to conceal the apparent entrance which only became evident as the company drew nearer.

Immediately they pitched camp and began a preliminary survey of the temple walls. No alternative entrance presented itself, nor any hint of how to gain access at all. By afternoon, axes and chisels had begun to deface the perfectly preserved carvings. Flat chunks of stone split away from the surface and the symbols of antiquity began to lose their meaning. The soldiers clung to ropes and ladders, working like ants on the face of the temple to widen the crevice around the massive door.

Varazin sat outside his tent sipping wine and watched the progress of his men. The dream of power and riches grew endlessly in his imagination. From where he sat, he saw already the golden spires of the great city he would raise to his glory on the plains of Lior. The afternoon sun began to sink and he thought how the spires would gleam towards the mountain peaks, challenging their might and authority. An instant later he heard screams and the sound of grating rock. He looked towards the temple in time to see a soldier fall from the top of the great stone door. His stomach tightened as he noticed the change that had come about. Pivoted horizontally half way down, the entire slab of stone that blocked the entrance had shifted. At the top it had unexpectedly swung out from the façade, throwing the soldier and toppling ladders. At the base it had receded and two openings had appeared, one at each corner, that led into darkness.

Varazin leapt from his chair and ran towards the temple. His Aide and Commander joined him. An officer assured them that the stone appeared safe, having shifted to the extremity of its intended limit. Varazin walked to the left hand entrance and stepped inside. A chill air greeted him. He called for torches which were lit at once and brought to him. Handing one to his Aide, Varazin beckoned him to follow and ventured within.

Slowly they groped their way to the end of a short passage that then turned suddenly back on itself. Losing sight of the light that filtered in from the entrance, Varazin hesitated and listened before moving on. Each step echoed and died in the musty air that clung to them. Again the passage ended abruptly, this time with a low arch leading off at either side. Varazin chose the one to his right, stooped and moved through it. Beyond the arch a new choice of paths presented itself. Holding the torch as high as the low roof would allow, he looked in each direction and strained his eyes to see where the passages led. Like all the others, blackness was the only clue they offered. Recalling the turns they had taken, he motioned to his Aide and carefully they retraced their steps. By the time they regained the entrance, the sun had disappeared beyond the mountains.

The temple was heavily guarded. Three soldiers were posted at each entrance for two watches and an officer patrolled the close vicinity. Other soldiers observed from nearby vantage points. The clear night was undisturbed except for the breeze that flowed smoothly from the mountains and chilled the sentries whose wandering thoughts entwined it with the shades of legend. Varazin dozed fitfully in his tent, a taper burning at his side. Occasionally he would wake, watching the shadows that flickered with the flame to rouse still more his agitated mind. Then something moved at the door of his tent. Irritably, he pushed himself up on one elbow and looked at the shadows that stirred in the corner where a piece of material was fluttering in the breeze. Again he sensed a movement.

"Who is there? Come from the shadows," Varazin shouted as he reached for his sword.

A figure stepped forward and Varazin froze.

"Tyrus!" he gasped as the blood drained from his face and his flesh tingled. Growing cold, he caught at his breath. "Tyrus!" he gasped again. "Ah! You died. I saw you burn. You died."

"Here I am, and here are you. If I am dead, Varazin, then we are both dead," Tyrus said, standing before him much as he had at their first meeting.

Varazin gaped for several moments. Then he leapt up, grabbed his sword and bellowed for his Aide. The ensuing pause seemed endless. Rushing to the door of the tent, he yelled again into the night. Footsteps came running as the Aide and Commander converged from opposite directions.

"Inside," shouted Varazin

The two men entered and stood aghast at the sight of Tyrus.

"How?" murmured the Aide.

"So much for our guards," ranted Varazin.

Tyrus intervened.

"Don't blame them, Varazin. How I came here is not important. That you leave is all that matters."

Varazin glared at the old man while the Aide and Commander stood close by.

"You didn't come back from the dead just to tell me that," Varazin said angrily.

"Your blasphemy and barbarity are your own affair. But if you would continue to rule, you must leave the temple and never again set foot inside," Tyrus warned.

"And why should I believe that you care whether or not I rule? I should have thought that you'd delight to see me dead."

"Not everyone is motivated by your strange principles, Varazin. I would not willingly see you destroy yourself like a child that doesn't understand what it's doing. Your life is as sacred as any. But what you do with it is up to you."

"That's right, talk to me like a priest. Do you still deny it? Tell me I'm like a child who doesn't understand and that you are the one who can help me. It's the oldest trick to gain what you want. On lesser men it might still work – but not on me, Tyrus. You don't think I'm touched by you high motives, do you?"

"I speak the truth, Varazin."

"The truth is that the more you speak, the more determined I am to walk from that temple and carry away your precious treasures by the cartload! You won't stop me."

"And where can you put your riches once you have taken them? There's not a safer place in the world than where they are now," Tyrus said.

Varazin sat and gazed confidently at the old man.

"I think I can arrange something," he said with half a smile.

"I see you're getting desperate for ideas to deter me," he added, laughing aloud.

"Here's another," Tyrus said calmly. "You will not listen to legends of phantoms?"

Varazin shook his head.

"What is it then that makes you so certain that there is any truth in the legends of treasure?"

"For countless years in countless lands the fabled riches of the Temple of Lior have been heard of by everything that lives. Whatever happens, Tyrus, I'll find out for myself."

"As you wish," said Tyrus with resignation. "But consider it."

"Chain him," Varazin ordered, turning to his Commander. "And make certain that he is guarded constantly by no less than three men. I hold you both responsible," he added, glancing at his Aide.

Chained to a tree, Tyrus sat placidly on the ground. The soldiers found difficulty tearing their eyes from his form and their minds from the inexplicable reality of his presence. The Aide, entrusting the prisoner's safety to an officer and two soldiers, took the Commander to one side and gave voice to his thoughts.

"What do you make of it?" he asked in a whisper.

The Commander shrugged.

"I don't understand it," said the Aide in a voice that seemed to hope for reassurance.

"Whether we do or not, he's real enough to stir up Varazin's temper," the Commander replied.

"He's sly," said the Aide. "But something isn't right about his arguments. He tries to instil doubts but they're not consistent."

"He won't put doubt in Varazin's mind," assured the Commander.

"No," said the Aide. "That's what I mean. It's almost as if he wants to egg Varazin on – to goad him to the very act from which he claims to dissuade him. As if he knows that the more he tries, unconvincingly, to stop Varazin, the more certainly Varazin will seal his own fate."

The Commander looked at the Aide and thought about what he had said.

"I don't know how his mind works. But even if we suggested it to Varazin, he'd say it was what Tyrus wanted us to think. Varazin will do whatever he will. We can only wait and see."

Every available torch and rope was stacked before the labyrinthine temple. The left hand entrance was first priority. Penetrating into the depths of gloom and silence, every path and archway was scored with an axe and lit with a torch as Varazin, his Aide, the Commander and an officer eliminated one by one the passages that led them nowhere. Cold stone and darkness were all that they found before stumbling out into the blinding light of afternoon. As soon as they had consumed the food that awaited them, Varazin was impatient for a second attempt.

Agreed on the same methods of marking and lighting, they entered on the right to discover a similar maze that led them back and forth and gradually told on Varazin's temper. However impossible it seemed to retain a sense of direction, the Commander asserted that the right hand side was a mirror image of the left. But the suggestion was not popular with Varazin who angrily refuted the implication that they would again find nothing. Whenever such a possibility arose, Varazin's thoughts turned back to Tyrus and he wondered what the old man knew. Then out of the gloom he came face to face with an altar.

Varazin gazed at the strangely carved stone that confronted him. The elaborate workmanship of its expansive design left him in no doubt of its purpose. Here was something that gave him hope, something that didn't reflect the emptiness of the left hand half of the temple that had led them nowhere. Bare of accessories, the beautifully chiselled motifs and symbols carved on the altar entwined its subtle shape and conveyed their deeply reverent feeling. Calling out, Varazin waited with his torch held high and felt a sense of power grow irrevocably in his body. So fine was the altar that he already envisaged it beneath the golden spires of the city of Lior.

The Aide came cautiously up to him and positioned torches all around them. The added light revealed an awesome intricacy to an even greater expanse of carving. It also showed that the altar appeared to form a solid end wall to the passage. Varazin studied the rock scrupulously for a way past the altar, convinced that there was more here than he was seeing. Only then did he notice the circular hole that bore into the wall some way above the altar itself. A moment later he was standing on the carved surface. Considerably taller than most, he was able to reach the hole and haul himself up. Commanding the Aide to pass him a torch and his sword, he crouched on his knees in the mouth of the tunnel. Tentatively he probed with the sword as he tried to determine whatever lay ahead. Then, thrusting the torch through before him, its flame warming the small tunnel considerably, he pushed it along the ground and crawled after it. The Commander joined the Aide as Varazin disappeared from view. The echoes of his movements were suddenly interrupted by a shout and even from where they stood, they heard his breathing grow agitated.

"Fetch me Tyrus. Fetch me Tyrus." The words boomed through the passages and instantly the Aide retraced his steps, leaving the Commander to affirm the order.

Varazin held out the torch and looked down from the far end of the tunnel to behold the innermost chamber. Bare stone was all that greeted him.

Judging the distance to the floor within, he lowered himself slowly down and found a firm footing within easy reach of the opening. Once inside the chamber, he walked to its furthest extremity, holding high the torch and searching every corner. Then he turned and looked back towards the tunnel. As he did so, his legs grew suddenly weak and he steadied himself against the wall to recover from the shock of what he saw.

Set back, directly below the hole through which he'd

crawled, was a carved alcove. Within the alcove, alive, breathing
and watching him with large unmoving eyes, stood a small boy.
Varazin felt his chest tighten and his attempt to exclaim resulted
in a mere hissing from his half-opened mouth. It was not the
visage of a small child that so unnerved him, for its delicate face
and large dreaming eyes were almost angelic and bore an expression of unimaginable innocence. What stunned him into shocked
silence was the presence at all of any living creature walled up in
stone and blackness. For countless moments, Varazin stood gazing
as if entranced until the torch grew heavy in his hand. The boy
looked back, unflinching, unafraid.

Varazin took the torch in his other hand and approached the
child. Recovering a little from his shock, he spoke.

"Who are you? What are you doing here?" His voice echoed
and sounded harsh. But the child remained unafraid and gazed
silently back at him.

Varazin thought for a moment and then made a sudden
movement towards the alcove but the boy did not flinch or move
a muscle.

"Living but fearless," Varazin said aloud and became hesitant.
"More sorcery?" he muttered.

Scraping sounds echoed from the tunnel above and a torch
flared. Then a ladder appeared which Varazin grabbed and
propped beneath the hole. Tyrus descended slowly, turned and
looked about him.

"Well, Varazin, have you found what you came for?"

"You've had a hand in this. I know it. No one makes a
chamber this difficult to reach and leaves it empty. Where are the
treasures referred to in the legends?"

"What greater treasure than nothing?" Tyrus asked. "Do you
not feel the freedom that accompanies it? And what greater treasure than silence, when silence is the voice of angels?"

"Legends aren't woven out of nothing," said Varazin.

"Except those that speak of phantoms?" Tyrus asked with a
smile.

"Is this your phantom?" Varazin asked, pointing to the boy who continued to gaze at him.

"Not mine, Varazin."

"What trickery is he? He looks alive enough but he's only the vision of some sorcery."

"Perhaps we all are," suggested Tyrus

Varazin glanced suddenly back at the child with a look of revelation.

"Of course," he breathed. "He's the perfect phantom – the innocence that hides everything. But what kind of 'innocence' is born of stones and locked in blackness? What evil have you worked, Tyrus?"

"There is no evil in him. Is that why he disturbs you?" Tyrus answered.

"You won't stop me," Varazin assured and glanced again at the motionless child who never once looked away. "The perfect phantom," he repeated. "Whoever could destroy such innocence? There's the test. Like the siren, he rouses pity and seduces the strong. But only when he's dead will he reveal the secret that he guards." Varazin drew his sword and approached the boy. "No violator can withstand him! So runs the legend."

"And legends aren't woven out of nothing, Varazin," said Tyrus, reminding him of his own words. "Can you destroy such innocence and beauty?"

"Innocence is innocence. But the essence of evil can deceive us with its pose," answered Varazin as he continued to gaze at the child. "But I'll make a bargain with you, Tyrus. It would seem that fear is stronger than rock. Only fear and superstition put about by priests have kept people away from here. The entrance to this temple yielded far too easily and the path that leads to it is well worn. Either I'm right about this siren," he said, pointing to the boy, "or you have removed the contents of this room by some means. Did you already know your way through the labyrinth? Or is there another way in?"

"There are many ways in – from every possible direction,

depending upon how much rock you wish to hew."

"Where are the treasures?" shouted Varazin, impatiently. "Either they've been moved, or this child obscures them and must die. Answer me, Tyrus. The chamber was empty."

"Was it, Varazin?"

"No more evasions. You don't frighten me, priest. Where are the treasures?"

"Standing before you," said Tyrus, indicating the child. "Is he nothing? Was he not here, just as the legend said? Here is the precious jewel for which you seek. Would you destroy it? It is the greatest of all treasures."

"Damn your deceit," bellowed Varazin. "I'll destroy you first."

"I thought you already had," Tyrus reminded him. "Do you not see? The temple is only a shell, an outer body. He is the life within it. There is no greater treasure."

"You won't make a fool of me, Tyrus."

"I speak the truth. You must believe me. Look at him. What do you see? Does he mean nothing to you?"

"You forget who I am," Varazin shouted. "None withstands me. Answer my question or he dies," he said, raising his sword.

"It is you, Varazin, who forgets. Think! Is that just any child? Do you not recognise him?" urged Tyrus.

Varazin hesitated. His face contorted as the boy looked impassively up at him and seemed disarmingly familiar.

"Do you not see yourself, Varazin? Deny not the child within yourself. If you destroy him, you're lost."

For a moment longer Varazin wavered. Then the golden spires loomed on the horizon of his mind.

"No. You're as much a phantom as he, deceiver," bellowed Varazin as he swung the sword and sent it whistling through the air to behead the child with a single stroke.

Torch and sword clattered to the ground with the echoing thud of the decapitated body. Tyrus stepped closer and slowly held out his own torch. Varazin's head stared up from where it had fallen in the alcove and blood spurted violently from his neck. The child was nowhere to be seen.

Tyrus climbed the ladder and returned to the Aide and Commander who were waiting by the altar. In awe they listened to the tale of Varazin's fate and each admitted, only to himself, that fear of the conqueror had been stronger than the fear of legends.

"Out there in the valley," said Tyrus, "Varazin's leaderless army awaits. To the east lie his conquered lands. Will you rule them or will you liberate them?" he asked.

The Aide looked thoughtful. He glanced at the Commander and wondered what loyalty he would gain from his troops when they learned the news of Varazin's fate. The Commander looked at Tyrus and wondered whether the Aide, when voicing his opinions of the old man's motives, had not in fact been hoping for this very moment. Tyrus looked at them both and spoke again.

"Liberate them and you liberate yourselves. Or will you fight, ever to remain the same?" he asked as he stepped by them and disappeared into the labyrinth.

STORM CHILD

A crescendo of thunder like ten thousand drums overwhelmed the entire forest and struck terror into every living form that heard it. Gales lashed the treetops and gnarled roots strained at their ancient anchorage as torrents of rain bit fiercely into the earth. Crackling swords of fire tore the sky and violent explosions shattered the calm of an anguished summer day.

The storm had seized the forest like a beast of prey that lurks with the patience of a sage and betrays no sign of its intent. Eleanor was trapped and helpless in the sudden onslaught and soon abandoned all hope of refuge from the driving rain that penetrated every leaf of the canopy above. Her small form was drenched in seconds as she hastened vainly to retrace her steps to the shelter of her parents' cottage.

With every flash that seared the sky the trees seemed taller, blacker and more menacing. Thunder crashed and rolled across the countryside like ocean breakers, crackling sharply just as it seemed most likely to recede. Eleanor's hours of wandering in her beloved forest had been brought to an abrupt and unexpected close. She loved her sylvan retreat as it had been in the serene stillness of only a few minutes before but now she was trapped amid the wild thrashing of trees in a storm more ferocious than any she had ever seen.

Looking quickly about, the rain streaming from her matted hair, she suddenly recognised the path she was looking for and rushed hopefully towards it. An avenue of swirling branches thrashed overhead as she battled against unexpected gusts of wind that darted at her from all sides. She stumbled but her fall was cushioned by a patch of long grass. Scrambling up, intent only upon finding her way home, her heart sank as all recognition eluded her. She had been sure that the way was familiar but in her panic all certainty now fled and fear rose within her as the leaden sky grew heavier still with the shades of dusk.

She darted first in one direction and then another but all her hopes were transient and vanished as soon as she reached out towards them. The storm rose to its climax and she was startled by a sudden crack as a heavy tree gave way in front of her and crashed to the ground. Her courage wavered, fear overwhelmed her and she finally knew she was lost.

In that fearful moment she tossed back her head in a last effort to rise above adversity and defy the powers that forged her despair. High beyond the wailing trees vast clouds skimmed the air like an endless flight of winged serpents, blackening and destroying everything before them. Almost blinded by the driving rain, Eleanor lowered her eyes again, her hazy vision following the line of a tall slender tree, severely bent in defiance of the storm. She traced it to the forest floor and was startled to see, standing silently by it, the figure of a young boy who stared at her with brilliant eyes.

Pushing back her hair with both hands, Eleanor blinked several times and gazed back at the unexpected onlooker. A crash of thunder boomed overhead and for a moment she was plagued with uncertainty. Frightened though she was, she noticed that the stranger seemed oddly unaffected by the fury of the elements and reassured her with a smile.

Stepping forward, he pointed a hand and walked towards a clearing in the wood. Eleanor's hopes rekindled as she hastened to follow him, running every now and then to keep up. At the far edge of the clearing the boy glanced back over his shoulder, gesturing to a path for her to follow through the foliage. As fast as she followed, she could never quite reach him as he constantly vanished from view just as she came to where he'd been waiting. After a few minutes, Eleanor recognised the deep rushing sound of the river that flowed through the forest a long way from her home. The boy turned and looked back again, beckoning her towards the sound of the water that rushed furiously beneath the abating storm. She realised with alarm how far she had strayed from the cottage and was grateful to be led back to a place from which she could find her way. Her father had always strictly forbidden her to go near the river and now she realised that she must already have crossed it at a point where it lay deep in a gorge and was barely discernible, perhaps far below some unrecognised bridge, camouflaged by leaves and branches.

Her trust in the boy who guided her out of the forest was unquestioning, perhaps because she had been so scared, and it wasn't long before that trust was confirmed. In the far distance she recognised the hill, surmounted by a circle of ancient stones, that lay some considerable way from her home. She had no recollection or any notion of how she had passed unwittingly over that forbidden terrain earlier in the day. Doubtless her father would have blamed it on what he scornfully condemned as her endless daydreaming but, however it came about, she realised she must now regain the opposite bank and her father must never know.

Arriving at the water's edge, she saw that the silent boy had brought her to a place where the river's breadth seemed impassable. Just for a moment she began to think that he would prove unequal to the task of guiding them safely across. But even as she thought it, the boy's nimble movements drew attention to a stepping-stone onto which he now leapt. Quite undaunted by the lashing rain and frequent gusts of wind, he looked round for Eleanor, pointed to the next stepping-stone and beckoned her to follow. She paused for a moment and looked timidly at the rushing water laden with leaves and broken branches as it swirled and plunged towards a narrow gap further on. But the boy's smile enchanted her and filled her with courage. Determined by the patient gesture of his hand she took an unsteady step onto the first of the wet stones and kept as close behind him as possible, her every movement reflecting his own. With increasing confidence Eleanor soon found herself surrounded by the surging tide. Precariously keeping her balance against the wind, she felt exhilarated as it blustered around her and began to enjoy this new sensation of daring and adventure. Her guide stopped now and then to allow her to catch up, each time giving her a reassuring smile before pointing to the next step on their precipitous path. For a brief moment the water rushed around Eleanor's feet but a second later she had leapt safely to the next stone. Then sooner than she could ever have imagined, it was all over. The river lay behind them and the boy held out his hand to help her safely to the bank from the last rock. This was as close as she had come to the strangely silent being whose appearance in the forest, in perfect harmony with his surroundings, gave nobility and grace to his lean and subtly elongated features.

Now for the first time she observed him more closely. His bright blue eyes, set in an angular face, sparkled at her and complimented the interminable half-smile that hovered on his lips; his complexion was intense and seemed to alter with the shades of his surroundings; his every movement displayed energy and strength, yet the hand that led her from the rock was as gentle as her own; his touch made her tingle with warmth; and his black hair, lush, fine and shiny, curled outwards against the rain. His delight in his natural surroundings was beyond question and Eleanor thought how out of place he would look in any other setting. Having brought her safely across the river to a path she knew, he smiled at her with a sympathetic gentleness that instantly reminded her – as if he too was aware – of the ordeal she would have to face when she returned home in such a bedraggled state. His hand grasped hers for a moment longer as if to give her courage and then he nodded towards the path she was to take. As their fingers parted, she turned and looked towards her home with trepidation. Then turning back with a fond smile, Eleanor wanted to thank him – but the boy was nowhere to be seen.

It was pointless to rehearse answers to the accusations she anticipated from her parents but nevertheless she did. It was her father she feared. She expected little support from her mother who, she realised, was as afraid of her father as she was herself. Experience had taught her to dread these encounters and she braced herself as she finally pushed open the cottage door. Once inside, her clothes clung to her and dripped pools of water all around. The icy stare of her father cast such fear into her that she prayed to be back in the forest, lost and alone. There was a long silence in the small bare room, broken only by the constant dripping from her clothes and the squelch of her shoes at her slightest movement. Her father pulled himself out his chair as her mother concentrated on her sewing with an exaggerated display of indifference. Eleanor waited for the words she'd predicted and steadied herself against the sink just inside the door. But plainly the words had already been spoken and the verdict reached. Eleanor stumbled back against the door as her father's broad hard-skinned hand beat at her head and followed her every writhing attempt to avoid it as she crawled on the stone floor and tried to make a dash for the furthest door that led to her room upstairs. As the blows fell, his harsh voice began to bellow a stream of insults and obscenities. She knew them well. Then came the inquisition.

"Where the Hell have you been?"

Eleanor had learnt that it was easier to answer and hasten the ordeal, especially since her every hesitation increased the threat of renewed violence. Still stunned from her beating, she resolved to tell exactly why she came to be home so late.

"I only went for a walk in the forest," she answered, resentfully.

"You've been gone all afternoon. How many times must you be told about being out so long?"

"I was caught in the storm. I tried to keep dry but it was impossible, so I hurried back as quickly as I could. But I got lost. The storm came on so suddenly. I couldn't help getting wet," she added, irate that her parents should expect otherwise.

"Well where did you go, then? How could you get lost, unless you went somewhere you shouldn't?"

"I don't know how it happened. Anyway, I met a boy and he showed me the way back here."

There was a stunned silence as everything in the room

seemed to run down and even her mother's sewing became visibly laboured.

"A boy? What d'you mean?"

"Yes, a boy. He showed me the way back."

"Well, where is he now?"

"He only came as far as this side of the river, then he went back." Instantly Eleanor realised her mistake.

"The river?" bellowed her father. "If you've been across the river, I'll thrash you, my girl."

Instinctively she raised her arms to fend off another blow but it didn't materialise and her father turned away in exasperation. Eleanor resigned herself and tried to speak calmly.

"Before the storm, I wandered into the forest. I didn't think I was anywhere I hadn't been before. Then the rain started and I was soaked in no time. I must have crossed to the other side of the river somehow while I was trying to find my way home."

"She probably crossed that little bridge by the ravine," said a voice as fragile as the piece of cotton its owner was threading.

Eleanor's father grew red at her defiance of his most explicit instructions.

"That's almost half way to the village. Well how in God's name did you get back again, girl?"

"Shh!" mumbled Mother at the mention of God.

"I told you. I met this boy and he showed me the way back. We came across some stepping-stones that brought us to the bottom of the lane that leads up to Bardens Farm"

"You never did, you lying little bitch. There's no way across the river there."

"There is," insisted Eleanor.

"Shut up. Where's this boy you met, then? And what's 'is name, a?"

"I don't know."

"You don't know," boomed back the sarcastic response she'd expected. "You do everything you're told not to and you're a liar as well. It's about time you spent more of your energy here, instead of going off on your own, dreaming your life away. You're fourteen, girl. You're useless. What do you do all day long? You just dream about the place, always going off into the forest, always arguing and doing things you shouldn't. You're no use to man or beast. I suppose you didn't think of us sitting here wondering where you were when you were out just now? Couldn't you look where you were going? Open your eyes girl, instead of dreaming about all day long. And I don't want to hear any more about any boy. Do you hear? From now on you stay in the garden where we can see you. Now go to bed. You're a useless, selfish little bitch."

Eleanor knew that this was the final verdict. After the beating came the inquisition, then the lecture, then the judgement, and then confinement to her bedroom without food. At fourteen she had become quite stoical about it. She left the room and went upstairs without a word.

"Don't you even have the manners to say anything when you leave the room?" her father shouted after her.

Eleanor looked forward to the relative peace of her own small room where she could recover, undress, dry herself and nurse her wounds, both physical and emotional. She was miserable and hungry but both were much alleviated as she turned her thoughts towards a new interest: the smiling, friendly – and she thought handsome – boy who seemed to know and understand how she had just suffered.

The following morning Eleanor stepped barefoot onto the wet grass. She was sleepy and her golden hair hung in disarray around her young face as her eyes grew accustomed to the light. The tangled trees looked wild and distressed after their ordeal and the ground glistened softly. Abundant summer flowers cupped the rain, miraculously recovered from the fury of the winds. Only those most exposed had been sacrificed, their scattered petals and broken stems strewn like jewels across the garden.

The velvet softness of deep red petals gently caressed Eleanor's feet as she wandered slowly across the large garden, away from the cottage and towards the pond, and the crystal-sharp air began to dispel her tiredness. Memories of a restless night contrasted with the serenity of the morning and nothing stirred except the delicate sounds of droplets that fell from trees and flowers, giving perspective to the depth of silence. Eleanor stood before the large pond that lay at the centre of the garden. She gazed at the still reflection of a brightening sky. A falling leaf floated slowly upwards from the depths of the clear water and met itself as it touched the surface. A solitary ripple circled outwards as the leaf drifted gently towards the mirrored image of the branch it had abandoned and Eleanor became aware of the birdsong that always brought her such pleasure.

On the other side of the garden she saw the songster blackbird perched on top of the old oak tree, from which was suspended her swing, motionless on saturated ropes. She inhaled several deep breaths which fully roused her to the day and as the sun pierced the thinning clouds she watched the first faint wisps of moisture rise into the air above the glistening garden. Gazing across at the oak tree, her dreams merged with reality as the images of the morning enwrapped and intertwined them. Her gaze fell upon the swing and fixed itself there. Not a breath of air stirred but the swing was swaying gently back and forth, its thick ropes creaking on the branch as traces of steam curled around them and vanished into the shadow of the great knotted tree. With her thoughts unfocussed and only half-formed, something attracted her attention back to the pool. From the corner of her eye, she thought she saw a figure at the edge of the water, then she heard a faint splash. She quickened her step towards the pool just in time to see multiple ripples floating on the surface as if something had dived swiftly from view. Intently she searched for a form or a shadow within the clear depths but nothing revealed itself. A sound of light laughter startled her and drew her attention to the willow that overhung the far end of the pool. There she saw the slender boy, gleaming wet at the water's edge, standing amid the supple willow branches that reached down to the water's surface.

For a long while they stood and looked at one another, he in shadow, she in light, dreaming dreams mercurial and quiescent. Across the silver pool the songster blackbird flashed to serenade elsewhere. Eleanor stepped slowly along the grassy bank to where the willow stood, narcissistic, its draped elegance high above and deep below the calm aquatic mirror. As she moved, the veiling willow branches shifting across her vision, two familiar eyes sparkled from within the shadow, from within the pool, from within her dreams.

Standing on the threshold of the realm encompassed by the weeping tree, Eleanor looked within. She recalled the vision of the boy as he had first appeared to her in the storm. She pondered the fact that he too was alone. The slender limbs of the tree that moved gently to and fro now parted. He slipped between them, she stepped within, he in light, she in dreams. The garden teemed with life and beneath the weeping willow nothing wept but only smiled in the dark intimacy of a whispered pact.

In the time that it took for the songster's image to flash once more across the pool and perch again on the uppermost bough of the old oak, the spell was broken. Distracted by the bird's return, Eleanor glimpsed its black form as it swept over the garden. Out of the flutter of wings came the sound of her mother's voice. The morning had evaporated with the dew and Eleanor was required in the cottage.

"Your father's still very angry, you know."

"Yes, Mother. Whenever isn't he?" Eleanor's question had the desired effect of making her mother side tacitly with her father. And that was just how she wanted it.

Food was placed on the table for the two of them. It was the one meal of the day that Eleanor didn't mind because it was made bearable by the absence of her father.

"Anyway," added her mother, "he's said that you're not to go beyond the garden today. Try not to cause any more trouble, won't you."

"I'm quite content in the garden today," Eleanor answered with feeling. "It's been a beautiful morning."

"What have you been doing?"

"Enjoying the sunshine, the perfumes and the birdsong," she said wistfully.

"Hmm! Dreaming, you mean!"

"Yes, if you like to put it that way," Eleanor added with a smile. "I've been dreaming. And shall I tell you *what* I've been dreaming?"

Eleanor's mother was suddenly wide-eyed with interest at the thought of knowing exactly what it was that filled her daughter's mind from day to day.

"I'd be delighted to know, dear," she said in a way that Eleanor knew was designed to humour her.

"The difference with my dreams, though, is that they really aren't dreams at all. What might seem like dreams to you aren't always dreams to me, you see."

Mother looked a little doubtful as Eleanor turned to her food before continuing. "Well, you remember me telling you yesterday about the boy who guided me back here from the forest?"

Mother nodded cautiously.

"I met him again this morning and we've been together in the garden."

Mother made a curious noise as she swallowed her bread. "Oh, really?" she urged.

"Yes. You see, he's a… a sort of a prince, I suppose. He's very handsome," she added quickly. "Anyway," she went on before her mother could interrupt, "he doesn't have a home in the way that we know it. He just lives amid nature and has hundreds of friends who tend the trees and flowers and protect the insects, birds and animals. There are so many things to be done," she added vaguely.

Eleanor's mother sat open-mouthed at her daughter's ridiculous flights of fancy.

"I see," she said, humouring her further. "And what about

your friend, the one who helped you yesterday? What does he do?"

"Oh well, he's very special. He does what he likes. But he showed me some of his other friends at work in our garden this morning. They have a lot to do after the storm, you see."

"Yes, I expect they have," Mother responded sarcastically.

"Especially as there's to be another storm tonight," Eleanor added.

"Oh, really?" enquired Mother, hardly trying to hide her scorn any longer. "And how do you know that? *He* told you, I suppose?"

"Yes," Eleanor answered as if her mother should have known better than to ask. "Anyway, I can see that you don't believe a word I'm saying, so I might as well not bother."

Realising that Eleanor's feelings were hurt by her mocking tones, her mother reluctantly decided to indulge her, rather than risk completely destroying her dreams with unkindness.

"I'm sorry, Eleanor. It's just that another person's dreams – even my own daughter's – are often very hard to understand," she said, trying to make amends. "And then you say they're not really dreams at all, but something else altogether."

"Yes," Eleanor replied.

"That makes it even harder. And where do all these creatures come from?" Mother asked without conviction.

"They serve Pan, the great nature God," Eleanor answered.

Mother fell instantly silent. Country folk were superstitious and never talked lightly about the nature deities. Her daughter was barely fourteen and not likely to have heard about such things, least of all from her father.

"Who told you about Pan, dear?" she enquired.

"*He* did," Eleanor answered.

Mother grew pale and worried. "Now listen to me, Eleanor. If you start talking like this in front of your father, you know what to expect."

Eleanor sighed at the mere mention of her father and tried to turn her thoughts to pleasanter things. Her memories of the morning were bright, fresh and alive compared to the atmosphere in the cottage. She pushed her chair away from the table and got up.

"I'm going back into the garden," she said. "He loves my swing, you know."

Mother was implacable.

"Who?" she asked, coldly.

"The boy, of course," Eleanor said.

"Really?" All her mother's sarcasm returned with her inability to assert control. She disapproved of her husband's methods but was undermined in Eleanor's eyes because she did nothing to counter them.

"Yes. After he'd been swimming in the pool this morning, we played on my swing. He was delighted."

"Swimming?" Eleanor's mother struggled to assimilate so many revelations. "He went swimming? In the pool? In our garden?"

"Yes. He wanted me to as well but I can't swim. He said he'd show me but I was too scared."

Mother looked shocked as she tried not to imagine how her daughter's friend might have looked when he went swimming. She couldn't bring herself to face the question burning in her mind. Now she *had* to believe it was all fantasy, and prudishness forbade her to think otherwise.

"And he likes your swing?" she said with undisguised scorn as a way of changing the subject.

"Oh, he *loves* it," Eleanor said, caressing the words as she disappeared through the door.

Mother rose slowly from the table and began to clear away the plates. A peal of laughter rang out from the garden almost, she thought, like two distinct voices. All her daughter's fanciful stories raced through her mind as she stepped to the window and peered out. Brushing her sleeve across the pane, her eyes widened with disbelief. A curious tingling sensation swept over her and she felt as confused about reality and fantasy as she'd always imagined her daughter to be. Jumping delightedly about the oak tree was Eleanor, while the swing surged back and forth with no visible occupant.

Mother's sewing achievements for the rest of that day were more than a little erratic. Eleanor had been called in early to tea and, as it seemed that her father was going to be later than usual back from the village, had gone to bed before he was home. Despite Eleanor's revelations, her mother had found the fresh summer day a welcome contrast to the storm of the previous afternoon. Nevertheless, her daughter had unnerved her and she welcomed the thought of her husband's return as she sat with the window ajar and, at the first sound of his familiar step, hurried to serve his meal.

In no time at all she found herself pouring out to him all that Eleanor had said: their lunchtime conversation; her mention of the nature deity, Pan; and with much reluctance, the disturbing scene she herself had witnessed from the kitchen window.

"I'm more and more concerned about her, dear," she finally confided. "She keeps on about this boy she's met. Have *you* ever said anything to her about Pan or nature gods?"

"Not me," her husband replied. "I don't know where she'd hear such things. You know my view. She spends too much time on her own. Too much dreaming about the place and not enough hard work. Can't you find her more things to do? Must I do everything in this bloody house?"

"Well you don't encourage her to be with other children, do you?" Mother ventured. "She can't be with other people if you won't let her go into the village on her own. I know it's a long way but..."

"Now don't you start on me," he interrupted. "I think I'll go and have a word with her." He walked to the foot of the stairs before turning back to his wife. "Are you sure about that swing? I mean it being empty and moving?"

Mother looked sheepish. "Yes," she said eventually.

"You must be as bloody mad as she is, then."

"And something else," she added, to distract him from that point, "she said there'd be another storm tonight because *he* told her so."

He was thoughtful as he climbed the stairs and seemed to have lost the edge that characterised his usual sense of certainty and control over everything.

Eleanor was lying awake and staring into the darkness as she heard his footsteps outside her door. Ungently it opened and her body tensed.

"Why aren't you asleep?" he demanded.

"Because I knew you'd come and wake me."

"Oh you did, did you? Now what's all this talk that's been frightening your mother?"

Eleanor didn't answer. There was the smell of inquisition in the air.

"Well, come on. What's it all about?"

"Hasn't she told you?"

"Yes. About forest creatures and this boy who's supposed to have brought you home yesterday. And where did you hear about Pan?"

"*He* told me."

"Who?"

"The boy."

Eleanor's father sat heavily down on the edge of her bed, pinning her legs under the covers.

"Now you look here, my girl, this is your last warning. We've had enough of all this fancy of yours. If either of us hears any more about forest creatures, or Pan, or this boy you keep on about, you'll stay locked in this bloody room until you learn to know better," he warned, raising his voice and his hand at the same time to emphasise his intent.

"But they're my friends," Eleanor protested, struggling to

free her legs and tensing even more for the physical violence she expected.

"Damn you, girl. Will you shut up about it," her father bellowed.

Seeing him lose control again, Eleanor took courage.

"Are you frightened, too?" she asked pointedly.

Her father was taken aback and instinctively she seized the moment to go on.

"You *and* Mother? Just because you can't see them?"

"You have too much your own way," he interrupted, his subdued tone telling Eleanor that her perception was right. "Look at the way you wandered off yesterday," he added weakly.

Eleanor bravely ignored him and resumed her previous tack.

"So long as you refuse to look, you'll never see them. They won't come to you just to satisfy you that they exist."

He looked restlessly about the room.

"You should be thankful to them for bringing me home," Eleanor continued, "...if you really cared whether I came home or not."

Suddenly her father had something to grasp, something on which to give vent to the emotion in which he was most practised.

"How dare you," he shouted as his hand smacked across her face.

Eleanor turned sharply away, resenting the imposition of his presence on her person. She thought of pointing out that hitting her seemed to be the only way he could show how much she mattered to him. But she thought better of it and stifled a sob, determined not to inflame his uncontrolled temper.

Poised to hit her again, he seemed for once at a loss to continue the conversation and the question that followed was weak and ineffectual.

"And what's this I hear about another storm tonight? What do *you* know about it? There are old men down in the village who could tell you when it's going to rain days in advance. Ha!

You'd make me laugh if you weren't so pitiful," he sneered as he lowered his threatening hand. "There'll be no storm tonight," he emphasised.

To Eleanor's relief he moved from her bed. Then he sighed heavily and paused. The sigh, she thought, was unlike him, and the pause was filled with the distant rumble of thunder.

The door banged shut and he stamped down the stairs. His wife looked up expectantly as he passed through the kitchen but chose to ignore her and quell his temper in the garden.

Outside the air was sultry and another far off rumble from the direction of the hills did nothing to improve his mood. He made a snorting noise, wandered towards the oak tree and paused beside it. There had been a cool breeze as he arrived home less than an hour before but now the stillness was unearthly. No murmur penetrated the garden, no breath of air stirred a single leaf or blade of grass. Even from the small cottage no sound reached him. Had it been totally dark, he might have admitted to himself that he didn't feel quite at ease standing in the shadows beside the tree but the last glimmer of twilight made all the difference. He lifted his gaze to the dim sky where gathering clouds obscured all but a small patch of deepening blue.

A chill crept through the air and he shivered slightly as he became aware of a gentle creaking sound behind him, like rope straining on a bough. He turned sharply round, rather more quickly than he might have thought necessary. But the chill continued to creep steadily over him as he peered into the gloom and saw the swing, barely two yards off, swaying gently to and fro with not the slightest breath of air to propel it.

Everything he had heard that evening from his wife and daughter flooded into his mind as his gaze was riveted and his body transfixed. In cold terror he watched for several moments as the swing rocked steadily back and forth, creaking on the bough above. Then the two supporting ropes twisted slightly out of parallel and he was filled with the unbearable sensation that something invisible was watching him. He lunged at the empty ·

wooden seat. There was a thrashing and rustling of bushes. Frantically he grabbed the ropes to stop himself falling and a low branch whipped back into place as though something had darted off into the undergrowth.

Clinging to the ropes, he tried to rein in the phantoms that began to invade his imagination. He thrust the swing aside and stepped towards the bushes but everything beyond them was perfectly still. Thunder rumbled in the distance. Turning towards the cottage, he chanced to look at the ground. In the dying light he saw, directly beneath the swing, a curiously-formed pattern imprinted in the damp earth. He stooped closer, then recoiled in shock. The same marks led towards the bushes. Never had he seen anything like them: footprints, chilling in their form, elongated, cloven and clawed.

The patter of large raindrops sounded on the leaves above him and thunder rumbled in the forest as he turned quickly back to the cottage. Hastening across the garden, he looked nervously about. He glanced up at Eleanor's bedroom window just in time to see the curtain fall back into place. Fuelled by fear, his anger propelled him straight upstairs to demand an explanation.

"Well, do you believe me now?" Eleanor greeted him, sensing his unease and suddenly fearless of his rage. "I saw you under the oak. Did you think you could frighten him away from the swing?" she demanded defiantly.

"There was nothing there," he bellowed.

"So you couldn't see him," she said with satisfaction. "The swing was moving. You know he was there."

He granted her an explanatory reply. "The ropes on the swing were creaking. There wasn't a breath of air. After what you'd been saying, I…"

"And did you expect to catch something you couldn't see?" she questioned. "He's far too quick for you. He could follow you for the rest of your life and you'd never be fast enough to catch him. Perhaps he'll do that if you don't leave him alone," she added as a warning and felt more on equal terms.

"Who was it on the swing, Eleanor?" he demanded, suddenly shaken.

"My friend. The boy. The one who guided me through the storm."

"A boy you said?"

"Yes."

"Describe him to me," her father demanded.

"He's beautiful and he's handsome and he's kind."

"But he's not so clever," her father retorted. "When he ran off just now he wasn't so fleet of foot that he failed to leave any traces. Cloven footprints with claws... You call that handsome?"

"Yes," Eleanor answered emphatically. "And he's free. He doesn't have anyone to tell him what to do." Her voice was suddenly subdued, measured and unearthly and her features seemed flushed, sharpened and subtly elongated. "He does what he wants because he wants to. He serves Pan because he chooses to. And if he no longer wishes to, he is free to go. He is as free as the wind and the waves and he goes where he will. He rides the lightning, leaps from cloud to cloud, laughs above the storm, stands astride the chasms of thunder and swims through the torrents of rain that spiral up from the seas. And wherever he chooses to be, the creatures who tend the elements welcome him to their domains."

Eleanor's father looked at her with astonishment and fear as the voice that spoke these words bore little resemblance to that of his daughter. Rooted to the spot, he adopted a more moderate tone.

"Where did you learn about Pan?"

"*He* told me," she sighed, as she resumed her former self, weary of the same questions.

"So if he's as free as you say, why does he spend his time here?" he asked.

"I told you. If that's what he chooses, then that's what he does. He found me in the storm yesterday and guided me home. He's as kind and gentle as any friend I could want. Today he came to me again and we laughed together and shared our secrets."

"What secrets?" interrupted her father sharply.

Eleanor ignored him.

"He told me of lands and visions that you could never believe, of where he travels and the dwellings in the skies of others far greater than him. And he's told me of the joy that awaits those of us who yearn to reach the skies and be free. And that is why the storm will come again tonight."

Her father looked puzzled. "Why?" he asked.

"So that I may join him. He wants me to be with him – and so do I. Tonight in the storm I will be free to ride with him through the skies, to dwell in the cloud cities and be a companion on his travels."

Eleanor's father recovered himself and burst into laughter.

"That's the best one yet," he mocked. "Are you never going to come down to earth, girl? Just wait till I tell your mother. Ha! Whenever are you going to learn about real life? You dream so much when you're awake, it's a wonder you've any left for your sleep. Ha!"

She was used to the sting of his mockery and humiliation, and while it never failed to hurt, it spurred her in her resolve. Her father walked out of the room and she heard him call out to her mother as he went downstairs. No sooner had he gone, than she was out of bed and peering down from the window. The rain was falling steadily as thunder rumbled and the swing swayed gently back and forth. Eleanor smiled. Rushing downstairs, she found her father still laughing about the story she had told him – a bitter, mocking laugh. But her mother seemed less amused. For several moments Eleanor's presence in the room went unnoticed. Then he saw her.

"Back to bed," he bellowed.

A loud peal of thunder cracked overhead and Mother suggested that the girl was ill. Ignoring them both, Eleanor ran to the door that led to the garden and threw it wide open. The rain lashed down as the thunder built to an almost constant tirade.

"Your bed is the place for romance and dreaming. Go on, get up there," Eleanor's father shouted, as much to make himself heard as in rage. He rose to his feet, his voice filling the room.

Eleanor turned to face him, determined she would no longer be a prisoner to his violence and scorn.

"But Father," she called out confidently in a voice that silenced him. "You forgot about the footprints. They weren't a dream. What about those? You saw them yourself and you were afraid."

A series of blinding flashes lit up the trees for several seconds and Eleanor saw her parents look on in shock. On the far side of the garden the vigorous motion of the swing was visible from the cottage door. No longer was it mysteriously unoccupied, no longer was its relentless surging unexplained. Smiling with delight, exhilarated by the howling storm and waiting for her patiently, sat a creature whose countenance was far beyond their wildest imagining. At last they saw him: the boy of whom they'd heard so much and believed so little – bright-eyed, fair-skinned, his subtly elongated features graced with garlands and black hair that framed an angelic beauty so fine that all earthly languages were rendered voiceless.

As the incredible apparition vanished again into darkness, Eleanor's father was transfixed. Eleanor seized the moment. Rushing into the garden, she was momentarily lost from view as lightning sparked across the entire forest. Startled back to life, her father ran to the door. Rain fell like fire, thunder exploded and another blinding flash seared through the air. Enshrined in that flash, he saw Eleanor and the boy clasped to each other as the lightning streaked skywards and the vision vanished into swirling storm-clouds.

Eleanor's father raced into the garden and was instantly drenched. Frantically he staggered, trying to focus his eyes in the rain and darkness. Something tripped him and he only just managed to keep his balance as a flash of lightning lit the crumpled form on the grass at his feet. Stopping in his tracks he stooped over the body of his daughter, lashed by the rain. Slowly he picked it up and carried it back to the cottage. His wife looked on in dumb horror.

Blackened by the bolt of lightning, Eleanor's saturated body lay cold on the stone floor. After a long pause her father moved his hand slowly towards her eyes to close them for the last time. Then he hesitated and his wife saw him tremble.

"Look," he whispered.

She leant down to see.

Overhead an oil lamp imparted its dim flicker to the eyes of the dead girl. Beyond the flicker and deep within those eyes, as though etched by a blinding flash, the silent couple saw a boy's pale and delicate face staring out at them. They recognised it – angelic and garlanded, like something out of a dream.

ELEGY IN RED

The knight awoke in twilight. A glint of silver from his heavy breastplate fell upon the scarlet tunic that matched the plumes of his helmet, his boots and his flowing cape, and glowed eerily. He wondered whether he had been dreaming or whether he had only just begun to. Everything was hazy. His recollections loomed, swirled and vanished, elusive, poignant and red. Before him glimmered a vast marble floor where the shadow of his plumes fluttered like ominous black pinions.

He glanced about him, unable to determine the source of the strange luminosity to which, gradually, he was growing accustomed. Everything felt like a recurring dream that he'd had a hundred times before. All was familiar, yet the moment was unique. He found himself standing next to a high stone wall, some kind of castellated tower, and noticed another very similar further off in the opposite direction. They stood like watchtowers overlooking a vast confine in which rituals of life and death would be enacted. Then he noticed two more, pale and luminescent, at different points ahead of him on his horizon.

Scuffling echoes swept across the floor as many foot soldiers assembled and high ranking priests arrived to bless them before battle. When all had settled down, the crowned heads of state appeared, entering with a gravity and dignity befitting their high office. The foot soldiers confronted each other in two long rows and the ceremony commenced.

His eyes focussed on the regal beauty of the visiting consort, wife of the crowned head who stood opposite, silhouetted between the two distant towers on his horizon. He gazed above the head of the soldier in front of him and strained to see her exquisite beauty more clearly. But as he did so, a compulsion welled up within him, an ancient inbred instinct that hers was a beauty to be destroyed. Agitation possessed him as her pallid form enchanted him with its ivory spell and his mount grew restless, champing at the bit. He grappled with his compulsion and fought the division within him that both attracted him to her but urged him to kill.

The solemnity of the moment was enhanced by an endless twilight and the ritual ceremony was slow to reveal its invisible purpose. The haunting image of some half-remembered omen fixed him with its stare and rooted him to the spot. And so he remained for an indefinite time, languishing, while others about him proceeded with their own courses of action. The mood was charged with tension as foot soldiers adopted new formations, parrying and edging about in an endeavour to outwit and outmanoeuvre each other. Then he saw his opportunity and he spurred his horse to leap forward, driven by his own primeval compulsion. The object of his dark obsession was now within his sights. One of the white-robed priests left the side of his sovereign and a path was open to approach her. Unobscured and standing in the twilight that embraced them all, her beauty left him breathless. She turned to face him, acknowledging his rank and granting him due respect. Her pure white robe bore a diamond clasp that she stroked with her hand as he trembled in awe at the studied carelessness of her gaze and gesture.

A solitary foot soldier came between them. Impulsively the knight cast aside his caution and moved around the man-at-arms to finally approach the royal beauty before him. Instantly, she rushed and fell upon him, tearing the diamond from her robe to reveal a blade as elegant as herself, which now she drove with unexpected force beneath his heavy armour. He fell and his scarlet cape rippled on the marble floor like blood. In that moment, the foot soldiers, the robed priests, the heads of state, the castellated towers, and even the marble floor itself, ceased to exist. All activity was suspended and the only sound he heard was a monosyllabic click. "Check!" It reminded him of the ancient inbred instinct that had so recently possessed him and driven him in his purpose. But now it all seemed like a dream and he no longer remembered what that purpose was.

THE MESSENGER

From the courtroom, along the grey stone passage, out across the sunlit quadrangle, up the steps to the ante-room, through the panelled corridor, and right into the Great Hall itself, the King was pursued, pressed, charmed, implored, urged and criticised by a bevy of disgruntled, sour-faced Ministers any one of whom would cheerfully have hanged the defendant freed by the King just two minutes before. Jostling and raising their voices one above the other, they burst into the hall, and on sight of the throne set above them at the far end, finally remembered their respective ranks and drew cautiously back as their King walked ahead and seated himself before them. Dal, the Court jester, appearing as if from nowhere, instantly perched himself at the foot of the throne, thrust his chin into the palm of his hand and watched with amusement as the now less confident Ministers bustled and braced themselves for a more formal attack.

Ten Ministers voiced ten cries of dissent against the patient King and ten times as many amongst themselves in searching for the direst means of execution. Twenty Courtiers stated their views while thirty Knights confused the issues and completed the ultimate uproar. The Great Hall resounded with glittering opinions, rippling gestures and brightly coloured arguments all invoked by a reluctant King and a vacant gibbet. Through it all the King said not a word and Dal just smiled.

When finally the commotion began to subside, the First Minister stepped forward. "Leniency is all very well, Your Highness, but not in this case. The man was undoubtedly guilty."

"There was doubt," replied the King.

"Doubt or not, he'd let him off," murmured a voice in the crowd.

Dal glanced in its direction but the King did not respond.

"But Your Highness," continued the First Minister, step-ping closer, "if you give the peasants too much, they'll only take advantage of you. A stern ruler gains respect."

"And wealth to share with his Ministers," prompted Dal, who became the target for twenty venomous eyes.

"Our laws are too lax, Your Highness," claimed another voice. "The revisions made last Spring have undermined the very foundations of our security."

Dal sprang to his feet and danced once about the throne.

"Alack! Alack! Lax laws allow our lacks!" he chanted and cart-wheeled back to where he had been.

A minstrel in the gallery struck his tambourine and laughter spread around the hall. Immediately the Third Minister sprang forward and pointed to the gallery.

"There, Your Highness! See how far, in these times of leni-ency, respect for you is undermined. In your own Court, a royal minstrel presumes to punctuate with his tambourine the cavorting of your degenerate jester. Dal, we know, is immune from official censure, but has just *any* man the right to treat you thus?"

The King smiled indulgently, though none could tell what thoughts he masked. Then solemnly he stood and a hush fell on the assembly.

"I should like to be alone," he said at last. "The Court is dismissed. I will summon you later."

The surprised and slightly disappointed Courtiers filed from the hall with speculative mumblings. Dal scuttled amongst them, reappearing at random in a ubiquitous romp. Children laughed from beyond the door as the last of the Knights and Courtiers disappeared and the Ministers turned to follow.

"Gentlemen," bellowed the King, his voice booming across the hall while the Ministers turned as one man and Dal stared out from beneath a table. "What respect have you? Your hypocrisy is immaculate. Get out!"

Faintly hopeful expressions melted beneath the King's glare as rustling parchments and shuffling feet receded from earshot.

Dal was about to follow but glanced first at the King who nodded
and signalled for him to stay. The last Minister looked back as the
high doors were closed from without by guards with swords and
halberds.

The King sighed and sat down again.

"Bustling, hurrying, ten thousand things at once, advisers,
Ministers pressing for answers, bullying, arguing with each other
and then turning to me to take sides! I wonder who is King?
Harsher laws, sterner rule – all for respect! Dal, they think me
weak."

Dal nodded.

The King beckoned and walked to a door beyond the throne.
Dal followed as they entered, crossed a panelled chamber and
passed through an arch to a spiral stair. Ascending slowly, they
emerged on a balcony that overlooked the Great Hall. Every
movement echoed about them and Dal cast a questioning glance.

"They think me weak because I've changed. Spring! The
revision of laws. They don't like it," the King said quietly.

"Change is never popular," ventured Dal.

"Least of all when it thwarts the lusts of ambition. They'd
have me murder half my subjects and tax the others double before
they were satisfied. Time was when I might have done just that,"
he added, gazing down at his throne. "And my Ministers knew
it. They urge me constantly to make war; to invade, murder and
steal; to realise my every potential for greed and envy. They stand
to gain from it and they know all too well the weaknesses of
kings."

Dal looked up. "There's a rumour put about that says you're
mad."

The King smiled. "Of course! One always sees one's own
worst faults in others. But if I'm mad it's for all to see, imprisoned
in my royal cage. Can I make a single move without it being
known? I think they think me safe enough. Kings are dispens-
able, outnumbered and reared for convenience. I am the excuse
for their actions and the bearer of blame. A king's popularity is

dependent on his co-operation. Resistance is… madness. Before the Spring I had their full support. Now…"

The King sat on a low step and peered down between the pillars of the balustrade. Dal looked at him and neither spoke for a very long time.

"What a silence," the King eventually whispered. "This stone's so cold," he said, placing his palm against the step on which he sat. "How strange! Down there they call me 'Your Highness' – 'Your Highness' this, 'Your Highness' that. Tell me, jester, up here am I 'Your Lowness'?"

Dal gazed at the unsmiling face of the King and said nothing.

"Your Highness?" the King mocked in the tones of a Minister, and then promptly resumed his former seriousness. "Your Lowness! Lowliness! What is high or low when one is allured by such a silence?" He looked at Dal. "Speak to me, jester!"

Dal moved across and sat next to the King. Both gazed down on the Great Hall. Dal hesitated a moment.

"What happened in the Spring?" he asked.

★

The castle was resplendent in the melting snow, gilded by the sun that warmed the budding boughs and touched with glory the fluttering banners of returning victors. Laden with trophies, the army filed noisily into the streets of the walled outer city. Steam rose from panting men and horses, halberds flashed in sunlight, and the clatter of hooves and armour fought to be heard above the deafening cries of welcome.

The Ministers greeted the knights at the gates of the inner city and hastily called them to Council. The King learned the extent of his increased wealth and expanded territory and presided over the victory celebrations that followed. The reunion was especially lavish to mark the tenth consecutive campaigning conquest and already there was talk of a new venture that would expand the

Kingdom beyond the fabled range of ice-capped mountains that lay to the north.

Revellers challenged and fought each other deep into the night, arguing over their deeds, denying their cowardice, and delighting in the gory heroism of victory. The Ministers glowed with approval and gradually turned the conversation to greater glories as yet unachieved. The King left early. All the training of a destined youth for his inescapable title had never quite hardened him to the pitch required for such traditions. As the din of drunken brawling receded from his ears, the torch he bore flickered audibly and pushed back the shadows that filled stone crevices where he wandered alone on the battlements beneath castle turrets. He paused and looked out towards the land where men who had never seen him were subjected to his will. A voice reached him, carried on the sharp night air. Summoned by a messenger of the First Minister, he was tactfully reminded of his historic duty in honouring his knights with his presence for the closing ceremony.

His duty done, he wandered all night, restless and disturbed. At each turn he encountered a guard, half asleep, helmet askew, halberd out of reach, unsuspecting of his approach and noisily attentive in the resulting confusion. He wondered to whom they were loyal and stared as though he might learn from their expressions. But the castle afforded him no peace and as the soft dawn light began to seep into every crevice, a liveried footman came running to find him. Bowing, he handed the King a sealed message. The seal was one of the King's own, used only for domestic matters, and to which he had given Dal the privilege. He read the message: "The night is full of whispers. A strolling player is said to have wandered the streets and sung of an envoy approaching from the north, who travels swiftly and is expected by evening. None can establish his origin, and the minstrel, last heard near a tavern, cannot be found."

The King re-read the message and sent the footman to summon Dal. He knew his jester would not have bothered him with anything he thought trivial. But Dal knew no more than he had written. The news was told in every corner of the city and already the Ministers had arranged to hoist a ceremonial banner from the highest turret. Many an envoy had been received before in the Great Hall. What strange or special tune had the minstrel sung to kindle such excitement about this one? And why the unspoken sense of awe that urged his immovable Ministers to raise a special flag? Such questions went unanswered, since no other thought to ask them. A spell seemed cast on the city and everywhere people were distracted, hesitant and vague. No one found the minstrel again, though many searched and tried to recall the lines of his song. Then a short fanfare rang down from a turret on the outer wall where a trumpeter had been specially posted. It was late afternoon as the gates of the city swung open.

Surprise was unanimous when it was realised that the messenger came on foot and alone. With measured step he approached across the open plain that lay at the edge of the forest. None doubted his identity, even at such a distance. His nobility of gait and bearing marked him out long before the fineness of his attire became distinctly apparent. But instantly the Ministers were suspicious and began to wonder at their own unnamed concerns. It was inconceivable that ambassador or envoy from any monarch would appear unaccompanied and on foot before a foreign Court. The thinly disguised possibility that horses, soldiers and provisions lay hidden in the forest, gave the Ministers new confidence as they promptly despatched a party to locate the intrigue. But when, with movements suggesting the strength of mountains and a Lydian grace that charmed the eye, the stranger stepped within the city gates, none could believe that one so young bore messages less than auspicious.

Through the streets that led to the castle he was escorted by guards. His billowing cloak of deep blue fell luxuriously about his youthful body and matched the eyes that stared impassively from a finely sculpted face. His rippling hair was touched by the sun, warm, soft, golden. Beyond portcullises, up many a flight of broad stone steps, past gates, arches, guards, towers, they came at last into the presence of the King. Courtiers and Knights thronged everywhere as the First Minister rose to greet their guest. But the messenger stepped by him and striding to the centre of the Great Hall, stood motionless before the throne. The Minister was quick to follow and several Knights stepped forward in defence. With frequent glances at the King, the Minister stood between the envoy and the throne.

"It is customary that we announce our guests and that the guest in question concede to our formalities," he said, sharply.

The envoy looked at him and then at the Knights who stood close by.

"Wherever your journey began, it led to the Court of a King, in whose presence you now stand. It is usual to acknowledge that fact," the Minister continued in a slightly calmer tone.

The envoy returned his stare unruffled and then looked at the King.

"Speak. State your errand," the King commanded.

The envoy continued to gaze at him and said nothing. Patiently they all waited.

"You have our full attention," the King added. "We are keen to know what news you bring."

But the envoy, standing firmly, continued to look at him in silence.

"If you won't speak to a King, perhaps you'll answer a fool," said a voice from the crowd.

The envoy looked to where the voice came from and Dal, to the delight of the Courtiers who always enjoyed this particular trick, approached him from the opposite side.

"This is quite ridiculous," said the Minister, whose thoughts turned suddenly to the forest and a possible trap. "Our young envoy has travelled far, though with little sign of tiring. Surely he can't have forgotten why he came?" he said, dryly.

There was an outburst of uncertain laughter. Then Dal stepped before the envoy and looked up at him.

"I bow to you," he said, doing just that, "for you mock the King and all his Court better than I can mock his Ministers. I have to work to such an end but you do it with ease."

The envoy looked calmly down at him.

"State your business or leave," said the Minister, growing impatient again.

A footman stepped forward and handed a message to the King. He pondered it and then eyed the envoy with curiosity.

"It seems that you did come alone, after all," he said. "No threatening armies encamped in the forest, no tracks or evidence of anyone but you. The nearest settlement beyond our border in the north is a march of twenty weeks from here. You have apparently travelled all this way alone, on foot, without provisions and without purpose. Your endurance and capacity to present yourself here in a state of such restored composure is something of a mystery – unless of course you are the emissary of some civil disturbance closer by. Whoever has sent you, wherever you are from, it is in your own interests to speak. You have had the courage to come here alone. What do you want?"

Surrounded by the hushed assembly, the young envoy continued to look impassively at the King. No word, nor gesture, nor facial change did he offer that might afford them any clue to his purpose in their midst. Dal, lounging at the foot of the throne, shifted from one elbow to the other and continued to study the strangely impressive youth. Time wore on and tempers quickened. The First Minister sighed and spoke.

"To have come here without an escort was indeed an act of courage. But to have done so in order to mock was simple folly. You offend us and waste our time, yet perhaps we would not be wise to let you leave. When you do not return to your master, he will no doubt send a messenger more eloquent. May I suggest, Your Highness," he said, turning to the King, "that we find some comforting dungeon in which to house our guest?"

The King looked at the messenger and searched his face for some response.

"Why not," he said at last. "If no one comes, then perhaps our silent envoy will begin to change his mind. Guards!"

A sword slid from its scabbard with a lethal hiss and scuffling footsteps echoed about as men converged on the defenceless stranger. The youth turned suddenly and stared at the soldier who, brandishing the sword, faltered and looked with startled eyes on the noble countenance of his supposed charge. Every one of the soldiers stopped in his tracks, unwilling or unable to advance. For an interminable moment nothing moved in the silence of the Great Hall.

"If I may presume to suggest, Your Highness, our extraordinary messenger might be invited to impart his purpose in greater privacy."

The words rang through the silence for all to hear and the young envoy looked back again at the throne where, with a gravity reserved for just such moments, Dal was standing before the King. Despite outcries from Courtiers and Ministers alike, the King resolved to clear the hall of Knights, Nobles, Ladies, minstrels, soldiers, footmen and even the internal guards. The ten Ministers alone were allowed to remain, together with Dal, who once again had managed to earn their displeasure. All the while the young messenger stood silent. Indeed, one might almost have overlooked the vital role he played in all that went on around him, for as soon as the doors had closed on the thirteen men within, bitter dispute engulfed all but he and formality was thrown to the wind.

"How many more concessions are we to make to an insolent foreigner who mocks our Court and insults the King?" raged the First Minister.

"What spinelessness to suggest such an unprecedented measure," croaked the Second.

"And spinelessness in executing it?" asked Dal, glancing at the King.

"It belittles us all. An envoy requesting confidence would have had it granted," countered the Second.

"Enough of this," shouted the King. "I consider the request made on behalf of the envoy, and it *has* been granted."

"The onus is on the envoy to make such a request for himself," said the Third Minister. "It is universal policy."

"Except when I choose to overlook it," answered the King, sternly. "Now, instead of arguing with each other, it might be more to the point to give attention to the envoy whom we accuse of lacking manners."

The King gestured to the youth in their midst who showed not the slightest sign of weariness or fear. Nevertheless, the King undertook to reassure him.

"You have our ear and our confidence. You may speak freely," he urged.

But the messenger remained as silent and impassive as before. The moments slipped by and tension continued to mount.

"Is he mad?" stormed the Fourth Minister.

"We are," said the Fifth, calmly. "Thumbscrews? Rack?" he suggested with a hopeful smile.

"A gibbet would save a lot more time," answered the Sixth.

"Perhaps even twelve is too many?" prompted Dal, thoughtfully.

"What?" bellowed the First Minister. "Your Highness, you're surely not going to listen to this creature again?" he asked, even before the King had begun to think about it.

The King pondered.

"Does it matter?" he finally said. "You began the concessions. We might as well go on."

"Speak will you, you madman," ranted the Minister as he turned on the youth and grabbed at the neck of his cloak.

This act alone determined the King, while the youth took hold of the Minister's wrists and with perfect ease removed the clutching hands from his collar. The calm expression with which he accompanied the act reduced the Minister to silence – a silence that prevailed even as the King dismissed them all but Dal. Slowly the Ministers turned to go but before they reached the door, they were protesting again.

"For your own protection, Your Highness, it isn't wise for all of us to leave," said one.

"Such a mockery!" mumbled another.

"Who knows what might happen?"

"Whatever it is, it'll affect us all. It's madness!"

"Go," said the King.

The doors closed once more and all was still. The King seemed momentarily distracted but then gave his full attention to the envoy who confronted him. Dal sat on a low bench to one side, elbows on knees, chin in hands, eyes everywhere.

"See what a turmoil you've caused?" said the King with a friendly expression. "My Ministers go scurrying to tend the wounds to their bureaucratic pride while you, a total stranger, have the undivided attention of the King." He glanced at Dal, then added: "And his jester. That's an even rarer privilege. What brings you here? And on whose behalf?"

The envoy continued to stand and look and say nothing.

"How can you serve your master if you won't convey his message?" the King asked.

The messenger was silent.

"You know, even before you arrived we made concessions to you. My Ministers, no less, had a ceremonial flag especially flown to acknowledge your coming. I'll bet it's safely furled away again now! Didn't you notice your reception? You were expected, you know. You were heralded by a mysterious minstrel who sowed the seeds of curiosity in every street and tavern last night and then vanished with the stars. You've certainly made an impression! But why? For whom? To what end?"

In the silence that followed, Dal stood up, walked quietly the length of the hall and went out by the main doors. The messenger stood motionless. The King, seated on his throne, leant back and pondered for a long time. He remembered the previous night on the battlements and the moment when he had gazed out to the land where men who had never seen him were subjected to his will. Then he noticed the fine heaviness of the deep blue robe worn by the messenger, the elegant white tunic beneath, and the golden clasp about the collar, and the sandals made of soft leather that caressed his feet, and the strong limbs, and slender hands, and the pure gold of his scented hair, and the pale smoothness of his boyish face, and the well-proportioned nose, and the gently sensual mouth, the gracefully arching brows, and the cool blue eyes that penetrated him to the core.

"Well, I'm alone now," said the King. "Will you speak to me?"

The messenger made no effort to reply.

"If you think we are overheard, there's no way I can convince you otherwise. It's possible anywhere."

The messenger was silent.

"With everyone gone, I feel less impatient. But it can't last forever. How fast it's running out is difficult to say. Yours, of course, is exemplary. But then you must be enjoying all this! Are you satisfied to have undermined our formalities?"

The King fell silent again and let his eyes dwell on all the details of the messenger and his attire.

"I see no fear in your eyes. Is it because you are untroubled by all the commotion you have caused? Or is it because you don't feel anything at all? What a waste, that one so beautiful should not feel. Or is it that you are naturally without fear? Perhaps therein lies the secret of your nobility."

The messenger remained silent.

"I fear," said the King. "Not you. You pose no threat. Nor any man. But I fear myself. I fear the deeds of which I am capable. My Ministers send my soldiers to conquer new lands, all for me – and for them too, of course. The richer I am, the richer they are. But I let it happen. I grow powerful and rich without lifting a finger. Think what I might achieve if I raise my hand!" The King smiled. "Will you speak to me?" he asked quietly.

The messenger said nothing.

"I could have you killed," said the King. "Then what would you have gained? Perhaps that's what you want. How can I know if you won't tell me? But you could reasonably argue that if you asked me, I wouldn't do it. Life is funny like that – and so are kings. But I think you're not disposed to argue about anything!

"You're strong, but you look weak – or perhaps it is that you look gentle. The gentle are often confused with the weak. I wonder if you think me weak? I wonder if you confuse my patience with weakness? But my patience is running out. There isn't much left. I think you should speak to me before it's too late. We have conceded to you to the point of division amongst ourselves and, in the eyes of all, to the point of absurdity. The time has come for you to justify it."

The messenger remained unmoved and as silent as before. The King stood up and descended the steps before the throne. The hall had begun to grow dim and he summoned five footmen to light thirty torches set against the walls. While they did so, the King began to pace about, gazing at the floor and glancing at the messenger.

"Get out," he bellowed to the footmen as soon as he saw that the torches were lit. The great doors crashed behind them with a resounding echo that filled the hall.

"I must be mad," shouted the King to the messenger. "Everyone around me sees what fools you've made of us, and of me in particular. I should have listened to my Ministers. Avaricious as they are, scheming, ruthless, obsequious when necessary, they aren't my Ministers for nothing. I can't blame you because I've done it all myself. But I *do* blame you because I'm the King and I can do what I like."

The messenger turned and looked with the same impassive stare and the King gazed back with fascination.

"Look at you! I could run you through with a sword, or shout for my guards to hack you pieces, and you wouldn't stand a chance," he said, incredulously. "But I don't, and I don't know why. You stared like that at the guard who drew his sword on you. What is it that we see when we look on you and find ourselves defenceless? Speak, damn you, speak!"

The messenger continued to gaze at the King.

"What's so special about you, that you're heralded by minstrels? Why do we waive our every formality and greet you with banners? Do you cast the same spell wherever you go? Is it some clever trick that makes us all so weak before you? My jester seemed to afford you more respect than anyone. Are you a jester, too? How long are you going to stand there, just looking?"

Still the messenger was silent.

"It is said that the minstrel sang of your coming from the north. We don't yet know what lies beyond the ice-capped mountains but my Ministers have it in mind to find out. Is that where you're from? Do you come to warn us against the attempt? You're not exactly winning us over! What can you hope to achieve by rooting yourself to the middle of our Court and refusing to speak? Is it a silent protest? If I walk away and leave, will you still be here when I return, mute as the stones on which you stand?"

The King fell silent for a few moments and walked slowly along the hall towards the great doors. Then he turned and spoke again.

"There! You're nearer to the throne than I. Why don't you sit down? Go on. See how it feels to be a King!"

The messenger made no move but remained with his back to where the King now stood.

"What more could I offer you? And what greater insult could you offer me by not accepting?" The King paused. "It's true that I'm mocking you, of course. But it doesn't much matter which way you respond. You've won your game, so you might as well sit down. It's only a formality."

The King laughed nervously and walked back to the foot of the steps before the throne. As he turned to face the messenger, he trembled uncontrollably.

"Speak, or go," he suddenly bellowed. "Haven't you seen enough? Go! Go! Get out!" he ranted and lurched towards the messenger. But abruptly he stopped short, choking on his words, which dwindled to a whisper.

"Why are you here?" he breathed, almost pleading for an answer as the trembling overwhelmed him and he clutched at the figure to save himself from stumbling to the floor.

The ever-deepening silence was his only reply. The King staggered and gradually regained his composure.

"What can I do?" he said quietly. "We've come to this and your mockery is complete. The Court will never be the same again – at least the King will never be the same in the eyes of the Court. It's you, not I, who achieves things without so much as lifting a finger."

The King ascended slowly to the throne and sat down. The Great Hall glowed with the flickering light of torches as he stared at the messenger and became conscious of the low howling of the night wind. The cold dark stone loomed everywhere about them and shadows flickered upon the floor as the moments slipped by.

"You didn't come for nothing. I'll wait," said the King, in a low voice.

The shadows continued to flicker, the wind to howl, and the trickle of golden moments gradually widened its source to flow gently and swiftly throughout the night. The King sat and watched, and waited, and listened. The messenger stood silently gazing, the cloak trailing from his shoulders like dusk on the horizon. But the night found no place for words.

As the first rays of dawn filtered through high windows, the King stood and slowly drew his sword from its sheath. With a look half-distracted and half-pitying, he approached the messenger.

"What a silence. And I can't turn back," he said quietly. "It's you who makes me do this. I have no choice."

Stooping down, he placed his sword on the ground between them. Then he stood and gazed at the youth in silence. Their eyes locked and something more profound than words passed between them. Slowly, the messenger turned, gathered his cloak about him, and walked from the hall, out of the castle and away from the city.

★

The King looked distracted and tore his gaze from the emptiness of the Great Hall below.

"What was that?" he asked, turning to Dal, who was sitting beside him on the cold step.

"What happened in the Spring?" Dal repeated.

The King sighed.

"Nothing happened," he said slowly. "He only came because there was nothing to be said. He had only to be here." The King hesitated. "They think me weak, Dal. Will you come with me when I leave tonight? It's all arranged for when I reassemble the Court."

"When?" Dal asked with surprise.

"Early this evening, while my Ministers are arguing and waiting for me here. Did you ever know a King who arranged his own exile?"

"Nor one who ended it, accompanied by his jester," Dal grinned. "But where?"

The King smiled and pointed a finger.

"North!" he whispered.

LACRIMAE

All he knew – all he had ever known – was blackness. It enclosed him completely, stroking and caressing him with its deep smooth emptiness. Perhaps the only reason he had been able to perceive it was that by solitary contrast he had a vague and distant awareness of himself. Thus he knew he existed within the blackness. Then, he knew not how, he had begun to move. But free as he was to do so, never had he discovered anything that shared his apparently vast prison. In black emptiness he simply was.

And so he remained in his solitude until a new awareness dawned. It came very slowly from a source he could not determine. It began as a misty point of light, its proximity difficult to define, its behaviour erratic. Gradually it grew, emerging slowly from the surrounding haze. Then he perceived a dissolving endlessness of colours, seething and pulsating, before the first shapes appeared. The shapes, volatile and graceful, moved and paused with an independent harmony. Then the light began to recede as the mist gathered about it once more and it faded from his view. In black emptiness he watched.

He was haunted by strangeness, conscious of a feeling he had never before known. Thick blackness cradled him, brushing lightly, lapping gently, heavier, encroaching, stifling. Then the light came back – not emerging slowly as it once had, but simply there, bright, colourful, moving. Again he watched as the shapes within it mingled in elegant patterns, endlessly changing, fascinating him with their strangeness. He wondered how they would appear if the dissolving colours around them became static and cast only a single hue upon them. And even as he wondered, it happened. Still the figures moved, casting myriad reflections, but now they were tinted by only a single vein of colour. His fascination grew. He wondered about a different shade of colour and again the vision changed. Then he imagined a static pattern into which the moving shapes might arrange themselves. And so they did. Then he visualised the light receding once more and so terminated his vision. In black emptiness he wondered.

The vast blackness flowed around him with oppressive intimacy. Then he visualised the light – something within made him do so – and there it shone. Endlessly he watched it and toyed with it. Then he banished it. Again he summoned it. Again he banished it. Its source remained a mystery. But he controlled it, and thus he knew it was within himself. Yet still it was a mystery. And as he wondered how it had come into being within himself, it returned. Within the blackness in which he moved, there was within himself, a radiant illumination. He alone, imprisoned in blackness, imprisoned the light. He alone, imprisoned in endlessness, imprisoned endlessness. He alone stood between light and darkness and realised his aloneness. A rhythmic pulse sparked through him. In black emptiness he wept.

And as he wept, the outer blackness flared before him. Tears streaked into the emptiness, sparkling and falling endlessly. Their blinding lights darted, flashed, collided, shattered and plunged chaotically into the vastness. All around they flared and receded as they fell from him, curving and rotating in clusters, suffusing the blackness with a jewelled symmetry born of the vision he had seen within. Everywhere the lights shone brilliantly as they circled and rotated about him. Only then did he understand that they were the first objects to enter the blackness and that prior to their existence he had been the only occupant of the infinite prison. The vision still within him, he continued to gaze at the lights now suspended in the outer vastness. Everywhere he looked they were fully illumined. Not a single shadow eclipsed any part of them as he watched and moved amongst them. At last he was beginning to understand himself.

STARS AND CRYSTALS

For the Child within us all

It was Christmas Eve and Simon wrapped his dressing-gown tightly around him as he crept to the window where he scratched the crystals of ice from the inside of the panes to make a hole big enough to peer out into the garden below. The garden was dusted with a sheen of heavy frost that didn't quite qualify as snow. The giant apple tree right outside his window barely stirred in its sleep and in the vast still sky the stars merely twinkled and conveyed nothing of whether Santa Claus was yet to be seen speeding on his way to the excited child.

Simon looked back to the stocking hanging limply from the chair at the foot of his bed and hoped so much to see it bulging with parcels of every shape and colour – and especially to see the three balloons that Santa always left fastened to the top as his special finishing touch to Simon's Christmas treat.

He crammed his numbed fingertips into his mouth and, turning back to the window, exhaled his warm breath on them. The window became misted and he rubbed his pyjama sleeve over the small space so that he could see out again. Simon looked out at the glazed garden with its icicle flowers and sparkling lawn, a magical realm strewn with crystals, which seemed to float before him. Perhaps Santa Claus was hiding behind that big cloud that drifted slowly towards the bright moon. He watched it move closer as its small tentacles reached across the moonlight, throwing irregular shadows onto the frosted treetops and the sparkling lawn beneath. Strange patterns ran up and down the hedges, washing over the garden before the large cloud blotted out the light altogether.

After a minute or more of complete darkness, the cloud

moved away and the full strength of the moon beamed down again. Simon's eyes widened with excitement as he pressed his face hard against the tiny frosted aperture to confirm what he thought he'd seen. Yes, it was Santa Claus himself! He was standing in the garden below, just beneath the apple tree. Simon's heart beat so fast that he didn't know what to do. At last Santa had come to this very house. He must have descended from the cloud. Simon thought he should hurry back to bed and pretend to be asleep because he'd heard it said that Santa didn't leave presents for children who were still awake. But he so wanted to see Santa for himself and so just to be sure he wasn't dreaming, he rubbed his eyes and looked again. It wasn't a dream. Santa really was out there in the frost and ice – a tall, white-haired, kindly man, standing under the tree and looking straight up at that very window.

Simon couldn't think what to do, so he just stared – but he also knew that something wasn't right. There stood Santa in his long red coat and white beard – which was somewhat smaller than Simon expected – but there was no sack of presents. Perhaps, Simon thought, he had left it with his sleigh. He pressed his face even closer to the window and then, to his surprise and delight, the figure outside raised a hand and waved to him. For a moment he was transfixed. If Santa knew he wasn't asleep, then surely he wouldn't bring him any presents. But the wave became a gesture, beckoning to him to go down into the garden, and it was accompanied by the friendliest smile Simon had ever seen. It was so friendly that no doubt could possibly remain that this was Santa himself. Simon hesitated only a moment before he signalled back and hurried to find his shoes and overcoat in the wardrobe by his bed. Quickly he pulled on his socks, tied his shoelaces and, without removing his dressing-gown, huddled into the thick winter overcoat his mother had bought him only a few days before. Then he hurried back to the window to see if Santa was still there. He tapped a few times on the pane and the figure, still smiling, looked up.

Getting out of the house was something Simon hadn't even thought about until that moment. This was only the second time he'd come with his parents to spend Christmas with his Grandmother. He loved her very much and was delighted when he'd been told they were going to visit her for the second year running. Her big house in the country was the perfect setting for a family Christmas but now he had to remember what he could of its layout. The room he'd been given was at the rear of the house and he now recalled the narrow back stairway behind the servants' quarters just down the corridor. At the bottom was a door that let into the back yard and he prayed that it wouldn't be locked. He crept to his bedroom door and turned the handle slowly. Every little creak seemed to sound like a drum. Once outside his door, he tiptoed along the wooden corridor towards the stone steps that led down to the back yard. The door at the top of the steps was shut and a thin band of light glowed beneath it. As he approached it, he remembered that the curving stairs led past the servants' common room, then down another flight to a stone-floored reception hall, off which were the scullery, the pantry, a store room, an enormous cupboard – big enough, he'd always thought, to get lost in – and the main kitchen.

In the opposite direction from where he now stood on the landing, he saw the door that led to another spare bedroom – currently occupied by his Cousin Sarah, who always took the opportunity to make fun of him because he was the youngest and smallest – and the corridor leading off to the main front portion of the house where Granny slept and all the other adults who had assembled for Christmas.

A sudden guffaw of laughter from downstairs indicated that Uncle Bartholomew was still at the rum bottle, as he had been when Simon was packed off to bed, and it determined him to act swiftly. Instantly he turned back to the narrow stairway, slipped noiselessly through the door and sped, light-footed like a cat, down the stone steps to the first landing. His heart was beating faster now, not because he didn't think he'd reach his goal, but in case Santa Claus wouldn't still be waiting.

Just as he reached the servants' common room, the door burst open and Annie the cook came bustling out with a chuckle and plodded off down the stairs in front of him. Simon pressed back against the wall just a few feet above her. Of all the servants, she was the one least likely to give him away but even she wouldn't approve of his going out into the garden on such a freezing night when he should be in bed.

She turned the bend in the stairs and disappeared from sight below him. She had left the common room door wide open and Simon could hear others inside reminiscing about previous Christmases amid occasional laughs and a clinking of glasses. Guessing that Annie was likely to return, Simon had to decide quickly whether to continue down the next flight and take the chance of meeting her, or go back to his room. Risky as it was, he chose to go on. The stone stairs made stealth so much easier than the creaking boards in other parts of the house and in an instant Simon darted past the open door, leaping down several steps at a time with the aid of the banister rail and reached the hall below.

Annie was scurrying about in the kitchen humming to herself. Simon thought it dangerous to try opening the heavy door into the yard while Annie was still in the kitchen, so he hid in the only obvious place – and once inside the big cupboard he hoped he wouldn't really get lost among so many coats and jackets, each with its own distinctive odour. No sooner had he concealed himself than he heard the big outside door fly open and crash heavily against the wall. The voice that followed was all too recognisable and Simon pulled the coats closer about him.

"What ye doin' there, young Annie?" came the drunken bellow of Jack, the stable hand.

Simon feared him most of all the servants as he remembered how the previous Christmas he'd threatened to lock Simon in the stables unless he agreed to steal a bottle of brandy from Granny's sideboard. Had his agility not proved superior to Jack's drunken sluggishness, doubtless that's where Simon would have found himself for the better part of Christmas Eve, or at least until such time as his parents organised a search.

"You drunk again?" Annie chided. "It'll be the death o' ye."

"Ne'er mind that, girl. What's cookin'?"

"Nothin'. You missed yer dinner. There's some bread an' cheese there, if you want it."

"It's you I want," Jack slurred with a laugh.

Simon heard them scuffling just a few feet away and peered out through a slit in the cupboard door.

"If yer touch me again, yer'll get the feel o' this," Annie answered firmly as she brandished a rolling pin and made to go back upstairs. "Where you been, anyway?" she asked as she turned away.

"Just out! Makin' sure no-one's a doin' what they didn't ought. Is that Master Simon in 'is bed?"

"I'm sure 'e is, bless 'im. What's it to you?" Annie asked, protectively. "Now don't you go gettin' at that boy."

"Thought I saw somethin' at 'is window, that's all. Maybe you better 'ave a look," Jack suggested.

"E's all right. You leave 'im alone. Now go an' eat. We'll be up early in the mornin'."

Jack grumbled and shuffled around the kitchen as Annie started off up the stairs.

"An' don't 'e forget to lock up, Jack," she called back as she disappeared round the corner.

Simon didn't dare move for what seemed like an age as he waited and listened to hear what Jack was doing. After a lot of shuffling, a clatter of cutlery and some mumbled cursing, all was still. From the rough dank coats, Simon emerged slowly and looked cautiously about. The sound of heavy breathing reached his ears, then a loud snort followed by snoring. Simon peered round the kitchen door. To his relief, Jack was already asleep in his chair, still in his overcoat, sprawled across the table with his sleeve in a pool of Annie's homemade chutney that spilled from an upturned pot.

In a flash Simon had gone. The door to the yard was unlocked and since it looked as though Jack would be asleep for some while, he had no fears about getting back in later. Once outside, the cold air washed over him and he pulled at his overcoat to keep warm. The thick frost was now more like a thin covering of snow as he hurried through the gate that led into the large garden behind the house. A dim light lit a window on the first floor and there was another right at the top of the house. Against the brightness of the moon, which kept disappearing and reappearing behind the clouds, these house lights appeared insignificant. Simon saw the big apple tree that reached up just beneath his own window and quickly made off towards it. As he rounded the corner, standing there, just as he'd seen him before, was the tall white-haired old man with his small white beard and friendly smile.

At first the figure seemed not to notice Simon's approach and yet it was as if he knew of it anyway. Then he glanced at the boy and without any other gesture, turned away and began to walk off down the garden. Simon hadn't known quite what to expect when he came face to face with Santa Claus and the absence of some friendly greeting unnerved him a little. He hesitated, unsure whether to follow. After a few paces, as if sensing Simon's uncertainty, the old man stopped and turning round to look at the boy, he lifted a finger to his lips in a gesture of secrecy. Then his face literally beamed – almost, Simon thought, like the moon itself – and he appeared quite noiselessly to laugh as if the two of them were sharing some exciting and hilarious prank. Simon found the old man's gestures a delight and when he beckoned a second time, he followed without a qualm.

Treading delicately through the fine snow they set off, an awesome sight that might have come alive from a storybook: Santa leading the way in his long red coat, white-trimmed with the hood thrown back, passing through a silvery sparkling enchanted land, followed close behind by a little boy with ruffled blond hair falling over sleepy eyes, so fearless and full of wonder that every now and then he would skip a step or two and quickly have to save himself from falling flat in the snow. Simon thought of asking his new friend whether in fact he was Santa Claus but the question seemed too silly. It was Christmas Eve. Of course he was Santa Claus. But where was his sack of toys? Perhaps he really should ask – but he didn't. Maybe if Santa had spoken to him first then he might have questioned it. But he was so happy that he began to think of other things, such as where they might be going.

Santa seemed to sense his small friend's happiness and every now and again would look back over his shoulder with a beaming smile. They passed in this fashion over a little wooden bridge – made of only a few unguarded planks, on which Simon was particularly careful about keeping his balance – taking them to the other side of the stream that trickled out to the fields beyond the hedge at the end of the garden. They passed a number of tall shrubs, so dense that they blotted out the light, then past the old garden shed and right across the middle of the vegetable patch.

Over this last stretch, the ground was hard and uneven and Simon kept stumbling as he tried to keep up with Santa. He took his time so that he was sure of his footing but was suddenly plunged into darkness when, as if puffed out by a giant, the moonlight vanished behind a thick cloud. Coming almost to a standstill, he glanced up to make sure that Santa was still ahead of him, but the sight that greeted him turned him cold with terror. He froze, rooted to the spot. He tried to scream but no sound came. Looming over him were two leering eyes gazing out from a grotesquely disfigured face. Long arms in a tattered black cloak stretched out on either side as they threatened to lunge at him and carry him off into the night. The face grinned at him hideously. Santa was nowhere to be seen and Simon was alone with his terror. His feet lost their grip and his knees collapsed under him. The hard earth rushed towards him as he fell and the last thing he saw was the looming black shape towering above him. His head swam and all was darkness as if he had been enveloped deep in the black-cloaked embrace of the hideous creature.

Not daring to move, he cowered on the ground. It was slippery and his hands were numb. Just where he lay, a thick wooden stake was sticking into the hard earth. He grabbed it to pull himself up. Then he froze again sensing the hideous creature directly above him. In one brave movement, with all his strength, he thrust himself to his feet. His heart was pounding as he leapt back from the thing and darted swiftly away towards the house. But as he did so, his steps faltered and he forced himself to stop. In that moment the moon had beamed down again. Bracing himself, he turned to face the figure. The first thing he saw was Santa Claus waiting at the far corner of the vegetable patch. In between them stood the looming black monster with the leering expressionless eyes, known affectionately to all as Scraggy the Scarecrow. Simon sighed with relief and even though his fear was waning, he gave a wide berth to the harmless old guardian of the cabbages.

As he caught up with Santa the old man smiled reassuringly and pointed to a small gate. The clouds had cleared and everything was bathed in moonlight once again. The gate led out into a field beyond the garden. As they approached, Simon made a move to go on ahead and open it. Had he reached it in time, he would have held it open for Santa but, to his astonishment, the old man seemed to walk straight through it. Simon wasn't at all sure of what he'd just seen and when he reached the gate himself, he found it as real and solid a gate as any he'd ever known, with the latch firmly fastened. He decided there and then that he must have been dreaming. Once in the field, the old man led him just a few more yards before finally stopping at the edge of the stream they had already crossed by the little bridge in the garden. Here, where the stream was wider, he waited for Simon, who wondered if this was where Santa had left his sack of presents – but still none was to be seen.

The stream flowed smoothly at this particular point as it

rushed towards a steep decline that took it sharply away from view. Santa stooped over it, beckoning to Simon to do the same. The moon seemed to float on the water and the great shining orb, in its undisturbed solitude, infused it with its own sparkling light. Simon watched as the water flowed through the crisp white night and, just for a second, he thought he saw something move within it. He glanced up at the old man who simply pointed to the stream again. When Simon looked back at the water he saw a picture forming and as he fixed his gaze upon it, it came gradually into focus. Although the moon illuminated the water, the scene within it had a light of its own. Before him, in the smooth-flowing stream, was a summer landscape as vivid and detailed as reality. It contrasted sharply with his winter surroundings, as though he were looking through time into another world. He could see a hill with trees and grass, flowers, blue sky and birds, and even the butterflies that fluttered from leaf to blossom over an undulating pastoral land of complete serenity. Santa Claus looked at Simon and smiled. Simon smiled back.

"Where is that?" he asked, and the sound of his voice pierced the night air with unexpected melody.

The old man answered with another gesture towards the summer scene where now Simon saw his own reflection superimposed upon it. He wondered why he hadn't noticed it before and shifted a little to see it more clearly. But as he moved, his image remained still. Then to his even greater surprise, his reflection began to move with a purpose of its own. He saw himself within the summer scene and watched as he ran over the brow of the hill and out of sight.

The vision faded for only a second and was soon replaced with another. Now Simon saw himself sitting beneath a tree. His knee was drawn up and on it rested a large pad on which he was intently sketching. Try as he might, he couldn't see what he was drawing. All he could see was the pastoral setting and his own intense concentration on what he was doing. Then as quickly as it had appeared, this vision also vanished and all he saw was the moon and the rushing water that sparkled as it swirled away towards the sharp decline beyond. Simon looked up and suddenly felt cold. He was alone. Santa Claus had gone. He pulled his overcoat closely around him as he remained crouching beside the stream. It was the middle of the night and he knew he must get back to his room. Somewhere in the distance a church clock chimed twelve – it was Christmas Day.

Simon hurried back towards the garden as tiredness possessed him. When he reached the little gate between the garden and the field, he had a strange sensation of gliding beyond it without stopping to lift the latch – almost as if he'd passed right through it – but he was so sleepy that he really couldn't tell. Whether or not drunken Jack was still snoring into Annie's homemade chutney, Simon never knew, but there were certainly no unexpected hazards to rudely awaken the small lone figure as he made his way – almost as if someone were guiding him by the hand – back to his bedroom. Sleepy and unremembering, he threw his clothes on the floor, clambered into his big feather bed and snuggled down to the warmest, longest and most peaceful sleep he'd ever known on any Christmas night.

The sun was up long before Simon and it was only by persistently peeping in and out from behind the fast-moving clouds that eventually it succeeded in rousing from slumber the small figure sprawled carelessly across the big soft bed. Simon moved his head from one side to the other and stretched himself beneath the heavy gold-patterned eiderdown. Summoning the strength to open one eye, his view was filled almost entirely by an enormous blue balloon. For the first time in his life he had forgotten it was Christmas. He opened the other eye and yellow and red balloons completed the picture. Suddenly he was wide awake, the sun filling his room, melting the frost on the windows so that it ran in long twisting rivulets down the panes. Leaping up, he crawled down the bed to a fat stocking crammed with gifts. He hauled the stocking onto the bed and dragged it to his side as he got back under the covers. Detaching the three balloons, he gave them a gentle tap, propelling them into the air and back to the foot of the bed.

One by one he pulled out the parcels, shaking them to hear if they rattled, squeezing them to feel how soft they were, weighing them in his hand and turning them at all angles to try to guess the contents. Coloured paper of every shade and pattern adorned the mounting pile of presents as he pulled them all out onto the bed before giving in to the temptation to open any. When they all lay before him, he savoured the moment of choosing which one to open first. Of all the different patterned papers, only one gift was wrapped in paper with pictures of Santa Claus. That one, he decided, was special and should be left until last. In no time at all the wrappings were falling away and the floor around his bed became a rustling, rainbow sea of paper and glittering ribbon.

Outside his door and all along the passage he could hear more and more activity as the household sprang to life. Cousin Sarah came running from her room, passing his door as she excitedly showed some presents to one of the busy but willingly responsive maids who was attending to some last-minute decorations at the top of the servants' stairs. Others came and went with trays of tea and cutlery for the breakfast table and everyone greeted everyone with cries of "Merry Christmas! Merry Christmas!"

As the excited cries filled the house, Simon sat in his bed rummaging through the wrapping paper to make sure nothing had been overlooked. Then he came to the gift with Santa's picture on it. He didn't know quite why he'd decided it was special. Perhaps because it was the only one of its kind – and that was reason enough. The parcel was wide and tall and flat with a lumpy bit at one side. Simon shook it. It rattled a little and was slightly bendy. Then curiosity got the better of him and all those smiling faces of Santa fell to the floor, wreathed in the rainbow sea. His first reaction was one of puzzlement. The big flat bendy thing was, of course, a drawing pad – and it was very big, just like a real artist would use. So he made an easy guess at the bulky object wrapped separately inside. Yes, it was a box of pencils, paints and brushes. The box itself made him gaze in wonder. It was made of the finest polished mahogany and like nothing he'd ever seen. These were not on his list to Santa Claus but he was instantly excited by them, perhaps because they were so unexpected, and straight away he decided that this was the best of all his presents. At that moment there was a tap at his door and Annie's friendly face appeared.

"Oh, you're awake then Master Simon, are yer?" she greeted him as she came in. "And a very merry Christmas to yer, m'dear," she said fondly, taking hold of his head gently between her hands and kissing his brow.

"And a very happy Christmas to you Annie – the very best Christmas you've ever had," he responded in his happiness.

"Bless you, m'dear. Thank you," she said as she saw all the wrapping paper lying about and the mound of presents he had received. "Looks like you been a very lucky young man, Master Simon," she beamed. "Anyway, it's ha' past eight, yer know. Time you was up an' about," she added as she went over to the window and straightened the curtains. "Young Sarah's been runnin' around for an hour already."

"Annie?" Simon asked.

"Yes, m'dear."

"What did you get for Christmas?"

"Oh, yer don't get presents at my age. Christmas is for you youngsters."

"You must have got something."

"Yes. I made m'self some special cakes just for the occasion."

"That's not right. Someone should give you something."

"Now don't you go worryin' yerself about that, young Simon. Your Granny sees to it that we 'ave all we want – and especially so at Christmas. Now it's time you got up and got ready for yer breakfast. Yer Granny'll be wanting to say Happy Christmas to you 'erself. She'll be wonderin' where you got to. Now come on, I'll tidy up this mess an' then I'll fetch you some water."

Annie bustled around to the far side of the bed and began to pick up the Christmas wrappings.

"Goodness me!" she suddenly exclaimed. "Fancy leavin' yer clothes all over the floor like that, Master Simon."

She picked up his overcoat and dressing gown. "What'd yer mother say to that? An' just look at these shoes – they're soppy wet. How'd yer get 'em like that?"

Suddenly he remembered his dream of the night before. But no, it wasn't a dream. Or was it? He recalled a vague impression of being in the garden at night... and by a stream... and meeting Santa Claus. But as he looked at the wet and muddy shoes that Annie held out before him, his memory snapped sharply into focus. He *had* been out the night before. Santa had waited for him under the apple tree. Then he remembered the scarecrow – and going through the gate that led into the field.

Annie looked perplexed and more than a little suspicious as if she was expecting some kind of explanation.

"Well..." Simon began. Then a thought occurred to him. "Annie, where's Jack?"

"What's that got to do wi' these?" Annie half smiled as she held out his shoes. "What you been up to, Master Simon?" she asked, partly in fun and partly out of concern.

"It's a secret. Promise not to tell, if I tell you?" And without waiting for the promise, Simon concocted a story about planning a surprise for his parents that necessitated his making a brief excursion into the back yard earlier that morning.

"Ah, so yer 'ave been out already, 'ave yer?" Annie said with a smile. "I thought it was odd for a youngster like you not to be up early on Christmas morning. Now don't you worry yerself. I won't tell anyone."

"I thought I might see Jack about when I was out, but I didn't. Where is he?" Simon asked again.

"Still abed, I don't doubt. 'E came in last night wi' far too much drink in 'im. Not the first time," she mused. "A real rogue, that'n. An' what's more 'e spent half the night sprawled over kitchen table an' wasted a jar o' my best pickle. Anyway, no good standin' 'ere gossipin' about the likes of 'im. I'll get these dried and cleaned and fetch yer water, then you can get on down to breakfast."

Left alone with the knowledge that the previous night's experience was a fact and not a dream, Simon thought more about the parts he could remember. One thing he recalled vividly was Jack's drunken entry and his view of him asleep with his sleeve in Annie's chutney. And if that was a fact, as Annie had confirmed, then surely everything else must also be true. He went to the window and looked down to where he'd first seen Santa Claus beneath the apple tree. Just then Annie returned with a large jug of steaming water, which she poured into a basin.

"There yer are, Master Simon. You'd better hurry. They're all getting ready for breakfast." And with that, Annie left him to his thoughts.

"Well, if it isn't Master Simon – the late Master Simon, in fact," greeted the tediously ever-jovial Uncle Bartholomew, as Simon entered the room for breakfast. After his Christmas greetings to Granny and his parents, he seated himself in the only available chair which, unfortunately for him, was in between the uncle in question and Cousin Sarah.

"Well, babies need extra sleep," was Sarah's first uncharitable remark of the day.

"Now then, Sarah," remonstrated Aunt Mildred.

"Oh, leave her alone," chimed in Uncle Bartholomew. "She's only having some fun. Isn't she old chap?" he added, turning on Simon and confirming by the smell of his breath that he'd already been at the rum – a fact known, but never mentioned, by everyone.

As the two maids flitted about removing and replacing various pots and dishes, Simon studied the faces around the table. His father and mother sat together and were too familiar for him to note more than their mere presence. His Aunt Mildred was, as she'd have been the first to admit, "a bag of nerves" when she had to tolerate Bartholomew on festive occasions, while their daughter Sarah delighted in playing off one against the other and invariably had her own way at all times. All the others present were of a generation yet further removed. It was Granny that he loved best of all and whose stately and resolute refusal to be involved in the petty disagreements of those around her on these occasions impressed him profoundly. Apart from her, there was her slightly younger brother and his wife, neither of whom seemed to affect or encroach upon his child's world; and finally, Granny's sister, who was always kind to Simon but quite deaf and so willing to help in running things that she seldom seemed to be present.

Breakfast passed for the company of ten, peppered with the essence of Bartholomew's rum wit, the sarcasm of Cousin Sarah, glances of criticism and concern from his father and mother respectively and much anxious sighing from Aunt Mildred. If it hadn't been for the servants, and especially the thought of Annie with her homespun kindness and her homemade cakes, Christmas was in danger of proving a rather dull affair for Simon. But then he remembered his most exciting gift.

It was to Granny that he ran with his treasured polished wooden paint box and the big pad of special paper, bubbling with energy and enthusiasm as soon as breakfast was over. In the heavily draped lounge, he knelt on the thick carpet by her favourite chair. As Granny expressed her admiration for the exquisite paint box, Simon's mother looked quizzical as she and his father joined them. Then Granny picked up the thick pad of heavy paper and flicked through it in a cursory way.

"And did you do this?" she suddenly asked with great pride as she held the book open at a page near the front.

"What?" asked Simon with curiosity, knowing that he hadn't yet used the paints.

"This lovely picture of the trees and flowers," Granny answered.

Simon knelt up to see what she was referring to. A tingling sensation swept over him and he grew very confused. Once again, the dreamlike experiences of the previous night came flooding back to him. The picture that Granny was holding before him was identical to the pastoral vision he'd seen in the moonlit stream – the hill, the trees, the flowers, the blue sky, and even the butterflies.

"And who gave you that for Christmas, Simon?" his mother asked as she peered over to see the picture.

"Santa left it in my stocking."

"Really?" she said, glancing at her husband who was slowly shaking his head.

"Yes. It was the best present he brought me. Look," he added, holding out the box of paints.

"But you didn't do that picture, did you?" she continued with surprise.

Simon would have liked to have claimed it as his own but had to admit that he hadn't done it, which only left him wondering how it came to be there at all.

"No," he said at last. "It must have been in the book already."

"Well now, how could that be?" his mother queried.

Granny had turned her attention to some presents of her own while Simon's world spun in confusion. He so wanted to tell them where he'd seen the picture before but that would mean admitting that he'd been out the previous night. Then he thought of a way to do it by saying that it was all a dream he'd had. And so he told them the whole fantastic story. His mother and father listened intently and Granny put down the book she had only just taken up as Simon began to relate the night's adventures, inter-mittently emphasising – perhaps just a little too much – that it was all the most remarkable dream.

"But Simon, dear," interposed Granny suddenly, "you can't surely have been dreaming. You say you walked across the vegetable patch and you were frightened by old Scraggy," she laughed.

"Yes, that's true," Simon said earnestly.

"But last year when you came for Christmas we hadn't put Scraggy up there. He's only been there a few weeks. So how can you know about him unless you've actually been outside?" She was plainly intrigued and amused and her good nature bore no trace of reproof for any such action.

Simon felt himself blush at being caught out, although he valued the further confirmation that he really hadn't been dreaming. Now his only worry was the anger of his parents as the truth began to emerge. Already he noticed his father's accusing look and so he began to tell his story all over again, just as it had really happened, taking care not to involve Annie's complicity in drying and cleaning his shoes when more easily he had managed to hoodwink her.

As the story unfolded for the second time, Simon noticed sceptical looks give way to expressions of intrigue. Every now and then his mother would exchange a meaningful glance with Granny while Simon was asked for a third time to describe the exact appearance of Santa Claus, right down to his kindly eyes and his irrepressible smile.

"Well!" exclaimed Granny when it was all told again. "That's a very strange tale indeed. It's a wonder you didn't catch your death of cold out there in the middle of the night. What do you make of it, dear?" she added, turning to her daughter.

Simon's mother thought for a moment while he waited nervously for her response, anticipating the likelihood of a scolding, rather than any real interest in his adventure.

"I think you should show me where you went with Santa Claus. Will you do that, Simon?"

Relieved by her seemingly genuine interest, Simon readily agreed and sped off to his room to fetch his coat and another pair of shoes.

In the broad light of day, old Scraggy the Scarecrow looked as friendly and harmless as any crow would have liked, yet still Simon couldn't help but keep his distance. The latch on the little gate that led into the field was covered with ice, making it difficult to open, and when they reached the stream, the water was still flowing as fast as it had been the night before.

"This is where we came," Simon announced, unaware how concerned his mother was at the idea that her child had ventured not only into the garden but beyond it. "And that's where we saw the picture – in the water. The moon was shining too."

"And what did Santa say to you, Simon?"

"Nothing. He never said a word. But I wasn't frightened. He was ever so friendly and he was always smiling."

"Didn't you ask him where he was taking you?"

"No," Simon answered as if it was a pointless question.

His mother gazed around them in every direction as Simon stooped over the stream and began to prod with a stick at the glistening ice. He chipped away at it until some broke off and fell into the water. Ice crystals, sunlight and splashing water delighted him as they sparkled and reminded him of the moon and stars he'd seen there the night before. For a moment he saw his own reflection in the smooth-flowing water and smiled at himself. His smile was returned just like any ordinary reflection. Then he saw another smile. Beaming up at him from the stream was the face of his companion who had vanished so suddenly the previous night.

"Look!" Simon shouted. But his mother had walked away and when Simon looked back again, he saw only the smooth flow of the water as it rushed away out of sight.

"Well," said Granny, "and what did you discover?"

"Just an ordinary stream," said his mother with a note of scepticism.

"If I thought you were playing a trick on us, Simon, I'd know just how to deal with you," his father interrupted in a manner with which Simon was all too familiar.

"But what about this drawing in the book, dear," Mother countered. "You know Simon couldn't have done that. He's never been good at drawing or painting. Remember his school report at the end of last term?"

"Yes I do. Bottom of the class in most things – except inventing stories," his father said as he eyed Simon suspiciously.

"Well, his English is good. Isn't it Simon?" Mother placated.

"Well never mind all that. Poor Simon doesn't want to talk about schooling at a time like this," Granny intervened, coming to the rescue as she got out of her chair. "Now you just come along with me, Simon. I've got something to show you," she added with a secretive air.

Simon leapt up, only too willing to escape the uneasy atmosphere that invariably clung around his parents when they were together for any length of time.

"And you come along too, dear," Granny called back to her daughter as she reached the door. "I think there's something you've forgotten."

Simon was disappointed that his mother was to be in on the secret but excitedly followed Granny's careful steps as she led them through the main hall and up the big flight of stairs that branched in either direction half way up. Simon ran ahead and waited on the first landing until he knew which way Granny was leading them before running to the top stair where he sat and waited. Granny smiled at him and looked almost as excited as he was. As she reached the top stair, she took hold of his hand and led him towards her own room. Simon's mother entered behind them as Granny was rummaging in a drawer.

"Now it's in here somewhere," she muttered aloud. "Ah, yes! Now then, Simon, sit on the bed and close your eyes."

Simon readily obeyed as he heard her slow footsteps approach him.

"Now open your eyes."

Simon's jaw dropped and for a few seconds he was dumbfounded by the framed photograph that Granny held before him.

"But that's Santa Claus!" he exclaimed. "That's him. The old man in the garden last night. I saw him. You never said you knew him too."

Simon leapt off the bed and took the picture from Granny.

The white hair, the beard – too small for Santa Claus – the kindly eyes and the warm smile were all there, gazing at him like a long lost friend. As Simon went on exclaiming, Granny showed the picture to her daughter and then gave it back to Simon who ran with it out onto the landing.

"Well, dear, perhaps you were too young to remember just before your father died," Granny said, turning to Simon's mother. "Your brothers would remember him like that, being so much older than you – it's a pity they're not here this Christmas. Every year your father would go out into the garden and dress up as Santa Claus in a red coat that I made for him especially. Then he'd come in and creep around the house filling all the children's stockings. And just in case they were only pretending to be asleep, he'd always make sure he wore his red coat, so as to convince them that what they might see from under the covers really was Santa Claus." Granny laughed at the memory. "Your poor brother Arthur was so convinced, that he went on believing in Santa until he was twelve."

Simon's mother smiled but immediately looked puzzled. "But that means Simon actually saw his grandfather last night! He recognised the picture straight away."

"Well, why not?" Granny said with a fond smile. "I've often thought he's been around the place with me all these years since he went." She looked at her daughter. "He was a loving man, you know."

At that moment Simon returned with the photograph and a revelation deduced from a little reasoning of his own.

"This isn't Santa Claus. It's Grandad," he said bluntly.

Granny and Simon's mother looked at each other, then at him.

"Yes," Granny said at last.

"How did you know that, dear?" his mother asked.

"It says on the back 'Charles William Crofton'. Crofton is Granny's name too. Does that mean he's a ghost?"

Back in his room, Simon felt not only excited at having seen a ghost, but even more pleased with himself for having not been frightened by it. He decided this ghost was his friend and if all ghosts were like Grandad, then he rather liked them all. And now that he knew who the visitant was who led him on his adventure beyond the garden, he found it hard to forget the kindly face that never once startled or frightened him. He'd even forgiven Scraggy for being so inconsiderate. With the old man's face still very much in his mind – and which he'd seen twice again that morning, once in the photograph and once in the stream – Simon took up his drawing pad and paint box. First he sat back on his bed and looked at the picture that was already in the book and which he'd seen the night before in the flowing stream. Then he flipped the page and picked up a pencil. As the face hovered in his mind, he flicked the pencil back and forth, outlining and shading different areas. Fragments of scenery came into his imagination and he became totally absorbed in what he was doing. Suddenly the door opened and Annie came in.

"Oh, I'm sorry Master Simon. Didn't know you was 'ere. Thought I'd just look in an' open yer window for a while – but not t' worry, m'dear."

Simon looked up in surprise. A moment passed before he recognised the friendly cook.

"I just made some special cakes. Fresh out the oven they are. Would yer like me t' bring yer some?" As she said it, the smell of baking wafted in from the corridor and Simon was back to reality.

"Oh, yes please!" he said.

"Won't be a tick," replied Annie and was gone.

Simon looked at the drawing pad that lay before him with a new picture freshly done and his eyes widened with disbelief. For a long while he gazed at the landscape that presented itself but he only fully comprehended when he realised that he was still holding the pencil in his hand. A strange sense of serenity over-came him as he placed the pencil very gently on the table at the side of his bed. His parents were right when they said he'd never managed to create anything remotely intelligible in his art classes at junior school – but now it seemed there was no other way that the picture in front of him could have manifested, except by his own hand.

The door opened again and Annie presented him with a small plate of assorted homemade cakes. Simon tore the picture from the pad.

"And this is for you," he said gleefully. "Happy Christmas, dear Annie." He leapt from the bed and threw his arms around her, unable to make them reach at the far side. Annie was over-whelmed and Simon knew that this was the best Christmas he'd ever spent.

Christmas dinner was long past and the guests had sprawled themselves around the lounge to sleep off the effects – all except Cousin Sarah, who had gone off the play with her new toys. Uncle Bartholomew had thoughtfully dozed off within reach of the sideboard, where his dreams bestirred him sufficiently from time to time to reach out and top up his rum glass. Amid the sighing and snoring of the replete adult forms that littered the room and with the warm gentle crackle of the log fire and the soft ticking of the clock for company, Simon worked almost obliviously with his paints. He had found himself a secluded spot, lying safely out of sight on the thick-carpeted floor behind the big sofa that was arranged diagonally across a corner of the room. Never before had he derived such pleasure from using pencils and brushes. At half past four, as one of the maids tiptoed through the room to collect empty cups and glasses, Simon was putting the finishing touches to yet another picture – not just a drawing but a fully-coloured landscape with trees, horses and an old cart by a windmill. He looked at it thoughtfully and was as astonished as he was pleased.

There was a sudden lurching movement and a heavy sigh from the other side of the sofa behind which Simon was ensconced, as Aunt Mildred stood up and, without seeming to recognise anyone, shakily crossed the room and went out. Simon began another sketch. The interruption by his aunt seemed to be the cue for a collective stirring of bodies and, as his pencil skimmed over a fresh page, groans and yawns rose all around him. The twang of an armchair spring announced the revival of Uncle Bartholomew who immediately stood up and poured himself a drink, which he took with him as he left the room.

One by one, the adults, oblivious of Simon on the floor behind the sofa, peered drowsily at one another and tottered along to the dining room for tea. It was only after he'd heard the hall clock chime the quarter to six, that a voice echoed Simon's name. Paint splattered a new page, filling out pencilled lines, washing over denser areas, pin-pointing significant details, as another scene came to life before him. The clock struck six-thirty and Simon's name had been called twice more but he was too absorbed to care. Once or twice a maid had looked in from the doorway to see if he was there as new shapes and forms coalesced into yet another picture. Finally, Simon leant back against the wall behind the sofa and the pencil slipped from his tired hand. His eyelids grew heavy as the new picture blurred and refocused before him. He leant forward and tore the large sheet from the pad to place it with the others. The long sharp tearing sound pierced the silence just as Uncle Bartholomew came searching for him.

"So there you are, old man. What on earth are you doing down there?"

"Painting," Simon answered and wished that his uncle was sufficiently interested to ask if he could see the results.

"Oh, really? Well, they've been looking all over for you. You'd better go and see your ma, old chap, unless you want a walloping."

Simon picked up his paintings and walked through to the drawing room, where he could hear the general chatter of his elders. Granny greeted him immediately.

"And where have you been all this time?" she asked with a patient smile.

"Only painting," Simon answered.

"Well then, let's see what you've done, shall we?" Granny urged.

He was aware that his parents had said nothing and it was clear that he had been the subject of teatime conversation since all the adults seemed to be eyeing him with some curiosity as if they expected him to transform into a bat at a moment's notice. Even Cousin Sarah kept a respectful distance and refrained from any derisive comments. Ignoring all but Granny, he fumbled with several pages from his book as he laid them out on the floor in front of her chair. The old lady gasped.

"Goodness me! I knew it. I thought as much. It's your Grandad, sure enough."

There was a general commotion amongst the elders as they craned their necks to look at Simon's work. Since none of the pictures he'd painted was a portrait, he was baffled by Granny's exclamation.

"It's not Grandad," Simon answered. "They're just ordinary pictures."

A moment later, Annie was ushered into the room carrying a bundle of rolled up pictures under her arm. Granny asked her to spread them out and then she turned to Simon.

"Annie showed me the beautiful drawing you gave her today. Your Grandad was so fond of painting. All his life he wanted to have the time to devote to it so that he could develop his talents. It was only at the very last that he started to do anything – when he was very ill. In his last four weeks he painted four pictures. He was so pleased with them but so sad that he couldn't have done it when he was a young man. He said, if he'd painted those four pictures when he was young, he'd have been a famous artist by the time he was thirty. Pictures were always his great passion in life. Look at them," she said with a gesture.

Annie spread out the pictures on the floor. They were almost identical to four of the pictures that Simon had painted. There was a general flurry of excitement around the room and even the dullest senses were stirred as Simon knelt in the centre facing Granny. Amid the chatter and speculation that arose, he thought of the kindly old man dressed as Santa Claus. He knew that it was his mother and father who had filled his Christmas stocking and he knew it wasn't they who had placed his most treasured gift there. In a world of his own he thought of these things and wondered why he'd never before been able to draw or paint so well. Amid all the whispered excitement, Granny rested her head back in her chair and smiled contentedly as she looked at Simon and spoke.

"And he always used to say," she told him quietly. "If only I could give my children a real gift. Not just something that Santa brings in a sack – but a gift in the truest sense."

As Annie was busy gathering up the pictures from the floor, Simon got up, kissed Granny on the cheek, and slipped away to his room.

With his book and paint box under his arm, he flung open the door and couldn't help but exclaim aloud. He tossed the book onto the bed where it fell open at the page with the already completed picture of the scene he'd witnessed in the stream on Christmas Eve. Then he climbed onto the bed and took the book on his knee. A candle flickered nearby and he rubbed his tired eyes as he looked again at the picture – the hill, the trees, the flowers, the butterflies. But now there was something else. On the brow of the hill was a figure – an old man walking away and looking back over his shoulder. Simon moved it closer to the light. It was just as he had expected – the white hair, the beard that was too small for Santa Claus, and the friendly smile that he had come to know so well in less than a day.

"Thank you," Simon breathed. "And a happy, happy Christmas."

He reached out for his pencil and skimmed it across the next page. How easily it came to him now – the sureness of each line, the lightness of touch. Somehow he knew just how to realise the forms that he envisaged. His head filled with images and ideas for so many pictures that he wanted to paint and he was impatient for the morning in order to begin.

But tiredness was overwhelming him. He put the book gently aside, climbed from his bed and darted across to look out of the window. Night had fallen outside. The big apple tree reached up to his window and nothing stirred in the brightly moonlit garden. Gazing out, he shivered as he marvelled at his most treasured Christmas gift and looked at the empty space beneath the apple tree. The stars flickered and sparkled and crystals of frost had begun to form on the window panes.

ECHOES

The young pianist looked at his mutilated fingers. Each one was smashed, swollen and bloody. Ligaments were ripped, movement impossible and the pain excruciating. It was the first time he had found the courage to look at his hands since his captors had ejected him from their makeshift torture chamber. As he sat in the large bare room to which they had taken him, he wept with the knowledge that he would never play another note. He remembered his first recital and the enthusiasm of the reviews that had launched his career a mere two years ago. The echo of an étude hung fleetingly in his memory, instantly replaced by the crack of rifle shots from the firing squad in the castle courtyard outside, whining, rebounding and echoing to remind him of his fate. He remembered Natasha, the young woman he had first seen at his public debut, for whom he had privately chosen his encore. And he remembered how, three months later to the day, coincidence had brought them together, and how quickly they had fallen in love. Only a week ago she had fled from soldiers and been shot down just as he turned the corner to see her sprawl headlong at his feet. Instantly he had caught her up in his arms. In their shared agony, he convinced himself that he saw a glimmer of recognition in her eyes. A moment later she was dead and he arrested. Arrested for what? It didn't matter. His social background was reason enough. Militant ideologies were only ever concerned with their own power and self-interest and in tyrannising those they branded tyrants.

A scream echoed in the corridor outside. For a moment it was the scream of Natasha as she fell on the street corner. Then he was back to reality. A helpless woman was being dragged to await execution in the yard below. He wondered who it might be. Several of those rounded up for interrogation had familiar faces – faces he had seen in the streets of the small town before the sudden occupation. Another volley exploded from the firing squad, followed by long echoes and that momentary stillness that hung in the air before everyday sounds resumed. He looked at the bare walls of the large, wrecked and looted room that served as a temporary cell until they were ready for him in the courtyard below. He tried to imagine what warmth and joy might once have filled this room – a warmth and joy that had already earned their possessors a place in the queue for execution.

Cautiously he tried to get up from the rickety wooden chair he'd found in the room. His body was weak, aching with the pain of several beatings, and his hands felt as though they were on fire. The chair clattered to one side, filling the empty room with its echo as he finally managed to stand up and keep his balance. He froze for fear the noise would attract further malicious attentions. The echo seemed interminable as another sharp crack from the yard below enfolded echo upon echo. Doors banged in the corridor outside his room. A shout, something being smashed to the ground, another shot from the courtyard, each reverberation overlapping other echoes. Spent cartridges clattered to the ground, then another volley from the soldiers in the castle yard. His hearing was amplified, the echoes swamped him and he felt nauseous and cold. He tried to hug his arms across his chest. His fingers were growing numb but convulsed with pain if he accidentally touched something. He limped to the shuttered window of his room but could discern nothing in the courtyard below. The nausea overwhelmed him and he doubled over but was too weak even to retch. The echoes re-echoed through his whole being as he remained motionless, waiting for... relief? ... release? ... a miracle? He could not have said. His world was totally destroyed. He no longer cared for the loss of possessions or the destruction of his home. He had suffered more than he would ever have believed he could bear as they had slowly applied the pressure that cracked, then snapped, his fingers. They knew his profession and it gave them a special relish for their task. But what drained his will above all was the emptiness left by Natasha. In the full flowering of their love, imbued with the creativity and sense of beauty that each inspired in the other, to be wrenched apart and so ruthlessly destroyed was the most insupportable pain of all. He thought of the firing squad that awaited him and as he did so, another volley rang out, echoing endlessly. With the echo surged the nausea. He craved oblivion. He pictured himself standing before the firing squad about to be executed. He'd heard that they didn't bother to blindfold anyone. He saw a gun barrel pointed directly at him. Despite his longing for oblivion, he flinched involuntarily at the thought. Then all he saw was flame and all he heard was the echo. Then it occurred to him that he wouldn't hear the echo at all. All he would hear would be a sharp crack, a dry, dead report, cut off in mid-sound. The bullet would reach him and he'd be dead before the long echo had begun its elaborate reverberations from wall to wall, up, down and across the castle yard. He would hear nothing of that. For a few moments he was intrigued by that strange thought. Then he remembered holding Natasha at the moment of her death and wondered whether she had seen his face and heard his brief farewell.

The door of his room flew open with such force that the porcelain handle shattered against the wall. Two soldiers threw him across the room towards the corridor. He lost balance and hit the floor as they kicked him and shouted to him to get up. Pain possessed him completely. Stumbling along the corridor, they kicked and prodded him from behind until they reached a flight of stairs. A moment later he was trying to pick himself up from the landing below. Somehow he hadn't passed out during the fall but he did so as they kicked him down a second flight of stairs. He found himself in the castle yard, brutally thrown into a rough wooden hut with several other prisoners. The cold air roused him enough to feel his face, burning and swelling. He staggered and wanted to be sick. Shots rang out with their familiar echoes as he slowly began to perceive his new surroundings. The makeshift windowless hut contained the next consignment for the firing squad. People huddled together, groaning, sobbing and terrified as a door at one end of the cramped space opened and the next victim was randomly hauled out.

In the darkness of the hut the echoes were louder, punctuated by sudden glaring light as the door was flung open and uniformed arms grabbed whoever came closest to hand. Some hung back, avoiding the area close to the door as if somehow they would escape execution. Their fear was tangible and terror haunted their faces. Others were more resigned to their fate and stood in front as if to protect those behind them.

The door opened at the end of the hut and light poured in as two soldiers, shouting abuse, grabbed the next captive. Then the door slammed and they were plunged back into darkness. As many eyes refocused in the gloom, the riflemen despatched the woman who had been amongst them trembling with fear only a minute before. Out of the echo, a voice in the hut murmured, "They're doing it the slow way here. In the cities they're using gas." Light streamed in again as the speaker was dragged from the hut. The pianist caught a glimpse of many faces lit momentarily by the sun, so many possessed by fear. The stink of sweat and urine filled his nostrils as the door slammed shut. Fear was not his own overwhelming emotion. Instead it was anger and a numbing despair at decades of intolerance, manipulation and greed that had led so inevitably to such a place as this. What could there be to fear about oblivion? He welcomed it. Another echo resounded and light flooded the hut as a barely living captive was hauled out. He saw the face of the man who now stood between him and the door – an old man with kindly eyes and a noble head. The door slammed. A pause, then execution and a persistent echo. The pattern, indelibly printed in his mind, gained momentum in its repetition. The door opened and the kindly man stepped into the clutches of the soldiers. Darkness. Shots. Echoes. At last it was his turn.

Light blinded him. He stepped as best he could into the yard. They grabbed his arms and he was half-marched, half-dragged to the courtyard wall that towered above him. It was an ancient wall, mellowed with centuries of weathering into something of character and beauty. Now it was scarred and pocked with bullet holes as though it had itself been condemned to death. Fresh blood and other fluids were smeared all over it, glistening and running into the ground. Wet tracks lay all over the sandy earth where innumerable corpses had been dragged away for mass disposal. Two soldiers pushed him against the wall. One of them secured his ankles. No blindfold was offered. He glanced fleetingly at the sky and thought of Natasha. Quite involuntarily he shut his eyes so that he might see her more clearly. He preferred her to oblivion. The shots rang out.

The echo hung in the air and he saw three riflemen lower their guns. He stood there confounded. What had gone wrong? They had fired – but he had heard the echo. Suddenly the castle yard was full of people milling about, looking fearful and bewildered. It was like a dream. So many people were suddenly just there. Where had they come from? He stepped forward. But how could he with his ankles bound? Something was wrong and everything was different, so wonderfully different. He was shocked that it took him so long to realise that he had no pain in his hands, or anywhere in his body. His senses were turned upside-down. He looked at the ground in front of him, at his own body, mutilated and inanimate. Two soldiers rushed up and dragged it away by the ankles. He looked again at his hands and saw no cause for pain. He tried to wake himself from this strange dream but wondered why he should want to. A face in the crowd caught his attention, an old man with kindly eyes and a noble head. His was just one among many faces that were all now strangely familiar. Their bewilderment was the same as his own and as he watched them, they grew more real than he had ever known them. The soldiers carried on their task. Increasingly they looked more like apparitions, oblivious of so many crowding the courtyard. His senses and perceptions had sharpened as dream and reality changed places. The life he'd led seemed like a dream, a dream that had become a nightmare, but now he felt so wide awake. It was a sensation he hadn't known for years – not since his birth. In that moment he relinquished all grief. His thoughts were no longer confined to the mechanical and rational. Now they became insights and impressions of the subtlest nature. Now they were crystal clear. He asked himself why he was standing there. He had no reason to stay. He was free to go. He should have realised sooner, as soon as they fired at him and he heard the echo.

The echo of an étude swelled in his mind, together with the image of she for whom he had played it. At the same moment, the wall behind him became curiously insubstantial. Prompted by this memory, with the lightness of air and the swiftness of thought, he made to go in search. Surely Natasha, too, had found freedom from her pain? And then he saw her. The mound of corpses lay just beyond, spectral and grotesque. The soldiers threw his own lifeless body headlong towards the pile. It fell sprawling at her feet the moment she appeared. Instantly she stooped down and tried in vain to take it in her arms. But as he approached her, moving easily through the crowd, her own confusion evaporated and she looked up and saw him.

MOON PROPHECY

Dedicated to Dorthe Rosefalk whose art inspired it

She watched from the edge of the high forest. Far below, a rocky gorge led towards the plain. Beyond, distant mountains appeared grey and sombre as dark mists began to swirl about them. A glint of silver caught her attention from a nearby turn on the path that rose from the gorge. Her horse shifted its weight beneath her, the faint jingle of its bridle swallowed in the damp silence. Alert and still, her keen eyes scanned everything from within her finely-sculpted face that remained impassive beneath the burnished bronze helmet of her kind. Again her horse shifted restively and she pulled lightly on the rein. Obscured from the path by trees, she watched and waited. A drop of moisture from an overhanging branch anointed her and trickled across the ancient protective symbols etched upon her helmet. A moment later, a mounted, armed knight came fully into view. He rode slowly, not from exhaustion, but with grace and ease, unchallenging despite the lance he bore, and unsuspecting or unconcerned of attack. Beneath a gleaming silver helmet his complexion was gold. He looked, she thought, somewhat out of place, as if he belonged in another, far distant part of the world. His clothes were fine and rich, yet devoid of the gaudy colours that many noble houses adopted and enjoyed. He passed within a sword's length of her, his horse patiently following each slight curve of the path.

Sentient as always, she held her breath, while her mount was highly trained to seem almost invisible at such a moment. Her eyes exchanged defence for curiosity, following his every movement as he receded higher up the mountain path. She watched until he was almost beyond sight before cautiously edging off in the same direction, still under cover of the foliage.

His leisurely pace was disconcerting, almost inviting her to endanger herself by venturing closer than she normally might when tracking an intruder. Her guard was as much against her own impulse to rashness as it was against the stranger's sudden perception of her presence. At the first hint of dusk, she grew weary of the added vigilance that then became so necessary but shortly her patience was rewarded as the mysterious figure came to an abrupt halt and dismounted. His horse remained motionless and quiet. The knight ventured a short way on foot and, leaving the path, walked towards the thickest part of the forest. Instantly, she too dismounted, tethered her horse and stole swiftly closer. She saw him slip between the undergrowth as though he knew the ground intimately. A moment later she heard a voice and grew alarmed that someone else could be so close without her knowledge. A few brief steps in that direction and she understood at once.

She had always wondered about the ancient caves that let into the mountainside, reputedly used over the centuries by hermits. Once she and two companions had searched in some of them to discover whether they led to another aspect of the hillside but all the passages ended after only a short distance against walls of rock. Once she had come alone at a time of great danger to seek advice of the legendary hermits who were said to inhabit the caves but again she had found no one and left unrewarded. Never had she the slightest hint of any occupants, yet now it was as if the knight had been expected. The knight showed due deference to the one who greeted him, remaining at a short distance from the hermit who sat in isolation at the mouth of a cave.

"Why do you seek me?" she heard the hermit ask.

"I thank you for receiving me," the knight replied and cautiously added, "I come to ask what you have seen beyond this day?"

"Then you cannot have come without some suspicion of my answer," the hermit said.

"That is true."

"And if you suspect the worst, is it not strange that you arrived without haste or caution?" the old man asked.

"So it might appear, except that I had reason for such a display. The symbols of protection upon her helmet are well known to me, for they originate in the place from whence I've come. Had I used all swiftness, she might not herself have followed me but merely despatched an ally who might have failed to find me."

The knight turned slowly towards the foliage nearby, from where he knew he was observed.

"There are no enemies here," he announced. Ready to defend herself, she revealed her presence. "And that of which we speak is of great concern to you. Indeed, but for your courage and wisdom, there may be no hope. Please be with us."

Approaching further, she listened to what they had to say. The knight showed great concern, sadness and resignation. The hermit was calm and distracted. Then he addressed her.

"I was saddened that you did not find me when you came before. I spoke but you did not hear. Your heart was too heavy with fear and hatred." He smiled kindly.

"I believe I understand," she answered calmly and he nodded in recognition.

"And what of tomorrow?" the knight asked the hermit, who paused for a long while before answering.

"I see a death," he at last replied, slowly and sadly. "It is a death that means more deaths."

"Whose death?" the woman asked.

"Yours! But not you," he added reassuringly.

"Then it is true," the knight reflected with grave concern.

"Your worst fears I must confirm. At last it has happened. The neglect has been prolonged enough. It may be centuries before the world can be restored and healed," the hermit pronounced. Then he looked from the knight to the woman and observed them both in silence. "If there is to be any hope, each of you must place complete trust in the other."

Then the old man stood up and made a sign towards them.

His face seemed to glow, his hands also, and as they watched, his entire form dissolved into the air before them. Neither could move until he was completely gone. A sudden breeze stirred the trees around them and then all was still.

"Do you understand?" the knight asked as he turned to face her.

She searched his face, studied his expressions and found nothing to distrust.

"Some things. But not your worst fears," she replied.

They returned to their horses, meeting again on the path, where she signalled him to accompany her. After a short ride in silence, they turned into the forest and she guided him to the camp where other outcast women had established themselves, united in their independence. His presence caused initial alarm, anger and suspicion, but she who brought him there was their leader and she soon assuaged the rising commotion. She invited him to her private quarters, took off her helmet, and bade him do likewise and be comfortable.

"And do you understand why we live here?" she asked.

"Only too well. I hoped you knew that."

"I do, otherwise I would not have brought you here. But why did you come to the hermit? Why did you let me follow you? What news do you bring? And what of your fears?"

He walked the length of the canopied shelter and turned to face her.

"Our astronomers say that a familiar and long-known star has vanished from the heavens. Those who welcomed it each evening can no longer find it. Does that seem preposterous?"

"Once, in distant legend, a new star appeared and the wisest of men knew why," she said, fixing her eyes upon him. "Yes, I do begin to understand," she added with a heavy heart.

"The earth will run with blood until it is unrecognisable. The sun will flare and scorch and blind, and none will notice when the moon is swallowed up, hurtling down to whence it came... Everywhere, men are primed for attack. But there's not a border left to take or a land left to conquer. So what will they do? I see only carnage and self-destruction. So much suffering distilled in ignorance and despair."

"And you?" she interposed, pointedly.

"I am one of those, not unlike yourself – though for different reasons – who is exiled from his fellow men."

A glimmer of a smile crossed her lips. "You seem to live well. In fact, royally, if I may say."

"Because of my attire? You could not have chosen a less apt word. I left a kingdom to come north, but that was many years ago. One night, I slipped away in company with my most faithful advisor. I could no longer endure the deeds of men. But it seems we were observed with interest and without our realising it, were steered, prompted and led towards the mountain retreat where we have remained ever since, and from which I travelled only yesterday."

"And yet you still fear for tomorrow," she observed.

"Yes, I do. I could never have continued in the world I left behind. Over the years our messengers had brought ever more disturbing accounts. I regret not at all the things I relinquished to be here today. There is a madness in the world as though it has been cast under an evil spell. Beyond the plain that you can see from the edge of this forest, all at once, everywhere, men are gripped with a malevolent restlessness. They are abandoning everything, possessions, families, principles, to roam the land, threatening each other, fighting without pretext, killing indiscriminately. Such baleful collective impulses are not unheard of in species other than humankind. But we have entered a dark era of malevolence and violence and our astronomers have nothing hopeful to tell us."

He paused and listened a moment to the night. Then he took a step closer to her and, looking tenderly at her increasingly anguished face, lowered his voice.

"No one is leading them. It's happening by itself, of its own volition, like a sudden raging fever. I said they abandon their families. But they kill them first. Children and women are the first to die in every case."

She recoiled in disgust.

"Yes! You know why you are living here. Did you not foresee it? Why, against all other instincts, are these women here? How many have risked death to exile themselves from man at large, from his domination, indifference and abuse? He has forced you to fight even to defend your own existence and freedom."

"And why do you come to us now?"

"I come to ask your help." He paused and looked at her steadily. "A counter-balance must be invoked."

She fixed him with a stern gaze that seemed to mock him as she understood.

"And the dead brought back to life?" she enquired with mournful humour. "Has man finally succeeded in crushing the feminine principle so thoroughly that he has extinguished it even in his own soul? Is that what the hermit meant by a death? Is that what your astronomers have witnessed?"

"And like the child that he is," said the knight, "having broken what he does not understand and banished that which frightens him, he suddenly realises that he's lost the one part of himself without which his existence is unthinkable and untenable – and his despair takes the form of rage."

"And what can I do about that? What can woman do to save a man who wishes dead the very essence of her being? Why do you come here?"

"The ancient helmet that you wear did not pass to you by accident. You understand the symbols wrought upon it. You understand more than you acknowledge to me. You have possession of a secret lore that only your kind can invoke. You knew, when the hermit spoke to you today, why you did not find him once before. You know it was because of the hatred you carried there with you. But you have since learned to overcome that hatred and see the folly of man from your unique vantage point in the order of things. And man, though he exiled you here, has still not learned even this much and so he is destroying himself. By his own folly he has made you the stronger. And that is why, if you can still live without your hatred, you are the one who can help him. I do not speak for myself – that much must be clear, since I too am an exile – but I speak for man. I believe, in time, his rage will give way to remorse."

Endless columns of men formed an army more massive than any that had ever gone to war. It was an army already exhausted and defeated, a seething of spent potential migrating aimlessly towards wilderness. Like one vast, wounded miscreation, it blindly groped its way out across the plain towards the rocky wastes beyond. Faces: gaping, staring, haunted, vacant, some seeking, some straining hopelessly to comprehend the overruling instinct to which they found themselves enslaved, some fearful, some racked with guilt and pleading to they knew not what, all weary, disillusioned and plagued by an overwhelming restless-ness. It was an army possessed by the soul of madness and futility, hopelessness and degradation. It was its own quarry, its own enemy, its own victim. From its ruthless, war-hardened heart, oozed the black aura that drew it irresistibly to the barren places of the earth.

When the women from the encampment left the forest and gathered on the rocky promontory that overlooked the plain, the army already spanned its extremities. For so long as they watched, it continued to seethe in its hopeless, limping progress. There was no beginning and no end and the air grew heavy with a fetid odour rising from the deadened clatter of dragging, shuffling, staggering impotence. The despairing howls of pain and fear that now and then pierced the day, were nothing less than the echoes of Hell itself. Here were the mourning millions who stumbled away in their own funeral procession, here was the grief of nature made manifest, here was the death foretold in the mountain cave. And here too was born in the onlookers, the realisation that only nature herself could heal the wound in man. Through evolution alone, step by laboured step, might the balance be restored.

The knight, incredulous at the dimensions of greed and ignorance manifested below, tore his gaze from the plain and looked at she who led the women. The evening sun touched the graven symbols on her burnished helmet and each understood that they were powerless to intervene. All that could be done was to encourage, promote and condone in their hearts the natural courses of recovery that they themselves might never live to see.

As this new era dawned upon the earth, a pale crescent moon appeared high in a sky of deepening blue. He watched as the women moved instinctively together in a circular position. Their leader dismounted and motioned them into a ritual formation before making signs known only to the initiate and at once he knew that her learning was pure.

She uttered undeciphered words while those around her created the forms through which their meaning might manifest. Twilight embraced them as their chant rose high above the plain, sweetening the air and shimmering against the mournful drone that rose constantly from below. Their rite unfolded in delicate patterns of flowering symmetry, attuning to the firmament and culminating with an entreaty to higher powers. And then they were silent and still.

In the gathering darkness, she who had invoked their ritual looked round to where the knight had been. Discreetly he had left and in the distance, tracing his way slowly across a hilltop, she saw him pause and gaze at the darkening sky. For a moment she watched him and then lifted her own eyes to where he looked. Poised beyond the crescent moon hung the evening star, shedding its light across the plain, bright, inscrutable and numinous.

LAST RITES

Dedicated to the many 'undead'

Like swarming ants, huddled black shapes jostled and darted against the red sunset. A few solitary figures stood away looking on and the only sound to be heard was a shuffling of feet. A moment later, from the centre of activity, there arose a cumbersome jagged outline. One final scurry and the moving shapes dispersed to reveal the heavy black form of a cross leaning slightly to one side and cutting into the brightest rays of the setting sun that glowed from a distant hilltop.

Father Gerard watched as the cross slumped into the hole prepared to support it and pieces of damp earth fell from it like a shower of black rain. He turned and made his way back to the old monastery to report to the Abbot on the day's progress.

"Father Gerard! And what good news have you to report this evening?"

The Abbot raised himself from a carved wooden chair and leant against his desk on which were strewn scrolls, papers, books, pens and a large pot of violet ink. He was a fairly tall man, more rotund than was good for his health and with a smooth, barely wrinkled face beneath a mop of irregularly cut and slightly greying hair. His voice was more raucous than appearances would have led one to expect and his greeting the same as it had been every day at this hour for years. Father Gerard sighed imperceptibly and only then seemed to gather his thoughts together.

"Work on the excavations progresses well, my Lord," he began.

"Father Gerard are we, in perpetuum, going to enact this daily ritual concerning forms of address? I am to you, Father. And you are to me, Father Gerard."

"Very well, Father."

"It is less formal and I am too old for the solitude of so grand a title. You say the work goes well?"

"Yes, Father. Digging is complete and we are now at a stage for the masons to commence laying the foundations."

"Our little community has a high standard of masonry. It always has had. The work will be complete in no time at all. You realise, Father Gerard, that this extension to our building means that we can enlarge our order by a substantial number of novices. I am leaving you a much enlarged community and a significantly larger responsibility as well."

"As always, you talk of leaving us as if the day were already come."

"I speak as I feel. My health could be much improved. I may not look it but I'm an old man. The community I leave behind me will not only be larger but will have considerably greater potential than the one I inherited."

Father Gerard turned and wandered to the tiny window by the Abbot's desk. His lean face assumed an expression of gravity which might have been provoked by his superior's talk of failing health. Then he turned and spoke.

"There has been a certain amount of excitement and speculation today amongst our brethren concerning a discovery made on the site of the new extension."

The Abbot was startled. "Oh?"

"Late this afternoon, while digging near the edge of the proposed site, Brother Andrew unearthed a heavy wooden spar which had been buried at least six feet under the ground. He dug around it but finding it of considerable length, enlisted further help. Eventually, the entire structure was revealed to be a cross, seven feet tall. It was lying horizontally and seemed to have been placed there intentionally."

"Why do you say that?"

"Its position in the earth was completely flat. The cross itself has a small carved motif along its edges. The likelihood of such a relic being buried for no reason at all seems remote. But that it should have been done with such apparent care, leads me to believe that some specific purpose was intended."

The Abbot mused on what he had just heard. "Where is the cross now?"

"I told them to dig it up and erect it beside the site. That was the last thing they did before work finished this evening."

The cross looked more impressive in the early morning light than it had the night before. As activity recommenced on the site and the masons began their task, the sheer size of the unlikely discovery, along with its decorative design, attracted much attention and provoked a certain amount of whispered speculation.

Father Gerard had just walked out to examine the relic more closely when Brother Andrew arrived breathless at his side.

"Father," he began in an agitated tone, "I have something to show you."

"What's the matter, Brother Andrew? Calm yourself."

The young monk, in his excitement, tugged momentarily at Father Gerard's sleeve and hastened him away across the site to where he had been working. They arrived at the hole where the cross had been discovered. The other monks were busy elsewhere on the site. Brother Andrew exclaimed and pointed into the hole. Father Gerard's eyes widened perceptibly but he concealed any other hint of surprise.

"It looks like a grave, Father."

"What is so remarkable about that, my son?" he asked, glancing at Brother Andrew from the corner of his eye.

"It wasn't there last night. And now it's empty."

"Yes, it does look like a kind of rough coffin," conceded the Father. "Are you sure you didn't overlook it last night?" he continued and looked straight into Brother Andrew's face.

"Most positively, Father. Ask those who helped me dig up the cross."

"Has any of them seen this today?"

"I haven't shown them, Father."

"Good. And neither shall you. Fill it in."

The monk looked at Father Gerard in surprise.

"I mean, of course, just fill it up to the level we require."

Father Gerard became agitated and sensing that Brother Andrew was contemplating an objection he eyed the monk reprovingly.

"Father?" Andrew asked awkwardly.

"Yes."

Andrew hesitated, uncertain whether to continue, but finally went on. "The cross has caused quite a lot of speculation amongst our brothers."

"Quite so. The crucifixion of Our Lord has been the inspiration for men far greater than we to question, examine and re-examine their purposes and motives. That, surely, is why you are here today?" replied Father Gerard, deliberately choosing to misunderstand, in the hope of discouraging the young monk from further questioning.

But Andrew responded, perhaps out of a certain sense of panic, by being more direct.

"What I mean is that particular cross over there, Father." He pointed as he spoke. "Why was it buried here? It's big, heavy, and useless six feet under the soil. Last night many were asking why it should be here. Speculation got the better of them. Many talk of it having been put here to lay an evil spirit."

Father Gerard looked sharply at Brother Andrew. "Is that so?"

"Some say, a vampire."

Father Gerard was startled by such a word and surprised that Brother Andrew could bring himself to use it. He replied with emphasis. "You know of course that such a thing is not possible. Therefore, do not waste your time participating in such worthless conjecture."

"But Father, even though I laughed at them then, isn't this grave further proof that they might be right?"

"Proof? Vampires? Huh! Unenlightened secular superstition

breeds this kind of scurrilous notion. If this is the state of the minds in our community, then the time is ripe for more invigorating and intensified concentration on our lessons and vows. Let me hear no more babble of this kind. Do you understand me, Brother Andrew?"

The monk looked sheepish. "I'm sorry, Father, that I have allowed my thoughts to be distracted by the idle talk of others. But one fact remains. Last night neither I nor anyone with me dug deeper than was necessary to remove that cross. The grave you see now was still hidden under the earth."

It took some while for Father Gerard to decide whether the Abbot should know about these latest developments on the excavation site but he decided that the weight of a word from the Abbot about the folly of superstitious gossip among the brothers might be beneficial in allaying fears and dissipating any rising sense of panic. He caught himself wondering why such a reassurance from the Abbot should be necessary and then convinced himself that it would be aimed primarily at young novices who might otherwise be distracted by the fears of less responsible brethren.

When the Abbot heard of the new discovery and absorbed its implications, he sat back in his chair and looked for a long while at Father Gerard. "And what do you think?"

"Above all, we must put a stop to this wild speculation about vampires."

"Yes, Father Gerard, you've already made that plain and I shall, as you suggest, give some reassurance on that point. But having directed the minds of others towards a denial of superstition, I'd be interested to hear your own views on the subject. You tell me how such a magnificent cross came to be buried thus – and for what reason?"

Father Gerard's eyes darted from one place to another. "There is no such thing as a vampire. We know that. It is true that local superstition entertains such ideas, and many more, but we know that they're bred of ignorance and fear, like all superstitions."

"So how do you explain the grave you told me of?"

"There is no reason why, having dug so close to this cavity, the earth didn't simply cave in during the night."

"Interesting." The Abbot smiled. "But the grave was unoccupied, you say. Curious! Come, Father Gerard, are you sure that you aren't trying to fool yourself?"

"You talk as if you believe it."

"Let us say that there are many things we do not know. I don't know the answer to this mystery and neither do you. I suspect that idle chatter is infectious since you seem so eager to provide some kind of explanation to satisfy both myself and yourself. All we can do is discourage the present rumour. We cannot offer an alternative."

"But by not providing any explanation, however tentative, we shall only cause further speculation and be made to look ineffectual in our authority."

"I disagree. No explanation, along with an order for silence on the matter, is preferable to a transparent excuse that will fool no one. I suggest that you make sure that Brother Andrew is silenced, by my order, and make it known that I am aware of the situation. As for the building plan, I want all attention devoted to it and, with enthusiasm engendered, we shall simply forget about the negative occurrences of late and direct positive devotion to the expansion of our brotherhood in the name of God."

Slighted at the suggestion that he had been infected by the gossip within the community, Father Gerard walked purposefully back to where Brother Andrew was working and made known the Abbot's order of silence. The monk nodded his understanding.

"Have you filled in the hole?"

"Yes, Father. I did it before anyone else could see it. I have been asked why you think the cross was buried here. I told them of your disbelief in vampires."

"Good. And remember not to mention it again."

As Father Gerard walked away another monk approached Andrew. "Well, are they taking it seriously yet?"

"He told me to say nothing more about it to anyone," Andrew replied.

"Then they do believe it!"

The Abbot put down his pen and raised himself from his chair, muttering something as he did so. Deep in thought, he wandered over to the window and opened it to take a breath of air. He noted with unexpected pleasure that the breeze that greeted him was mild. The rustle of a few trees nearby attracted him. His face lightened, he glanced at the half-finished sermon on his desk and decided to take a walk. Only that afternoon he had told Father Gerard that he had little or no inclination to venture out these days but taking his cape, he passed along a stone passage and out into the garden. Beyond a high iron gate he saw the black outline of the cross, slumped slightly to one side. Taking a key from his pocket, he let himself out of the gate and walked slowly towards the cross. It was silhouetted much as it had been during the sunset on the evening it was first erected and the Abbot's imagination needed no prompting to add the detail of a human form suspended from it.

Standing next to it, he placed his hand on one of its rough and crumbling corners. He remembered that Father Gerard had told him that the cross bore an unusual pattern along its edges. He looked closer and found it, lit by the sinking red sun. A thought flashed across his mind. He ran his fingers over the carved pattern. His memory was working hard to convey something. The design extended along the entire edge. This was not a cross that had been hastily constructed. The wood was of fine quality and the craftsmanship excellent, although time and the damp earth had badly rotted it.

He pondered the design, a triangular pattern that overlapped and interlocked with a secondary almost circular motif. It was unusual indeed and unlike anything he had seen within an ecclesiastical context. But he *had* seen it before. Then his memory broke through and in that moment he knew exactly where to find a reproduction of just such a design.

Imperceptibly, the sun had slipped from sight as the Abbot had been peering at the carving. He blinked as he realised how intense the darkness had become. Recalling the current rumour inside the monastery, he half-smiled, looked quickly over his shoulder, shivered and made to move back towards the big iron gate that marked the boundary of consecrated ground on which the monastery stood. As he locked the gate behind him he paused once more to listen to the rustle of the trees. In the distance an animal cried out.

Back in his study, the Abbot hung up his cape and sat heavily down in his chair. He looked quizzically at the unfinished sentence of his sermon and brushed it aside to rummage in the tiny compartments of his desk, full of all the losable objects he had put there for safe-keeping. He opened several small drawers that lined the back of the desk before his fingers lighted upon the key for which he searched. The library to which he now hastened was always unlocked but the key he carried was necessary to reach certain volumes that were not available to novices and monks. Behind a thick wooden door which now swung open, shelves of long-neglected volumes and loose papers confronted him. He removed them, one armful at a time, knowing exactly what he sought. Almost two hours had passed before he finally recognised the volume he recalled from distant memory and placed it on the table before him. He peered at it in the dim light. He was right. The edges of the front cover bore an identical design to that which adorned the cross.

A usually particular man, he bundled the strewn papers back behind the heavy door and locked it. Then he picked up the elusive volume, pushed it under his arm and walked slowly back to his study. Once there, he scanned through the pages, many of which were loose and disordered. He recalled having read much of this volume before but now, as recollection followed recollection, the dim memory of what he was really seeking began to dawn.

The book he was holding contained the voluminous

ramblings of his predecessor's predecessor, a somewhat eccentric
Abbot who had obtained his post largely as a result of his prolific
sacerdotal writings. It seemed almost as if his urge to write had
been compulsive, even obsessive. Amongst many theses, essays
and articles, the Abbot recalled there had been a diary kept with
scrupulous regularity and it was to this that he now directed his
attention.

As he searched among the multitude of loose pages crammed
inside the book, he caught frequent glimpses of the motif that
adorned the cover. The design was, he recalled, an original
pattern created by the writer of the book, which had apparently
pleased him, and that he had used to identify and decorate many
of his papers.

He turned another page to reveal a section of the diary. A
note at the top indicated that it was continued from page 44. He
examined the page before him. It detailed the day's services; a
conversation with a young monk, Brother James, on the virtues of
obedience; an account of his struggle to complete some sermons;
mention of an intended visit by a Bishop, whose name was illegible; and much minutiae. The handwriting was very small and
neat but displayed several interesting graphological quirks that
seemed to underline the eccentricity of the writer. Occasionally the manuscript appeared to have been written by a decidedly
unsteady hand, perhaps one feverish with excitement, anger or
expectation, as in the case of the visiting Bishop's name, but for
the most part it was quite legible.

The Abbot pondered for a moment as if trying to recall a
particular section of the diary. He turned a few more pages. The
content was vaguely familiar but its significance eluded him. The
name of Brother Mark kept catching his eye. He turned another
page and there it was underlined. Then he remembered that
there were incidents recorded here that related specifically to this
Brother Mark whose name the author had always underlined.
This was what he had been seeking.

Taking a pen, he jotted down the page numbers on which

any reference to Brother Mark appeared. Large sections of the diary were interspersed with several other completely different narratives. Finally, with the diary sections located, he commenced reading. The first fleeting reference to Brother Mark was on page 75.

It read:

> Today <u>Brother Mark</u> was received. We talked.
> He seems not only intelligent but zealous – a rare
> combination.

The next reference to Brother Mark didn't occur until page 193:

> Father Selwyn informed me today that <u>Brother
> Mark</u> has, of late, been showing a distinct lack
> of interest towards his devotions. It seems that
> his former zeal has waned steadily in the past
> month, that he has become easily distracted and
> frequently displays an anguished demeanour.
> Plainly, this latter is not due to religious passion.
> He has excused himself from attending most of
> his obligations, including Communions, on an
> inordinate number of occasions. This is such a
> sudden change of heart for one who has shown
> great promise in our brotherhood for over a year.
> I have asked Father Selwyn to keep me informed
> of young <u>Brother Mark's</u> progress.

Then on page 202 the Abbot had devoted much space to a lengthy interview with Brother Mark following a further report by Father Selwyn to the detriment of the young monk. The Abbot seemed to have been struck by Brother Mark's intellectual potential and even conceded an originality of mind in excess of all others within their community. This, he pointed out, was:

> …in addition to having matured into a strikingly
> handsome young man whose physical excellence
> has been in no way subdued by the excessive
> plainness and simplicity of his garb and monastic

environment. In fact, the effect of his surroundings serves only, it seems, to make him shine
out from them, imbuing them, in turn, with a
distinct dowdiness.

The Abbot smiled to himself and turned to the next page.
He noticed that one or two other names in the diary were also
underlined. This caused him false hope once or twice when he
thought he had found other pages relating to the monk in question. Then he discovered a further entry of some significance:

Father Selwyn confided to me his belief that
Brother Mark's continuing distraction from
devotion is due to an unhealthy interest in
another of our number. He dates the decline of
zeal to a day shortly after the inception of eight
novices. His suggestion is preposterous and I
cannot accept that this over-simplified explanation could possibly apply to Brother Mark who,
of all people, would not let such a distraction
undermine his exemplary start to a monastic
vocation. If, however, Father Selwyn is correct
in his belief, then Brother Mark must be warned
about the temptations of the flesh and his obliga-
tion of obedience to his superior in so grave a
matter. I have suggested to Father S that Brother
Mark should be watched. I will see to it personally that he is.

These last remarks struck the Abbot as sadly amusing and he
scanned the pages for further references to the monk. His name
was immediately apparent a few pages further on:

Today I concealed my presence at a vantage point
near the altar in our chapel in order better to
observe Brother Mark. It was, however, to no
avail and I was unable to detect any action on his
part for which he might be criticised. Certainly,
I could not have failed to notice him among the

congregation since, as I have previously stated, his intensely ambient individuality appears to permeate every corner of his surroundings. Father S has again spoken to <u>Brother Mark</u> about his apparent 'distress' and, he tells me, has offered to personally instruct and supervise him. (My wily assistant seems never to overlook an opportunity.)

The Abbot knew that there was much in this vein in the diary but his memory still nagged him to locate the information that would verify some facts that he believed he already knew. He focused attention several pages on before looking again for the name of Brother Mark. Then, on page 430, he read:

Father Selwyn is somewhat gleeful today, though he would be embarrassed if he thought I had noticed, since he informs me that he is sure he has finally identified the object of <u>Brother Mark's</u> attraction. The one in question is, apparently, Brother Robert (perhaps that is not so surprising). Father S claims to have seen <u>Brother Mark</u> approach Brother Robert at a moment when neither of them can have known they were observed. Although he could not hear what was said, gestures and expressions led Father S to believe that Brother Robert was either fearful of, or offended by, <u>Brother Mark's</u> solicitation. I understand that the exchange was brief but agitated. Father Selwyn's own zeal in pursuing this... [the word 'quarry' was crossed out and substituted by 'matter'] leads me to think that his offer of personal advice and guidance to <u>Brother Mark</u> was perhaps over-forcefully declined! I have never doubted <u>Brother Mark's</u> astuteness and intelligence. In spite of that, I fear he will find that he has thereby fallen foul of Father S.

The Abbot was weary but his nagging curiosity forced him to scan a few more pages. Page 448 yielded the following:

> At last Father Selwyn has ceased his pretence not to gloat. In an over-excited manner he informed me today that matters concerning the discipline of <u>Brother Mark</u> are coming to a head. He over-heard the boy talking to Brother Robert and quoted the following remarks from their hasty conversation. <u>Brother Mark</u> was heard to say: 'It is more than infatuation. I dare to admit that I am in love with you.' To which the response was lengthy: 'Dear Brother Mark. I wish I knew what to do. I recognise that there are some amongst us who would go so far as to sacrifice their vows to be in my position now. You must be aware of that yourself. Believe me, I am grateful for your love, but I cannot return it in the way you need. I have thought deeply about what you have previously said. May God have mercy on you.' These remarks, which Father S seems to have committed to memory with a disconcerting precision, make it plain that I can rely upon him to be thorough in doing <u>my</u> work. Already, I understand, he has taken <u>Brother Mark</u> aside and, with outward friendliness, has asked him why he will not unburden himself. He even went so far as to suggest the confessional there and then! I fear that such enthusiasm will only serve to put the boy on his guard. On the occasions of his regular confessions, <u>Brother Mark</u> has not once alluded to his emotional difficulties.

The Abbot had ceased to find amusement in the pages that he now read and noted also the writer's increasing tendency to refer to Brother Mark as 'the boy' – a familiarity not in accordance with an Abbot of integrity. His suspicion that the writer

himself had a frustrated interest in Brother Mark seemed increasingly justified. In spite of the fact that Father Selwyn appeared as
the object of the writer's jibes, there was an underlying sensation
that the Father's evidently fanatical and unsubtle personality was
being used as an object onto which the writer could project his
own weaknesses.

On page 461 the Abbot read an account from which it
was plain that Brother Mark has sent a note, via another of the
brethren, to Brother Robert. The note had been intercepted by
Father Selwyn and acted as the damning evidence when, as related
a few pages later, Bother Mark was summoned to see his Abbot:

> In response to my summons, <u>Brother Mark</u> today
> attended an interview at which Father Selwyn
> was also present. I questioned the boy about his
> numerous absences from the chapel and his infe-
> rior and inadequate approach to any task he was
> set, from simple daily domestic duties, to the
> sacred devotions that form his whole purpose in
> this community. After many inadequate responses,
> which added further fuel to my argument, Father
> S, at a nod from me, produced the note written
> in the boy's hand. Although surprised, <u>Brother
> Mark</u> remained insolently aloof, whereupon
> I was forced to draw his attention to the sin of
> pride.

Turning the page, the Abbot discovered what appeared to be
the original note in question. It was a tiny scrap of tattered paper
on which the handwriting, though bold in character, was faint in
impression. The Abbot laid it out carefully as if strangely in awe
of handling such a significant triviality. It read:

> Brother Robert, I respect your feelings and am
> grateful for your gentleness towards me. But I
> have reason to suspect that we were overheard
> when last we spoke together. I dread that I have

led you into an ill-fated association. Please be
watchful – and forgive me. Mark.

The poignancy and resignation of the note made the Abbot
pause for a moment before returning to the diary:

Father S charged him with lustful, selfish and
irreverent intent towards Brother Robert but
the boy denied all and persisted in his isolation,
doggedly refusing to warm to offers of sympathetic counselling from Father S and even from
myself. Father Selwyn's presence might have
been inhibiting to <u>Brother Mark</u> and perhaps
served only to anger him the more. One had to
admire the boy's unflinching courage in the face
of so ruthless an enemy. Father S proceeded to
heap abuse and accusation on him but the boy's
face was for the most part impassive, even serene,
though occasionally observable was an inevitable
flicker of hatred. Fortunately, Father S can easily
survive such feelings – no doubt experience has
taught him how. I informed <u>Brother Mark</u> that
henceforth he is to avoid the presence of Brother
Robert whenever possible and that I expect him
to make renewed efforts to establish himself once
again in the esteem of the entire community. I
also instructed him to visit me in my study (every
second day to begin with) to tell me how he is
progressing. I will then see about reducing the
necessity of such visits. His attitude was hostile,
which is regrettable, but I believe he will change.
He ventured the insulting remark, no doubt made
in the heat of bitter frustration, that with us as
God's servants, God need not fear for His reputation as being all-knowing. Father Selwyn, unable
to contain his venom, struck the boy across the
face but appeared, nonetheless, ineffectual.

Hereafter, references to Brother Mark were invariably written in the characteristically more shaky hand, suggesting a degree of emotional involvement rather than objective detachment. There followed a list of instructions and duties for Brother Mark to observe; a list so comprehensive that time for non-devotional thought would have been at a high premium. These additional demands were effective only in intensifying Brother Mark's already anguished state. Determined in their decision to force the monk into a role of obedient conformity, the plan to suppress and obliterate his fundamentally natural emotions was ruthlessly applied.

The diary showed evidence that success had been obtained insofar as the regular visits to the Abbot were concerned. Accounts of their conversations and the prevailing mood were recorded in every detail. The name of Brother Mark appeared frequently on page after page until it even began to creep into contexts where it was plainly irrelevant, while in other reports there was now a significant *lack* of detail quite uncharacteristic of the writer hitherto. It seemed that at first Brother Mark's efforts towards his devotions were pleasing to his superiors but evidence of the pressures that were being applied to him soon became starkly apparent and an unexplained change of mood prevailed:

> Brother Mark today missed the evening service. I
> have ordered him to be placed in an isolated cell
> well away from the rest of the community. His
> food will consist of bread and water only, and not
> even this on the Sabbath.

This abrupt and concise entry startled the Abbot as he shifted on his chair and moved the book into a better light. Following the profusion of previous references to the monk, this entry seemed ominous and too extreme for the named transgression to be its only provocation. But there was no evidence of any other misconduct on the part of Brother Mark. The extreme change of mood persisted in the form of scattered, curt and isolated notes:

> After a week of solitary confinement and a diet

of bread and water, <u>Brother Mark</u> remains unre-
pentant. I have ordered the treatment to be
continued.

And then, a few pages later:

Repeated insolence and abuse by <u>Brother Mark</u>
is reported to me by Father Selwyn. Father S
suggested flogging. I agreed.

The Abbot noticed that the writer had now abandoned the
over-familiar and inappropriate references to 'the boy' and had
consistently reinstated his formal name of Brother Mark, which
he continued to underline throughout. Then the following note
caught his eye:

The flogging of <u>Brother Mark</u> seems to have
taken effect. Although I did not order it, Father
Selwyn saw fit to leave him in chains even after
applying the whip, only allowing a brief respite
and the freedom of his cell in order to eat. Today I
summoned Brother Robert for an interview. We
discussed his development here and I suggested
that he see me again in a week. A timid but
pleasant boy.

This last comment struck the Abbot as the beginning of
something more sinister.

References to Brother Mark were not to be found for several
pages and when his name did next appear, it was with the news that
he was to be allowed back to his old cell and encouraged, under
supervision, to resume an active part in sacred community life. It
was not clear from the diary whether Brother Mark's attitude to
his superiors had changed, whether his will had been broken, or
quite what had caused the decision to reinstate him. The writer
Abbot's interviews with Brother Robert had continued to be a
frequent feature of their cloistered life and it seemed that the latter
was being afforded occasional concessions and privileges.

The Abbot rubbed his eyes, leaned back in his chair and
pondered for a moment on what he had read so far. It had been

many years since he had discovered the existence of this unlikely book and in the meantime he'd almost forgotten about it. But re-reading the diary now, he tried to cajole his mind into revealing to him the significance that he was sure it bore on the black-ened wooden cross so recently discovered beneath the ground and which now stood resurrected just beyond the monastery gates. Sensing that the answer was not far away and in spite of his fatigue, he persevered into the night, scouring these obsessively meticulous and revealing jottings. The next reference took the Abbot by complete surprise and the handwriting was at its most enraged:

> As instructed by me yesterday, Brother Robert took the service this evening. Brother Mark was allowed to attend for the first time since rejoining the community. He had been subdued all week – I believed he had learnt an important lesson. Apparently not. During the service...

Here the handwriting became illegible. The next words that could be deciphered read:

> ...crying out, blaspheming, threw himself at the altar, thrashing wildly, desecrating and tearing down the cross itself. His strength can only have come from the Devil. No man could propel himself to such feats when, only a week ago, he was suffering physical exhaustion. Lapsing back into his weakened state, his energy spent, he was immediately overcome and returned to the lower cells. God protect us from this evil.

Without doubt, the entire monastic community had been shaken to its foundations by what was plainly the act of a man pushed beyond the point of his endurance. But hatred and fear only engendered further hatred and fear. Incensed, the writer Abbot was now determined to destroy Brother Mark:

> Father Selwyn came to see me this afternoon. Brother Mark's condition is extremely weak

following the punishment meted out. I understand that he has been crying out for mercy for
many hours. He is anathema. Tonight we will
excommunicate him.

On the following page his fate was sealed:

Today I took pleasure in visiting <u>Brother Mark</u> in
his Hell. I always suspected that Father Selwyn
had been zealous in his application of punishment. Now it is all too clear. I recoiled from
the thoroughness of his methods. The creature I
witnessed bore little resemblance to the <u>Brother
Mark</u> who was last seen defiling our chapel but
the punishment has been eminently commensu-
rate with the crime of sacrilege. News that he
had been excommunicated was received with the
most fearful groan – an anguish that conjured the
torments to come. It would not have been appropriate to witness his physical expulsion from
the monastery without some personal memento
from me.

Again the writing became too shaky and excited to decipher.
The entry concluded as follows:

...whereupon, Father Selwyn was aided in dragging him up from his cell and ejecting him from
our hallowed premises. I must now take it upon
myself to talk with Brother Robert, whose distress
of late has been causing me some concern.

The Abbot thumbed through the next few pages but found
no further mention of Brother Mark. These events, he noted, were
recorded in the winter months and the survival of the expelled
monk under those conditions would be utterly impossible in his
weakened physical state. He felt certain that there had to be at
least one further reference to Brother Mark somewhere. It was
inconceivable that the writer would omit the fact that Brother
Mark's body had been found. From the description of Brother

Mark's condition at the time of his expulsion, it seemed unlikely that he would have had the ability to so much as crawl out of sight. The Abbot's memory kept hinting at something that spurred him on. It was this last elusive entry that he now sought, and that he almost feared to find, that would provide the key.

Scanning the pages that now began to blur before his eyes, he was sure he'd caught sight of the name of Brother Mark. His heart leapt and he realised how caught up he had become in the fate of the young monk. The reason Brother Mark's name almost eluded him was that, on this occasion, it had not been underlined. He blinked several times as he moved closer to the page:

> Father S came to me this morning and told me
> that Brother Mark's body had been discovered
> by the edge of the wood. There was a fine layer
> of frost on his habit and on his face. Father S
> seemed agitated and I suspected that he had been
> shocked by his own handiwork. However, he
> was so for a very different reason. He told me that
> on the neck of the corpse were two large bloated
> wounds and that the body had been drained of
> every vestige of blood. He is surely now in the
> Hell to which we rightly consigned him.

The Abbot clenched his fist. His memory was complete. He soon found the passages that he now recalled having read many years ago. The writer Abbot had ordered that Brother Mark be buried. He also decreed that the desecrated cross from the chapel be laid along the top of the rough coffin to ensure that he could never escape. Father Selwyn had suggested that a stake be driven through the monk's heart but his superior would not hear of it. One final reference appeared at the foot of the page:

> Brother Mark has been buried outside our walls,
> a fate he brought upon himself. He will find
> no rest cut off from Holy Mother Church. I
> witnessed the burial myself and...

Here the writing became shaky and illegible again. The entry ended:

> Brother Cedric, returning from an errand to the village in the west, told Father Selwyn that the people there are behaving in a highly nervous and furtive way. They speak of many fearful disturbances, the howling of dogs and the bolting of horses, and whisper of a monstrous evil that passed close by in the darkest hours of the night.

The Abbot now knew everything he needed to discover. His thoughts drifted back to his walk earlier that evening in the dark when he had placed a hand on the curiously carved cross. A moment later he was asleep in his chair.

Father Gerard tapped briskly at the Abbot's study door and received a weary response.

"Good morning, my Lord."

"Good morning, Father Gerard," replied the Abbot, not bothering to get up from his chair. "I was reading until very late last night and I'd appreciate as little trouble as you can manage today."

Father Gerard looked at the large and bulging tome that was still lying on the Abbot's desk. He raised his eyebrows.

"Well, Father Gerard, what is it?" the Abbot enquired a little impatiently.

"I'm sorry, Father. I just came to ask you what you think we should do with the cross that was retrieved from the ground during our excavations?"

"What do you think we should do with it, Father Gerard?"

"I'm not sure. This morning, I suggested to some of our brothers that we take it down. With some renovation, maybe we could eventually make use of it. Perhaps in the cloister of our new premises."

"Indeed. Why not?"

"However, I couldn't help noticing a general reluctance to remove it. At least, for the time being."

"Oh?"

"I fear that in spite of your rule of silence on the matter, our young brothers are brooding somewhat on the origins of this cross."

"I see," said the Abbot, thoughtfully. Much of what he had read the previous night was still fermenting in his mind. "Perhaps you should leave it where it is for now, Father Gerard. Then, when the extension is complete, we'll think about employing it inside."

"Very well, Father."

"By the way, Father Gerard, would you ask Brother Geoffrey to see me? Thank you."

A minute later, Brother Geoffrey was at the door. "You wish to seem me, my Lord?"

"Come in. Are you familiar with the geography of the nearby villages?"

"Yes, my Lord."

"Good. I have an errand for you."

Work on the building progressed swiftly that day and there was little talk to be heard on the site. A generally subdued air seemed to have settled over the entire community. Occasional calls of instruction were the only voices that broke the monotony of shuffling feet, scraping trowels and grating stone. The cross remained where it had been placed, standing like a guardian, tall and gaunt, and many looked upon it as their only protection outside the monastery walls as dusk began to fall. The silence among so many was unearthly. It was not the silence of devotion and tranquillity but of nervousness and uncertainty. Its effect was to accelerate every effort towards the early completion of their task. As the sun began to sink behind the hill, that acceleration became more agitated and flustered and movements were more brisk, barely concealing a mood of unspoken panic.

As the monks finally filed towards the gates of the monastery, Brother Geoffrey came hurrying from the shadows of the wood and joined the end of the silent procession. Once inside, he went straight to the Abbot's study and knocked on the door.

"Ah, come in, Brother Geoffrey. Father Gerard was just leaving."

Father Gerard hadn't been aware of it but he withdrew accordingly.

"Well, Brother Geoffrey? You found the printer I described?"

"Yes, my Lord. Here are the books," the monk replied as he produced two newly bound volumes and placed them on the Abbot's desk. He was startled by what he heard next.

"Thank you. And what news did you hear in the village about vampires?" The Abbot's tone was hard to interpret and the monk became flustered.

"Yes, I know, I forbade any talk of vampires. But I think I'm entitled to waive my own ruling." He looked straight into Brother Geoffrey's eyes. "You may speak freely. What did you hear?"

"On no fewer than a dozen occasions today I have heard mention of dogs howling in the night or cringing close to their masters. Someone said he heard a tapping and scraping at his window and then a sound of groaning, like a wounded animal, but he was too terrified to investigate more closely. They said that dogs were howling all around the village until just before dawn."

"Are you afraid, Brother Geoffrey?"

"Yes, my Lord."

"You are safe within this monastery. If you really believe there is a vampire, let me console you by telling you that, according to folklore, such a creature can only enter a building if it is specifically invited. However, once invited inside it may come and go as it pleases. If you wish, you need not go beyond our gates again. But I command you to be silent and say nothing of this to your brothers."

As the days passed, the sense of unease in the monastery was profound. What had been a bustling community was now like a silent order. The Abbot questioned any passing visitors personally, whether they were pedlars or travellers seeking alms. More than once he heard rumours of someone in a nearby village being laid to rest with a stake driven firmly through the heart. Men and women were treated in the same way if they were thought to have fallen victim to the vampire whose presence was now common knowledge in local settlements – but never had the creature been seen.

The building plan flourished as the silent black-clad workers moved like startled rodents around the looming cross that surveyed them. As each day drew to a close, reactions were always the same. At the slightest crack of a twig or the distant cry of an animal, all became still, ears were pricked, eyes darted and a paralysing sense of fear descended on them all.

The days ran into weeks. The mood that had gripped the monks seemed to lose its sense of unreality and so became the norm. Reports from the nearby villages now reached the ears of every member of the monastic community and what began as a guarded secret was now common knowledge. And so it was with much relief that the new buildings and cloister were finally completed and the Abbot called upon to bless them. Once the ceremony was over, and with no further necessity to work beyond the walls of the community, a sense of peace settled on the brethren and faces dared to smile once more.

That night, under the dim stars, a shadowy figure crawled swiftly to the top of the monastery wall, hesitated, and sped down the inside like a gigantic spider. And for the first night in a very long time, peace reigned in the surrounding villages.

Dawn broke and there was an agreeable sense of satisfaction and accomplishment in the monastery with the extra space and freedom that the new buildings afforded. It was a busy day – a day of cleaning and tidying and applying finishing touches. There was a general bustling of suppressed excitement. The Abbot received word that a dozen new novices would be arriving within the week. Letters were despatched, consultations held and plans prepared.

It was late that evening before Father Gerard found a moment to make his daily report to the Abbot. He was tired as he walked along a narrow stone corridor and happened to glance down as he passed a flight of steps that led to one of the many cellars. It was an ill-lit passage but in that fleeting glance he was certain that he had caught sight of a figure as it passed from view into the darkness on the curving steps. He stopped in his tracks to look again. A draught stirred a cobweb suspended in the gloom halfway down the steps and he felt the chill air as it reached him. He was puzzled that anyone would be going down to the cellar at such a late hour and since they carried no light, he decided that his tiredness had created the illusion.

But the next morning, Father Gerard learned that his was not the only mind creating illusions and something very unusual was taking place in the monastery. Three monks, in separate conversations, claimed to have seen a cowled figure roaming the passages of the building. One had approached the figure, which, glancing over its shoulder, had swiftly descended the stairs to the cellars. In that brief moment the monk, a middle-aged man who had spent many years in the monastery, had glimpsed a face but failed to recognise the dark, half-obscured features as belonging to any of his brothers.

During the service that evening the Abbot occupied a chair set to one side of the congregation. He had appointed an elderly brother to conduct the ceremony but began to wish he hadn't as the voice droned on, lulling him to sleep. His eyes roamed about the chapel, of which every corner was familiar in minute detail, before letting his gaze fall upon the symmetrical rows of monks. To counter his tendency to drowsiness he found himself idly counting the numbers of the congregation. All were present, aligned in six rows of ten, as was customary.

After the service Father Gerard appeared in a state of agitation at the Abbot's door and without preamble stated his purpose. "I'm afraid I have some rather disturbing news to relate."

The Abbot gestured for him to continue.

"I have heard three independent reports today of a stranger in our midst who roams the monastery at night. The brothers are becoming very disturbed. Unfortunately I was not able to stamp out the rumour before it became common belief. In fact, Father, I have to confess that I think I too have seen this apparition. It was when I was coming to see you at this time yesterday but as I was feeling very tired, I dismissed it as something from my imagination." Father Gerard's voice became shaky and breathless.

"Sit down, Father Gerard. I spoke once before about popular rumours being infectious and I perceived then that you were slightly offended. Dare I suggest that this is a recurrence of the same phenomenon?"

"I'm sorry, Father. You're probably right."

"Perhaps."

"If you'll pardon me for mentioning it, I've always been inclined to think that you entertain the possibility of some truth in this not so distant rumour of a vampire."

The Abbot smiled. "And you think there is a connection between this latest rumour and the one we have only just managed to quell concerning vampires?"

Father Gerard felt foolish and moved uncomfortably as he changed the subject. "Oh, I almost forgot. Brother Anthony is feeling unwell and asked me to convey his apologies for not being in attendance at the service this evening."

"Thank you for telling me, Father Gerard," he answered absent-mindedly. There was a prolonged silence. A moment later he was fully alert. "How many were in attendance?"

"Of course, there should have been sixty but on this occasion there were only fifty-nine."

There was another pause before the Abbot spoke again.

"I counted sixty."

"Oh, then..."

They exchanged glances.

"I wasn't mistaken. There was plenty of time to count and recount, which I did. I see I must be frank with you, Father Gerard. You are correct in supposing that I have given credence to tales of vampires. In fact, I have evidence. You must have heard the stories that reached here from the village. Can all those be wrong and we right? In my position I must be careful what I say, not least to avoid spreading alarm. But men don't bolt their doors against nothing. Perhaps a few will but you cannot ignore and deride dozens of villagers who do just that." The Abbot got up and walked to his desk. "The facts are in this book, if you care to read it. The vampire, unleashed by us, was once resident within these walls. It is perhaps natural that he would want to come back for vengeance."

"Vengeance?"

"He has much to avenge. But there are things that I don't understand. Assuming he *is* amongst us, how did he get in here? It is at odds with everything we know about these creatures. And how could such a being survive on hallowed ground or bear to be present at a religious ceremony? I believe he was in the chapel this evening sitting amongst the brothers. All I saw were sixty figures in black cowls. He could have been any one of them. There is something particular about this case. The folklorists themselves have only a few generally agreed facts. They are frequently in conflict and contradict not only each other but also themselves. I will give it thought tonight. Come to me first thing in the morning, Father Gerard."

That night a stupendous crash shattered the silence in the monastery. The sound came from the direction of the chapel and panic spread swiftly from cell to cell. The Abbot had been lying awake deep in thought and was physically jolted by the ominous sound. He scrambled from his bed, snatched his cape and hurried along to the chapel. Monks were peering out into the corridors as Father Gerard came running from the opposite direction.

Several people converged at once on the two entrances to the chapel. The sight that greeted them caused shock and terror. Oaths were uttered and some of the monks reached states of hysteria. Standing on the altar was Brother Anthony, tearing down the draperies and destroying anything that came to hand. Shattered on the ground was the vast crucifix that had replaced the one of a previous generation after it had been used to seal Brother Mark's coffin.

The Abbot shouted an order and Father Gerard raced towards Brother Anthony. Brother Geoffrey threw himself at the defiler's ankles and brought him down. Brother Anthony's head cracked against the marble altar and he fell instantly motionless. The monks crowded around and a horrified silence fell as Father Gerard, grabbing Brother Anthony by the hair, turned his neck to full view. Two fresh bloated wounds oozed blood that trickled onto the marble slab. Now was acknowledged to all, not only the existence of the vampire, but its presence in their midst.

In the remote hope of allaying panic, the Abbot quickly shouted for all the monks present to assemble in the chapel, while two others went to ensure that none remained in their cells. Then he motioned to Father Gerard to join him in his study. With the Father close at his heels he hurried back and closed the door behind them.

"Father Gerard," he began urgently, "this is not a time for seeking answers to our former questions. The facts are plain and we must deal with the situation here and now." He suddenly clutched at his chest, wheezing violently. Father Gerard rushed forward and helped him to a chair. It was several seconds before he was able to continue.

"Never mind this. I'll be all right. A thorough search must be organised and carried out now. We have enough brothers for such a task to be possible. Concentrate on the cellars. There is a maze of passages, vaults and cells beneath us and every one must be searched."

"Wouldn't it be better to wait until morning?"

"It's barely midnight now. In those six or seven hours, anything could happen. Arm yourselves with whatever you like. Anything! Every monk has a crucifix that he can use for his protection. I suspect the only reason Brother Anthony was able to destroy our cross in the chapel is because he has only just begun to make the transition from normal life to the realm of the undead. But the one who made him like that cannot bear to be touched by a cross. It will burn his flesh like the torments of Hell. The marks on Brother Anthony's neck mean he will also be a threat to us unless we bury him soon with a stake through his heart. If we don't act tonight, how many others will be infected in the same way and escape into the outside world? It must be done now. Choose those you can best rely on for courage and determination. Let them lead the others. Go. This is your hour. Prove yourself."

The Abbot gave a hasty dismissive gesture and gasped to catch his breath.

"One question, my Lord."

"What?"

"What made Brother Anthony desecrate the chapel?"

The Abbot replied with patience. "In legend, the vampire can hypnotise its victims. That is why they return and allow him to drink more of their blood. Terrified as they are, they cannot resist. It is only when they die through loss of blood and are buried without being laid to rest according to that legend that they too rise again as vampires. Brother Anthony was doubt-less carrying out his new master's instructions. Don't be fooled. Brother Anthony is not yet dead. Not until we drive a stake through his heart. Be cautious, Father Gerard. Now go."

As Father Gerard's footsteps faded away along the stone corridor, the Abbot slumped back in his chair and sighed. Whether for a brief moment he fell asleep, he was unable to tell. The next thing he heard was the sound of his study door as it closed and the click of the key in its lock. Before him across the room stood a figure in a monk's habit with the black cowl pulled over its head. The Abbot was startled into full consciousness. He blinked rapidly and tried to clear his throat. The figure turned towards him, lifted its head and walked a few paces across the room. The Abbot peered at the shadowy face, only half visible beneath the cowl. Then his direst suspicions were confirmed as he realised what was missing. No crucifix hung from the neck of this monk. The figure raised its bony hands and threw back the cowl.

"They won't find me, Abbot." The voice was hard and bitter and came from blood-flushed lips set in a young and god-like face of shadowy marble. Black hair curled about his head and everything the Abbot remembered reading began to make sense.

"Brother Mark?"

"Once it was so."

"And now?"

"One of the undead."

"How did you get in here?"

"You invited me – by choosing to build around my grave."

"And what do you want of us? Is it revenge?"

"I want blood. Let us say I foresaw an opportunity. There are more tunnels and rooms beneath this building than any of you know. I spent much time down there many years ago. Your brothers will be gone for hours."

"But how can you survive here in a religious environment?"

"It is a temporary measure. You might as well ask how you can be close to a fire. Only if you touch it will it burn. Otherwise it will merely keep you warm."

"I know your weaknesses, Brother Mark. You are vulnerable."

"You're not the first Abbot to tell me that. We are all vulnerable."

The Abbot looked straight at Brother Mark, whose eyes burned like coals and fixed him with an unblinking stare. There was a momentary silence.

"I pity you, Brother Mark. You were wronged and abused. What happened to you after your note to Brother Robert was intercepted by Father Selwyn?"

Brother Mark flinched at the mention of these names but the Abbot went on. "You were ordered to visit your Abbot every second day, were you not?"

Again Brother Mark's face contorted and he showed surprise that the Abbot knew about his past.

"In this very room," he snarled. "The Abbot knew everything about me and he exploited it. He was an insanely jealous and frustrated man." His lips contorted with distaste. "At first I tolerated his abuse, yielded to him and bargained my way through life, because I knew that if I didn't, my life would be hell. But it became too much. I weighed one hell against another and one day I defied him in the way he least expected. I fear that Brother Robert suffered for that."

"What happened?"

"He demanded more and more. He promised absolution in return for favours. He became obsessed with me. And the more he tried to love me, the more I despised him. The day I lashed out he had me confined. And every day he visited me, chained me and told me how much he loved me. Even on the night he excommunicated me and threw me out, he declared his love. He and his world and everything it stands for, you, and all the others like you, are hypocrisy personified. You create us and then you are first to condemn us."

"Us?"

"The undead."

"Your present state is not the work of your Abbot. I've read his diaries. I know what led up to your expulsion."

"They threw me out. They harassed me and beat me, they denied me food so that my body became weak, they tortured and mangled my emotions and then, as if that wasn't enough, they cast out my spirit into blackness. When they threw out my body I was undermined and vulnerable in every possible way. I was easy prey for the dark and evil force that found me. I am what I am because of them. One such as you damned me."

Brother Mark came closer, looming over the Abbot, who began to mutter in Latin and finger the crucifix around his neck. As he did so, Brother Mark picked up a heavy candelabrum. The Abbot pushed himself to his feet but a well-aimed blow sent the crucifix flying from his grasp. Beads clattered to the floor. The candelabrum landed heavily in the Abbot's chest and winded him. A wave of darkness overwhelmed him and he fell.

The Abbot stirred, clutched at his chest and tried to lift himself from the floor. Brother Mark was sitting over him and immediately stood up.

"Look at me," he ordered, and the old man was transfixed by his hypnotic stare. "Sit down, Abbot, and listen to me carefully. Your brother monks will be gone until dawn unless they are summoned. Shortly we shall go and ring the bell for service. It can be heard plainly in the subterranean cells, I assure you. Whatever confusion this creates, it will inevitably bring your Father Gerard running here. I shall be interested to meet him and you will introduce us. As your personal assistant he will be a necessary part of our plan. You will announce to the entire community that the search is off and that you have caught your quarry. You will decree a special service of prayers of thanksgiving for your deliverance, which will be held this very night. Prior to the service the brothers will be ordered to retire to their cells from whence they will be summoned one by one to receive a special blessing to be administered by you. You will receive each one of them in the secrecy of your private chapel. It will be a simple matter to initiate each brother in turn. By morning the task will be complete and the brotherhood will commence devotions of a different kind."

Brother Mark released him from his stare. Fully conscious of what he had been ordered to do, the Abbot emerged from the trance and raised a hand to the stinging sensation on the side of his neck. Blood trickled down his fingers as his gaze reached the abandoned crucifix lying on the floor on the other side of the room.

"Well, Abbot, I think you understand me now. And when our twelve new novices arrive in a few days we will be ready to receive them."

Brother Mark drew himself up to his full height like a lean, powerful and terrifying wild animal surveying its territory with all its senses primed. The Abbot was horrified that Brother Mark knew of the impending intake of novices and realised that his innate awareness and instincts were formidable and far-reaching. His own feeble attempts to resist what was happening were fruitless and his energy severely depleted, drained with the blood sucked out of him by infected fangs that had sealed his fate. Brother Mark turned back to the Abbot who now cowered under the gaze of his new master.

"It's curious that even after everything I suffered in this place, that hypocrite couldn't bring himself to mutilate my body with a stake. He must have known that even if the cross they placed on my coffin had not been removed, it would simply have crumbled away, and one day I would be free to return." He pulled the cowl about his head. "Now it is time to ring the bell. Fasten your collar, Abbot. Everything must be perfect for our special communion."

THE PRISONER

For countless years the prisoner had sat gazing at the wall on the opposite side of his cell. The chain around his ankle prevented him from his desire of getting close enough to study it in detail. He knew every crack and every individual stone of the wall in front of him and of those to either side, but he refused his captors the satisfaction of seeing him face the wall to which he was chained. He knew exactly how many links there were in his chain and he knew, without even turning around to look, exactly how they were fastened to the wall behind him. To taunt him, his cell door would sometimes be left open – not often, but sometimes. And he knew, or was sure, that it was seldom, if ever, locked.

He also knew that his food was imminently due. The door opened and the same cowled figure entered with a piece of bread and a cup of water. The figure stooped down and placed the food, ceremoniously, only just within the radius of his chain. Then it stood, and as it turned to leave the cell, the prisoner glimpsed the blind stare of the skull from beneath its cowl. That day the figure chose to leave the door ajar and thus the prisoner knew it would stay until the same time the next day, when once again he would receive his bread and water.

The sight of the door left open was agonising. He had lost count of the number of occasions on which he had been tormented so. To endure this torture and retain his sanity, he had devised a way of distracting himself. He looked at the wall before him and began once again to count each of its stones and each of its cracks, before reaching behind him to count each of the links in his chain. The open door taunted him abominably and his despair was overwhelming. He counted every one of the nine thousand stones. He counted every one of the nine hundred cracks. And then he savoured the counting of the nineteen links in his chain, knowing, without even turning around to look, exactly how they were fastened to the wall behind him.

Then panic seized him. He clutched at the air beyond his chain. He could bear it no more. The years of torment were too much. In desperation, and for the first time since his imprisonment, he refused his food and turned his back on it. And his gaze alighted on an unfamiliar wall – the wall to which he was chained and which represented for him his humiliation. Always, for countless years, he had stood firm and denied his captors the pleasure of seeing him face that wall.

But as he looked, his gaze fell upon the means by which his chain was fastened to it – *not* as he had always "known". He walked towards the hook over which the last link of his chain was placed and, sobbing, he removed it and departed from his cell.

LABYRINTH

At the end of his recital he bowed to an enthusiastic audience.
Stepping around the piano, with one hand on the dark wooden
body of the magnificent instrument, he saw clearly the faces
of those in the front two rows. So many times that evening in
response to the warm reception he won after every work – Ravel,
Debussy, Beethoven – he had seen the faces below and always
his gaze had been arrested by the same one. Once she had been
smiling, once distracted, mostly she was alert, attentive, intel-
ligent, and always she looked beautiful. No other word would
do – for him, she was beautiful.

He left the stage but the applause continued. After a considerable pause, he returned to the platform and bowed again. Then,
upon an impulse, he did something he had never done before.
He returned to the piano resolved to play a short piece of his
own as encore. There were a dozen or more options from which
he might normally have chosen but now it had to be something
special and personal that he would play for her. As soon as he
sat down, the audience fell silent and without announcement he
proceeded. Thick and complex chords grew steadily in volume by
way of introduction but upon their transposed repetition, a distant
melodic line could be heard weaving its way upwards against their
density and weight. As the piece progressed, the crescendo of
opening chords reached a plateau and soon began to wane while
the long translucent melody was gradually revealed in all its grace
and subtle beauty. The effect was of light shining out of shadows,
the freeing of something beautiful from dark confinement. The
heavy chords offset the beauty of an exquisite melody and the
audience was moved to warm applause. Again he took his bow
and looked directly at she who was the object of his encore.

Outside in the crowded foyer bar a few of his friends had gathered to welcome him with a drink. It was a small and intimate hall, used mostly for quartets and solo recitals, and the bar was shared by performers and audiences alike. With a drink thrust into his hand, he received congratulations from several friends and acquaintances who paused for a moment on the periphery of his group. Then jostled by the crowd and distracted by someone's passing remark, he suddenly found himself separated from those who had come to meet him as he was edged nearer to the middle of the bar. A moment later, several people turned to leave and a welcome space appeared at his side. It was then that he found himself just a few feet away from the face that had haunted him all evening. She was with a man and an older couple, all three of whom were talking politics. For a moment he met her eyes with his but had no excuse to speak and so he turned away. Still there were several people separating him from his friends and, unwillingly, he thought he should try to edge his way back towards them. He hesitated, glanced around again as if looking for someone in the crowd, and let his eyes pass once more in her direction. At that moment, she stepped towards him and began to congratulate him for such a sensitive performance. He was both delighted and relieved that she had addressed him and was quickly oblivious to anyone else. Despite her apparent boldness, she seemed instantly unsure and diffident as soon as she had spoken. There was a moment of awkward silence and then she spoke of his energy in playing the encore after such a substantial and demanding programme.

"What was the encore you played?" she asked.

"It's a piece of my own. It's called 'Labyrinth'."

"It's beautiful," she said simply.

"Thank you," he said, and wanted to add: So are you. "I call it 'Labyrinth' because the chords that begin it are like solid walls between which the melody weaves its way until it emerges. The transposition of the chords near the beginning is intended to suggest a labyrinth of several layers."

Again he found himself doing something he had never done before. He would never have presumed to explain a piece at such length to someone who hadn't asked. But once embarked, he had gone on, her apparent shyness enabling him to do so more easily.

"Forgive me. I'm being a bore. It's the first time I've played something of my own in public." He hesitated, then added, "I played it for you."

He smiled hoping she would believe him but painfully aware that it was the kind of remark that anyone might make to placate her shyness.

"No. That's silly," she said with slight embarrassment.

"I mean it. I saw you sitting in the second row and I played it for you. Normally I would have played a more standard piece."

"Thank you," she said, a little coyly. "And you're not a bore."

He took the plunge. "I hope I'll see you again. I rehearse here every Thursday. If you'd like to come, I'll make sure they let you in."

He'd said it just in time. As she was thanking him, the crowd suddenly impinged and they were loudly interrupted with effusive congratulations and the request for an autograph. A moment later he was whisked back to his own group of friends who were making suggestions for his next recital. He swallowed his drink, tried hard to listen but was hopelessly distracted and soon excused himself.

Next morning he surfaced slowly from a restless night and dwelt for several minutes in that curious region that lies between sleep and wakefulness. An image of beauty enticed and excited him – the beauty of her face. Music welled up inside him and several new ideas suggested themselves in a surge of creative energy. Behind it all that exquisite face looked at him – a face so empathetic to his innermost spirit that it was as if he had known her before, a face from a dream, a face that stirred in him the tenderest feelings, that moved him to gentleness and creativity, a face so sensitive and disarming, against which no deceit or falsehood could ever be contemplated, that opened his heart and bared his soul, a face he found more desirable and beautiful than any treasure, a face that inspired him, and that had listened so intently as he told her of 'Labyrinth'.

A moment later he was wide awake and threw back the duvet. He had overslept. He went to the bathroom and washed quickly. He had to collect a score from the bookshop on his way to rehearsal. Rummaging through his wardrobe, he decided he would just have time. He stopped to shave (he hated not shaving) before stepping out into the bracing air of a spring morning. Music filled his head as he walked down the street and the warmth of his reception the previous evening lightened his step, reminding him to check the newspapers for any reviews.

"I've come to collect this," he said as he handed a notification card to the bookshop assistant. The man produced the full orchestral score of Ravel's G major Concerto and offered it for his approval. The transaction complete, he turned to go and saw, looking in through the window, the shy face that had greeted him from sleep. Unaware of her until that moment, he noticed that she was holding a paper bag containing a purchase from the same shop and concluded that she must have just stepped outside, having been browsing between buying and leaving. As soon as he too was outside, he went up to her. She smiled, plainly delighted by this chance meeting.

"Hello," he said. "What did you buy?"

She drew from the bag Longus' 'Daphnis and Chloe' and watched him as he studied the title.

"That's a coincidence," he said. "Ravel was inspired to make a ballet of that story, and I've just bought his G major Concerto. I thought it was time I had my own copy instead of always using a library edition. I'm rehearsing it this afternoon with the orchestra. Would you like to come?"

"Yes. But I can't." She smiled a little, more to herself than at him.

"That's a pity," he said.

"But I'd like to hear some more of your own music sometime, if I may."

He wanted to touch her. She seemed so vulnerable, so sensitive and, even when smiling, a little afraid. It was the same curious combination of boldness and hesitation that he had noticed the previous evening.

"Of course," he answered. "But as I told you, I don't play my own music in public – not usually, anyway. It will have to be at the house of a friend. He lets me use his concert grand whenever I like. What about tomorrow afternoon? I can meet you by the theatre in the square. It's just around the corner from there."

"Yes, that would be nice," she said, distractedly.

He looked at his watch.

"I'm almost late for my rehearsal. I'll meet you tomorrow at three."

She nodded. He hesitated as she looked at him. Then he was gone.

Walking home from the rehearsal, he wondered about the coincidence of their meeting. The coincidence of their purchases was real enough but there had been something about her that didn't seemed surprised to see him. Might she have contrived it? But how could she have known where to find him? The more he thought about it, the more preposterous it became and coincidence seemed to be the only genuine answer. As he reached this conclusion, he became aware that all the time he was watching the faces of women as they passed him, watching them in a way he never had before. The more he studied them and the more he recalled to mind the faces of women he knew or had known, the more he realised that he had never seen anyone who affected him as she did – and it was far more than just her beautiful face. Now, too, it was her voice. It sounded in his mind, repeating little phrases he'd heard her use that morning and the previous evening. There was a soft musical quality about it and a cadence that was distinctly hers and nobody else's. Then a musical phrase sounded in his mind and he made a mental note to jot it down as soon as he arrived home.

The spring sky was growing dim as he let himself in but he didn't turn on the light. He enjoyed natural light for so long as it lasted and was loath to spoil the effect of its subtle changes as evening encroached. He threw down his jacket and went straight to the upright piano in the lounge. From beneath a pile of scores he extracted his own manuscripts and started to leaf through them. 'Fire Music', 'The White Garden', 'Nordic Impressions', 'Mystic Night' – these he felt were the best, and to them he added 'Labyrinth' before placing them together in readiness for the next day.

Then he paused, sitting at the piano, and turned to notate the melodic sequence that had come to him as he walked home. Instantly her voice was in his mind again and then her face – both with such persistence. Fragments of their two brief conversations surfaced in his memory and he was tempted to speak to her as he sat there alone. He resisted the urge to speak aloud but heard himself holding a conversation with her in his head. He found himself saying what he really felt while her responses seemed curiously her own, rather than those that he might have contrived. As they 'spoke', he wanted again so much to touch her, to very gently feel her soft cheek against the palm of his hand, to hold her in his arms and reassure her of his love... At last he acknowledged the word – to himself, if not to anyone else.

The doorbell rang and he suddenly remembered that a young woman he'd been seeing intermittently in past months had said she might call after his rehearsal. But he was too involved with his thoughts and feelings to want to answer the door. He was glad that he hadn't put on the light and continued to sit at the piano. Another ring was followed shortly by a folded piece of paper that fell through the letterbox but remained unattended on the mat. Then he lay on his bed and fell asleep.

It was a few minutes after the appointed hour that she walked up to him in the square and apologised for being late. It was a sunny day, mild and clear, and her hair was ruffled by the gentle breeze. She looked as lovely as ever and he was so happy simply to be with her. They turned the corner and walked for a few minutes along a broad street lined with large plane trees. The houses on either side were some of the most opulent in the town and it was to one of these that he led her. As they reached the front door, he took from his pocket a key and ushered her in. Plainly she had expected the friend to be present and seemed tentative about going into the house of someone who didn't even know her.

"Are you sure it's all right?" she asked as though they might be committing some offence.

"Yes, of course. He's away so much that he gave me a key. Maybe he wouldn't be quite so generous with his piano if he was here more often," he smiled.

She stepped inside but her diffidence persisted. To encourage her, he walked straight on into the music room and opened the double doors wide. A concert grand stood in the middle of the room, which was otherwise under-furnished with exquisite taste and large enough to accommodate a modest audience. The Persian carpet alone was enough to entice the most hesitant guest and on the wall at one end hung an Oriental scroll of extreme beauty and delicacy, depicting a river in mist flowing endlessly between mountains and trees. As he placed his scores on the piano she came slowly into the room. Straight away he offered to take her coat but she declined, preferring to keep it on. He gestured to a comfortable seat and perceived from her smile that her reluctance was more towards what she seemed to regard as their intrusion, than it was towards himself. She withdrew into the chair and pulled her coat closely about her.

Without further hesitation, he sat at the piano and opened the score of 'The White Garden'. Aware of her sitting just at the edge of his vision, he began to play. He didn't really need the score but kept it before him in case he decided to make an alteration. The piece was slow and dream-like and warmed the room with its harmonies. He glanced briefly in her direction when he sensed that she wasn't watching him and saw that she had relaxed and closed her eyes. As delicately as the Oriental scroll, the music unfurled and enchanted his listener. At the end he paused, not for comment or appreciation, but simply because the silence that followed was, for him, as much a part of the music as the notes themselves. Then he took another score – 'Fire Music' – a robust and flickering piece, which changed the mood completely and was enhanced by the contrast. Again he glanced at her but she was still in the same position with her eyes closed. He wondered whether she had fallen asleep but suddenly she opened them and was looking directly at him. Fleetingly they held each other's gaze before he looked at the score and then beyond it to a painting on the wall. Then she moved into his line of vision as she got up and went to the painting, looking at it with her back turned towards him as he played. She had taken off her coat and seemed as delicate and lovely as if she had been a lone figure in the picture. Then she turned around, looked at him for a few seconds and continued her path across the room while the music rose to its climax and subsided into silence. Now she stood gazing out of the window that looked onto the garden behind the house and he leafed through the score to find a particular movement of his 'Nordic Impressions'. It fell open at the 'Love Song' and he played it. She remained motionless as the last note faded.

"Is that enough?" he asked softly, but she appeared not to have heard him.

He stood up, moving the piano stool intentionally as he did so, the sound echoing and momentarily filling the room. But still she remained motionless and gazed into the garden. He walked over and stood by her side. But her spell was unbroken and he noticed that her eyes were tearful. Moving behind her, he could no longer resist the urge to touch her as his right arm encircled her waist and his left hand came gently to rest upon her stomach. For several minutes they remained motionless, his breathing synchronised with hers, as gradually she allowed herself to relax further into his arms. He wanted so much to whisper something soothing and took breath to do so, but no words came to him, save those he would not speak. Instead he held her closer with an affection that she alone could rouse in him. Then, very slowly and gently, she took his left hand and placed it on her breast. He responded with the slightest ripple of his body against hers, an acknowledgement of her trust and acceptance of his closeness. He felt his face against the fine silkiness of her scented hair and for a long while they stood exchanging the tiny impulses of warm tenderness and reassurance. But eventually she moved, turning in his arms to study his face as though she were searching within it. He kissed her forehead and they looked at each other again. Then slowly their mouths met and they kissed one kiss until it became the longest kiss that either had ever bestowed.

He took her hand in his and walked towards the piano stool. They sat together as he turned to the score of 'Labyrinth' – to where the delicate theme emerged in all its simplicity from the dark opening chords – and whispered "for you". It was certainly the most beautiful piece he had ever written and she let her head rest on his shoulder until the last note had died softly away.

It was some days later before he saw her again. The last members of the orchestra were leaving the platform and the conductor smiled warmly, congratulating him on his performance of Ravel's G major Concerto. Everyone was pleased and they had worked well together. The concert was that evening and this was the last rehearsal. He had invited her but she had been uncertain whether she could come. The conductor turned away and left him alone on stage in the empty hall. He looked out into the auditorium and, not seeing her there, sat down again at the piano and began to play for his own pleasure the concerto's *adagio assai*. It had about it a delicacy that reminded him of her and during rehearsals he had always played it with her in his thoughts. More than one person had told him that they had never heard it so subtly and sensitively played.

As the notes echoed in the empty hall she emerged from the darkened part of the auditorium and walked slowly towards him down the central aisle. He saw her but played on to where a flute should have taken up the theme – but there being no flute, he rounded off the phrase and stepped down from the stage. She smiled a smile that seemed as lonely as it was delicate and lovely. He went to her and kissed her lightly on the cheek but she turned her face slightly away.

"You seem wistful," he said.

"Blame Ravel – and your playing," she replied and sought his hand with hers.

"Coffee?" he enquired.

She nodded and they wandered slowly out of the hall.

The fresh aroma greeted them as they sat down opposite each other at a small table at the only good coffee shop in town.

"Were you there for the whole rehearsal?" he asked.

"Almost. You'd already started. I nearly didn't go in but nobody seemed to mind."

"I'm glad you did. I told them to look out for you. It's a beautiful work," he added.

"Yes."

"Are you all right?" he asked.

"Yes," she said but he wasn't convinced.

"Are you?" he emphasised.

She nodded.

He took her hand across the table. "What's the matter?" he asked.

"Nothing."

"Yes there is. Please tell me. It matters to me..."

She looked him straight in the eyes as he continued.

"...I care about you very much." It wasn't what he'd been going to say but something wouldn't yet allow him to speak from the very depths of his heart.

She stared at him and breathed deeply. "You know that I already live with someone, don't you?"

He wondered why he should have known, and yet somehow he had known, and it was no real surprise.

"Your companion at the recital?" he asked.

"Yes."

"Does that make a difference?"

"Yes," she said, uncertainly.

"Does he know?"

"Yes."

"And what does he think?"

"He's hurt."

"Then why are you here?" he asked as gently as he could.

"You invited me."

"I know. But you didn't have to accept."

"I wanted to," she said softly.

"Why?"

"Because I like you… and I like your music." She smiled a little.

"Is that all?"

She didn't answer.

Again he wanted to reveal his heart to her, yet he wouldn't.

"Do you have anyone else?" she asked.

"No," he replied quietly and clearly, and was aware of the word 'else'. "I'd like to see you again," he continued. "Would you like to spend the day in the countryside tomorrow? We could take an early train."

She hesitated a long time before answering. "Yes, I would."

He raised her hand to his lips and kissed it gently – first the back and then the palm, which was warm and a little moist. Much as he wanted to say, he could only look.

The concert that evening was a great success and as soon as he'd played the concerto he went back to his flat to be alone. He knew that she hadn't been present but despite that, he'd found himself seeking her face in the audience. As he played the slow movement, he wished he'd told her that he loved her. Yet he was almost afraid to, lest she mocked him for having known her only a short while and fled from what she might consider his rash insincerity. Whenever he'd come close to saying it, it was always something else that came out, or nothing at all.

Sitting in his flat, he picked up the note that his caller of a previous evening had posted through the door as he'd sat silent and alone in the twilight. He re-read it, aware of the considerable affection that existed between them. But that affection remained nothing more than what it was, dwarfed by the love that he felt for she who now seemed to be the one he had waited for for so very long. Slowly he tore the note in half and with that act, in his mind and heart, put an end to any further progress along that path. That very afternoon she had asked him whether he had anyone else and he had answered her honestly. It hurt him much to hurt another but in his heart he'd already known what had to be done.

Discarding the scraps of paper, he got up and walked to the piano. The score of 'Labyrinth' lay open upon it and he sat down and played it. Delicacy, grace, kindness, warmth, sensitivity and softness – these and a dozen more qualities filled his mind together with more than just the image of her face. As though conjured by the music, ever-present within that most beautiful melody, her very spirit came to him with a love that seemed predestined. As the last note of the melody faded away, he took up a pen and inscribed three lines on the score that now was hers:

"O my rose, I touch thy softest part,
For I am the breeze that caresses thee
And carries thy scent in my heart."

The train steamed into the tiny country station in the middle of nowhere. They were the only ones to alight and no one was there to look at their tickets. Pulling slowly away again along a single track, the last carriage disappeared around a bend, leaving behind only the sounds of birdsong.

In no time at all they were walking in seclusion. Gigantic trees burgeoning with new foliage were vibrant in the sun as they strolled beneath. They breathed deeply the freshly scented air and spontaneously spread their arms to welcome mild spring. And so they went peacefully together in warm and tender contentment. Beyond the wood, they came to a village and bought fruit, cheese, bread and wine before going on. By midday the air was warmer still and they sought a place to stop and eat. No sooner had they voiced their intention, than they came upon a ruined wall, beyond which a slope led down into an overgrown garden. They looked to see whether they were trespassing but found no sign to suggest that they were. No buildings lay in sight, merely the remnants of what had once been a cultivated garden belonging to a now non-existent home. As they ran down the slope beyond the crumbling wall, they felt the still warmth trapped in that sheltered spot. Taking her hand in his, they ventured further until they were beyond sight of the path. High shrubs entwined themselves at random with overhanging trees and beyond these they came to a small open patch of grass where they spread a blanket. They unpacked the food and wine but it was left unattended. No sooner had they sat down than each was transfixed by the other. Simultaneously they reached out and touched. He caressed her cheek with his palm and their lips met and opened. Endlessly they kissed and their bodies ached to be one. Each was the well-spring of such tenderness as the other craved and each quenched their scorching thirst in the embrace of the other. Then, in a whisper, she spoke the words that he so often had been afraid to speak, "I love you."

Their naked bodies merged and soft tenderness enfolded them. He touched her softest part and her smoothness inflamed him, the soft whiteness of her breasts, the silken touch of her hair, entwining limbs, and the gentle hands that caressed and welcomed and held him... and held him tighter until his flesh grew red, his body writhed with hers, and the exquisite ecstasy of their love possessed and overcame them both.

Deeper and deeper they sank into their love, into each other's hearts and, in stillness, lay in each other's arms as if they were one. And so at one were they, that all seemed insubstantial, and beneath the sun he found himself standing in a garden alone, with her in his heart. Then he looked up and saw amid the trees a white unicorn, which quickly darted hence and was gone.

He wandered at peace in the garden, his senses ravished by

the quintessence of all that he perceived. Never had he known such living colours, such noble forms, such vivid textures, subtle perfumes and vibrant sounds. The warm breeze carried on it a melody that caressed him, ever changing and ever renewed. It was more like paradise than anything he had ever imagined. But while love possessed his heart and communed with him about all that he perceived, he was not content to be there alone. He listened to the melody of the breeze, he gazed upon a myriad of flowers and then, in a moment of deep longing, he plucked the reddest rose. And he carried it with him as he walked on through the garden and came at last to a gateway. And opening the gate, he found himself upon a narrow path that led between two high hedges of such density that he could see not the slightest thing beyond them. And so he proceeded along the path of a labyrinth that soon twisted sharply back upon itself and then went off in a new direction. He followed patiently, walking on, turning left and right at every conceivable angle, traversing ever onwards in all the degrees of a circle. At times he thought the path would never end but he carried the rose in his hand and love in his heart and always he went on.

Then he thought he heard a sound of footsteps and looked sharply round to see who followed him. All he saw was the empty path. He hurried to the next turning but found no one coming towards him. As the sound of the footsteps came to him again, he stopped in his tracks to listen. They were close by and yet he could see no one. And then they stopped. In the silence that ensued, the perfume of the red rose caressed him. Then one last time he heard the footsteps as they receded and he knew that someone had passed close by him on the other side of the same impenetrable hedge. He resumed his journey, aware that he was not the only occupant of the labyrinth.

As he proceeded, the twisting convolutions became ever more frequent and hardly had he turned one, when he was imme- diately compelled to follow another in the opposite direction. And so it persisted until suddenly the high walls ceased and he found himself at the centre. And facing him, having emerged at the same instant from a similar path on the opposite side of the clearing, was she who existed in his heart. And she held in her hand a moonstone that shone more brightly than any he had ever seen. As the eyes of each fell upon the other's face, they walked towards a plinth poised above a limpid pool at the centre of the clearing. And upon the plinth she placed the brightest moonstone and beside it he placed the reddest rose. Then he turned to his right, and she to her left, and they embraced beside the pool. And as they bathed in each other's warmth and light and love, tasting the sweetness of each other's kisses, by the perfume of the rose were they enraptured, by the brightness of the moonstone were they quickened, and by the cool breeze were they caressed with a singular melody. And when in their reverie they at last drew apart, they noticed a third path that led into the centre of the labyrinth, and gracing its entrance stood the white unicorn with its golden horn sparkling in the sunlight.

Enchanted by the presence of that noble creature, they moved towards it as it turned about and began to walk slowly away along the third of the labyrinthine paths. When at first they did not follow, it paused and waited for them. Patiently it led them through numberless convolutions until they emerged together in an idyllic garden set upon the bank of a river. It was a place neither of them knew and the unicorn, once it had led them there, moved away and took to grazing silently nearby. All around them were trees abundant with gold and silver fruits while others were of colours they could not name. Flowers grew everywhere, some of which they knew while others they had never seen. Here the cool breeze carried a different melody and as they wandered together at peace among blossoms of every form and hue, they pointed out their favourites and came time and again to regard each other. Each felt the longing in their heart that had led them into the labyrinth to meet at the centre, that they might forever know and recognise their place together wherever after they might find themselves. And each knew that whatever trials were to befall them, howsoever they might be separated, and by whatever means they might seek to avoid the pain necessary to free themselves from other distractions, neither one would ever find rest or fulfilment until they were reunited. Wherever they were, they would find themselves irrevocably drawn back together with this same sense of belonging. And with that realisation, communicated without speech and passed directly from heart to heart, they looked at the unicorn who, turning towards them, walked up and lowered his head, not in enmity but in salutation, before galloping away from their sight.

Hand in hand they laughed together and as they did so, they became aware of a presence that stood beside them. And in that presence they grew strong and were filled with peace and insight. Turning towards it, they beheld what they could only regard as an angel, though he had not wings, yet he had all the appearance of such a fabulous being. Though he was youthful, yet he was wise, and though he was strong, yet he was gentle. And when he looked upon them and spoke, they heard not a voice, but they perceived in their hearts his meaning. Reaching out he took their clasped hands in his and informed them that it was their time of parting. Yet they were not to fear for they had already sealed their love. And so he counselled them: that each was to set off in opposite ways beside the river, she towards the source, he towards the mouth, and at the first opportunity, by whatever means, both were to cross to the opposite side. And when eventually they met again on the opposite shore, no matter what imperfections they discovered in each other, such was the nature of their love that every fault should be patiently soothed and lovingly endured, and so would they deepen and enrich their oneness. And as they understood this instruction, they knew that they had to obey. The angel reached up and plucked from an overhanging tree a golden fruit that was filled with honeyed wine. Opening it in two, he gave one half to each of them to drink. And then he said to them: Believe in the love that you have chosen and no harm will befall you. And so he departed. Knowing that it was for their ultimate fulfilment that they had thus been counselled, and that each moment they delayed would be a moment longer before their reunion, it was with much sorrow that they prepared to go their separate ways. Once more they embraced, tasting still the honeyed wine upon their lips that the angel had given them to ease the pain of parting. And eventually they did, neither one daring to look back.

As he strode beside the river he tried to perceive the nature of the dark land upon the opposite bank. All he could see were high black trees obscuring any hint of the world that lay beyond them. And as far as he looked in either direction, the same was presented to him. Eventually he came to a narrow landing stage where was moored a small boat with oars and straight away he recalled the voice of the angel. The prospect of the opposite shore was uninviting but he believed in the love that possessed his heart and he believed in she who was its object. And so he set out, as he had been instructed, and rowed towards the dark land. The current ran swiftly and took him somewhat downstream but he made good progress in spite of it. And as he neared the shore, the darkness there overwhelmed him and he remembered no more.

He blinked and rubbed his eyes in the sunlight as he heard her give out a little groan at his side. He looked at her. Instantly she propped herself up on her elbow and for a moment they stared at each other. Then she was in his arms hugging him as he hugged her. It was spontaneous and mutual and they held each other very closely, declaring their love.

"I had a strange dream," she said at last. And when she began to tell it, he was able to remind her of many small details. What she had experienced was like his own, and she too had glimpsed the unicorn before she entered the labyrinth.

"Is it any wonder that we are here now?" he said. "For so long I have avoided involvement. Now I know why."

"And for so long I have delayed commitment," she said.

Already he had freed himself to be with her. And as he held her close, she also knew what she must do.

TOWER SONG

Dedicated to Alan Hovhaness
in gratitude for your great gift to the world

The air was warm and hummed with summer sounds in the serene stillness of the place to which he had come. The old tramp heaved his aching limbs over the stile and stumbled wearily and clumsily to the other side. He sat down on the ground, took a deep breath and sighed deeply in the sun. Tall grasses stretching away in front of him swayed gently in the breeze and rustled faintly over the trickling sound of a nearby hidden stream. Insects buzzed, birds sang and wild flowers grew everywhere in profusion.

From where he sat at the side of the stile he could see two paths that forked away – one well-trodden that went down into the valley towards the river; the other to his left, neglected and overgrown, that led to the top of the hill where stood an ancient and crumbling tower. Standing like a sentinel that surveyed for miles the surrounding land, the tower was adorned with a wild and colourful tapestry of the most delicate blossoms that had ever chosen to enwreathe themselves in such harmony.

The old tramp savoured the strangely beautiful sight poised on the hilltop beyond the neglected path. His tired body – constant wanderer and witness to many exotic landscapes – had seldom seen such intimate poetry wrought by nature across its vast canvas of endless imagination. Together with the rich symphony of sounds that undulated softly through the air, the old man welcomed the sense of ease and tranquillity that seemed gradually to overwhelm him.

As he pondered the floral tower, he also turned his attention to savour the other wonders before him – the harmonious fusion of shades and colours, the intricacy of birdsong, the elegantly diving swifts, the ingenuity of the burden-bearing ant, the subtleties of fragrance and the measured delicacy of all movement when stirred by the infinite breeze. From within his lined and weathered body, his sharpened senses responded sensitively to every form that stirred. He savoured his life and his surroundings and he had gleaned much from countless treasured years of wandering. No experience had ever been wasted, even when sometimes he might have feared for his life. He had wandered over lands that others only learned of by his effort. His steps, through forests, across deserts, high over mountains, in fields and cities, running and elated, measured and weary, welcoming or departing, were the centre of his life. He had lived by the customs of the lands he inhabited, rejoicing or mourning, loving or weeping – and now he chose to rest.

He leant back peacefully against the stile as the breeze stirred his wisps of grey hair and cooled his tanned face. Then, from nowhere, the most delicate and exquisite sounds drifted on the air, capturing his attention and causing him to listen intently – first high in pitch, then low, swelling and receding, forming a strange and beautiful music that encircled the hilltop. Turning his head he tried to pinpoint the origin of the elusive sounds but as fleetingly as they had come, they vanished, and only the breeze stirred. A skylark let out its plaintive piping, rising in the air directly above him as he followed it with his gaze. Then once again, as suddenly as before, the same elusive sounds returned, filling the air with soft soothing chords, hovering and darting on the capricious breeze and just as swiftly dissolving.

The old man's senses were teased and he sharpened his efforts to recapture the magical tones. His curiosity enlivened, he longed for just one more chance to locate the exotic music. As if the very intensity of his desire had summoned it up, the

air instantly rang again with the limpid notes that had come
to haunt him. No longer were they faint and fleeting, making
him strain to hear them, but full and rounded, pure and strong,
with an elegance and delicacy that left him in awe of the musi-
cian's poetic mastery. From the highest piping, to the lowest
hollowed tones, the song of a mysterious flute rang through
the air with a reverence and enchantment that becalmed all
restlessness and made a telling distinction between the merely
tranquil and the deeply serene. Its mode he recognised as
archaic, with a curious chanting quality, yet superimposed
with a melody that he was convinced no mortal could ever
have conceived. The flute sang and filled the air for several
moments and the old man felt replenished and at peace. At
last the gentle melody receded, leaving him to ponder on the
strangeness of the occurrence that was unlike anything he
could remember.

As the soft harmonies faded away, he saw coming towards
him along the path from the valley, the figure of a young man
walking at a strong and steady pace. Watching him intently, he
tried to determine something of the character of the person
he was about to meet. As the youth strode effortlessly up the
slope towards the stile, he seemed alert to all that surrounded
him. He had seen the old man sitting there and several times
had looked straight towards him with a studied expression as
if he too were weighing up his fellow-traveller. Soon the old
man heard the sound of the youth's footsteps and a moment
later they were greeting each other.

"I haven't seen you on the hill before. You're a stranger
here," the youth observed with an engaging smile.

"Yes. And you too?" enquired the old man

"No. I know this country well enough. Have you travelled
far today?" the newcomer asked, observing the tramp's worn
shoes and small bundle of possessions.

"Not far. It's been hot and today I'm tired."

"This is a good place to rest. You won't often be disturbed here."

"The path down there looks well-used. There must be a fair number of passers-by," the old man said.

"Yes, passers-by, but that's all. No one will bother you. It's not a place where people usually choose to stop."

"Why not?" queried the old man as the youth decided to sit and lean back against the other post of the stile.

"It's the tower," the youth said looking at the old man and pointing up the hill.

"But that's the most beautiful part of the scenery here," the tramp said with surprise.

"Do you think so?" the youth beamed. "It's my favourite, too. Just look at those flowers – and not a single strand of ivy that dares to choke such a lovely building as that."

The tramp looked surprised and questioned why no ivy should grow there. The youth ran his hand through his hair and ruffled the dark curls that gave his tanned complexion a deep southern look.

"It's strange! I don't really know why – but it's right that it shouldn't. Poetic, really."

"Why?" the tramp enquired further.

"Because of its history. I like to find out about the old places in these remote areas. There's invariably some strange story to learn – and that's one of the strangest."

"Will you tell it to me?" the old man asked, his eyes twinkling with curiosity.

"Yes, if you like. Most people don't seem interested in such things. It's quite a climb up here and the local people have so many other distractions that this one doesn't seem very special to them any more. And as for the passers-by, well they just hear some ill-informed gossip and if they're energetic enough, they might come and take a picture and look at it when they get home."

The tramp snorted with disapproval, knowing only too well the kind of second or third-hand interest that many people generally took in their surroundings and the history of the very ground on which they walked.

"Well, let's forget about them. What's the story behind that?" the tramp asked as he looked from the youth and up the hill to the old stone tower with its exotic robe of cascading flowers.

"Well, how do I begin?" the youth smiled. "Yes, I know. Once upon a time…" he laughed. And the old man laughed back with an expression that, only to those who really knew him – of whom none survived – would have revealed that he felt he had discovered a friend.

"Go on," urged the tramp, looking pleased.

"There was once an old man who passed this way – perhaps not unlike yourself, except that this was at least two hundred years ago – and seeing the tower that stood at the top of the hill, he went to investigate. He found it bare inside but structurally sound and, being something of a hermit, he liked the idea of living there. So he made a few enquiries in the valley to see who owned it. The extraordinary thing was that not many people knew much about it, except for the fact that it had once been within the borders of an estate that had long ago been split up and disowned. Anyway, it transpired that due to some confusion about where the new boundaries lay, and the fact that neither owner of the two newly-formed estates wanted the trouble or responsibility for such a remote and useless folly, the old man came to an arrangement whereby he could live in it."

The tramp looked from the youth and back again to the tower, trying to imagine what it would be like to live in such lofty solitude.

"What then?" he asked.

"Well now, I'm sure you know what people are like! As soon as he had moved in, the villagers seemed to take a renewed interest in the old tower. They'd ignored it for years. But now with the presence of a stranger, not exactly in their midst, but who chose to visit them only once and then cut himself off from

172 Strange Tales in Fiction and Fact

their company, they found the idea of the old man living up here all alone too strange to accept."

The tramp gave his disapproving look again and the youth continued.

"Well, first the children, then the farm hands, and finally whole groups of villagers used to come up here – either at night or on Sundays – to look around and see how the old hermit used to spend his time. Their curiosity was really for want of something better to do and I suppose they saw him as some kind of potential amusement.

"So, in order to get rid of them, the old man decided to start the rumour that the tower was haunted. One night, he went down into the village amid stern and suspicious looks and let it be known – by 'confiding' at the local inn – that sometimes in the dead of night he was woken up by a fearful screaming and the shaking of his bed. And then he added, just for good measure, that he'd often seen a hooded figure walking down the path away from this very stile in the direction of the village."

The tramp suddenly convulsed with a fit of satisfied laughter and had to catch his breath to stop himself choking.

"Aah!" he exclaimed as soon as he'd recovered, "I bet that got 'em worried."

The youth smiled and hesitated long enough to make certain the old man was all right before he went on.

"To a point, yes. The wily old boy had naturally told the barman to keep it to himself, knowing that it would straight away become common knowledge throughout the entire village."

The tramp laughed again, amused by the predictability of human nature.

"Anyway, although his story had the desired effect for quite some time, eventually the more adventurous villagers – usually when they'd had too much to drink – took it into their heads to seek out the alleged hooded figure who some nights, so it was said, walked down the path towards the village. So once again the old hermit, wanting only to be left alone, had to contend with people staggering about in the bushes in the middle of the night looking for ghosts! And not only that. Some people still came here at other times because I suppose they couldn't really understand why, if the place was as haunted as they'd been led to believe, he should still want to live here.

"But then the rumour began to go around that if he *could* live here when it was haunted, there must be something about him that was even stranger than they'd first suspected. And it was then that people began to talk of witchcraft and the conjuring of devils."

The smile left the old man's face and he glanced again at the tower, then back to his story-teller, urging him to resume his tale, which he feared was about to take a more sinister turn.

"So what then?" he asked cautiously.

"Because of these new rumours, people once again began to shun the place. Except," the youth added in a lighter tone, warmed with a smile, "for the children."

The old man sensed that his story-teller had a fondness for children – that he himself shared – and he too dared to smile, if somewhat uncertainly.

"One day," he continued, "the old hermit was sitting in his tower playing his flute."

At the mention of a flute, the tramp suddenly interrupted. But then he stopped himself, not wanting to change the subject and urged his companion to carry on.

"Anyway, he was sitting up there," the youth pointed, "playing his flute. And as he did so a little group of children who'd decided to venture up here couldn't help but hear the sounds.

"You see, the inside of the tower is very big and since there's only an open flight of spiral steps all the way around to the room at the top, there's an extensive space in which any sound will echo. And that's what the old hermit liked to do. He'd sit at the top of the steps playing his flute into the vast well of the tower and listen to the sounds as they boomed out and echoed far into the fields.

"When the children heard the sounds, their first reaction was one of bewilderment. But they liked what they heard. There was nothing to frighten them and they forgot all about ghosts. Inevitably they rushed home to tell others and the word got about that there was a strange music to be heard coming from the tower. At first the adults were very sceptical and forbade their children to come back. But as you can imagine, one by one they did. And so it happened that the children would return home, unable to keep such a beautiful experience to themselves, and tell their parents of the strange music that they loved so much."

The youth paused for a moment and leaned forward, resting his elbows on his knees. The tramp looked at him as the tranquillity of the place they were sharing warmed him to the company of his new friend. He felt so much that he wanted to tell him about the music he'd heard earlier but decided to wait. The youth looked up at the tower, silently admiring its beauty, before looking back at the old man and continuing his story.

"Word of the mysterious music, which the children found so beautiful, became known all around the village. Of course, the children were scolded, warned not to come here any more and threatened with punishments if they did. It seemed, as far as the adults were concerned, that all this was further confirmation of the old hermit's sorcery. They began to worry that their children were being bewitched.

"But one of the older girls who'd heard the music, and was very distressed at being forbidden to listen to it again, had a younger brother who was dying. There was no hope for him and his mother had resigned herself to the apothecary's verdict. One day, when the mother was deeply distressed and the whole family knew that at any time the young boy might die, the girl begged her mother to bring her dying brother up here to listen to the mysterious music. She told her again and again, as all the children had, how beautiful and strange it was. In a moment of panic and anguish the mother picked up her child and let her daughter lead them to the tower. And sure enough, the old hermit was playing his flute to himself, very contentedly.

"Immediately the mother was enchanted by the sounds she heard. Her daughter was thrilled to be able to hear the music again and happy that her mother was so moved by its beauty. But after they had been standing here quietly listening for several minutes, the mother suddenly cried out. Her daughter turned to see what was wrong. Her brother was writhing violently in his mother's arms and she was beginning to sob."

The tramp was unable to resist interrupting. "What had happened?"

"The child had barely moved for a week and the music had had the most extraordinary effect on him. From that moment on, he began to recover and a few days later was completely well."

"But that's impossible!" exclaimed the tramp.

"Well, that's what the story says," the youth replied, patiently.

The tramp thought of the strange music he'd heard that day and was on the verge of mentioning it when his companion continued.

"As soon as they saw what had happened, the mother was overjoyed and word spread quickly of a miracle. In no time, people were venturing back to hear the hermit's music. Then they noticed the abundance of flourishing trees, flowers and wildlife in the vicinity of the tower and attributed this, too, to the strange music. And so it was that the villagers began to form a kind of cautious respect for the hermit.

"But no one ever saw him during all this time and when he, for his part, realised that they had begun to respect his privacy and could tell from their behaviour that they intended to leave him alone, he made no further efforts to repel them. He simply did as he wanted, which was frequently to play his flute, and let them come and go as they pleased – so long as they didn't come too near.

"Of course, news of the miraculous cure had travelled from this village to the next and far beyond. And so it was inevitable that in time more and more people began to climb the hill, bringing with them their sick and dying – though the climb itself must have killed off a good many. All kinds of people came from far and wide, especially on Sundays when they were free from the burden of working. Some days these slopes – just here, where we're sitting now – would see as many as a hundred people or more congregated beneath the tower to listen to the hermit's music."

The old tramp sniggered and put a hand to his mouth. "Talk about gullible," he laughed.

The youth looked at him impassively and his lips curled into a wry smile.

"Well, gullible or not, the fact was that dozens of them benefited and were cured. And not just from minor illnesses. Elderly people who were dying, children and parents, some with injuries, others with illnesses, were going away and recovering."

"And still no one ever saw the old hermit?" asked the tramp.

"No, not as far as I know," replied the youth.

"This really is a rather ridiculous story," exclaimed the old man. Then the memory of the strange flute music returned again to haunt him.

"Perhaps you might think so," the youth answered. "But maybe the end of it will show you that those to whom it happened certainly took it very seriously."

"So what happened?" the old man asked, his curiosity overtaking him.

"Very simple, really. As you can imagine, a lot of commotion resulted from all these events. Sunday was the only day that most people were free to make what had become something of a pilgrimage. And it was noticed that people were not attending their local churches as regularly as before. The word was about and everybody knew what was going on."

The tramp scratched his head as the youth continued.

"Consultations were held and it was decided that no less a person than a Bishop, together with two attendants, should visit the hermit. Quite a crowd gathered up here on the hill that day – but it was a very silent crowd. They feared the presence of the church dignitaries.

"After much argument and shouting through closed doors, the Bishop alone gained entry to the tower while his attendants remained outside. The hermit was questioned about his religious convictions and was plainly thought to be not only lacking in reverence and piety towards God – but to be in league with the Devil himself. It was not long before the Bishop found himself ejected from the tower and back on the outside of the door, calling frantically for his attendants to break it down. But they failed to do so and the Bishop, with obvious embarrassment at being so humiliated, turned his inquisitorial eye upon the villagers and dispersed the crowd with threats of hellfire.

"A healer in the community could only have gained his powers from the Devil, and for that the Church had only one solution. That night the tower went up in flames. It was professed that no one knew how – but certainly everyone knew why. The intensity of the glare was seen for miles across the surrounding countryside and quickly drew large crowds. The children, more than any, were distraught. They had come to love the hermit even though they never saw him.

"Though many – through fear of what they couldn't under-stand – thought it a good thing, others in the surrounding villages were shocked and horrified as the news quickly spread that the tower was on fire. Children screamed and wept and everywhere people were in panic. But none dared challenge the authorities they knew were responsible. Of course, there wasn't much to burn. The stone resisted the fire well enough, as you can see, though the intense heat, fanned by the winds up here on the hill, must have made it glow like a tormented spectre. Having finally broken down the door, they fed the fire constantly and it was a simple matter to stoke the flames inside, leaving no escape for the old hermit, whose fate was to be roasted alive."

The tramp's expression turned to outrage, all trace of his former frivolity now gone.

"So he died!" he exclaimed bitterly as the youth continued.

"A hideous death. But it is said that even then the hermit didn't show himself. Not once did he appear on the ledge at the top of the tower. Instead, so legend has it, he just sat inside and played his flute. His song echoed over and over through the roar of the flames as they licked higher around the tower, inside and out, destroying all but the stone itself.

"But after it was all over, there were many who said – though only in hushed voices, for fear of the churchmen – that the old hermit's music could still be heard. Many of the children who were here to see the last wisps of smoke swore that they could still hear his flute. And they refused to believe that anything so beautiful could have been destroyed in such a way. Never would they admit that he was dead, and again and again they claimed to hear his music whenever they visited the hill. And there are some who say," the youth added, "that it can still be heard to this very day."

The old man, having wanted all along to tell the youth that he had heard the strange and beautiful music, was so moved at that very moment that he was unable to do so. They both just sat in stillness as if each was listening for the haunting sounds. Then once again the story-teller broke the silence.

"The Church saw to it of course that the hermit had no burial place or memorial to preserve his memory or provoke any suggestion of martyrdom, but in its stupidity it overlooked that its victim had already been living in his own monument. He needed no other. And there it stands, adorned and more graceful than any. Perhaps what the villagers of two centuries ago observed about the abundance of nature within the vicinity of his music is borne out even now by the proliferation of all flowers, except the strangulating ivy, which still pay homage to his memory."

The two men, young and old, looked at the high stone tower, radiant in the evening sunlight. The breeze stirred the long grasses and the old man finally spoke – but only in a hushed whisper.

"I've heard it – the music. This afternoon, before you arrived."

"Is that so?" asked the youth. "There are still some who say they do."

"But you don't seriously think it was the music that cured the sick, do you?" the tramp asked.

"How else?" the youth shrugged. "Whatever it was, it happened."

"But it's hearsay – a folk tale. How can you know it really happened?"

"Was the music you heard today just a folk tale?" the youth asked. "And what did you feel when you heard it? You said you were weary today. Did you feel refreshed or replenished?"

The tramp hesitated for some time, grappling with the contradiction between his belief and his experience.

"Yes, as it happens, I did. But that was just because of... well... because it was so beautiful," the old man said, still unconvinced.

"Well, perhaps it does have some curative property then. But whatever it was, it caused enough of a stir to embarrass the Church into taking such extreme action," the youth pointed out.

"True. They burnt him alive – they were accustomed to such extremes for the slightest threat to their monopoly. But it still doesn't prove that the music produced anything but a sense of euphoria in the minds of the sick," the old man persisted.

"Can that be true of a dying infant? The first child who was brought here out of his mother's desperation? I think he might defeat your argument. And there were many others. But even if it was all in their minds, when a sick person is made healthy, does it really matter how, so long as it happens?"

"I suppose not," said the old man, resignedly.

"Anyway, I accept that you think my tale is only hearsay," the youth said. "Although you have admitted that when you heard the music before I arrived, you felt physically replenished."

"True," the old man replied, still a little sceptically.

The youth leapt to his feet.

"It doesn't really matter," he said as he stretched himself. "I don't really expect to convince you of anything – only to give you what I have to offer." He smiled. "And perhaps, too, I might be able to leave a small doubt in your mind. So you think the alleged cures were all in the sufferers' minds, do you? A figment of imagination?"

"I dare say," said the tramp.

"Then I too am a figment of your imagination. Because the music you heard today was mine."

The old man laughed nervously. "How? What do you mean?"

"We are not always what we seem. I was the hermit and this is my home. Through my solitude and contemplation, I discovered the art of healing with music. It was only after I reached a high degree of concentration and meditation that I had a strange dream – and in that dream I heard the music that you heard today. I memorised it and played it until I could never forget it. And you only heard it today because I was playing it."

The tramp laughed aloud. "But that's impossible nonsense. If your story is true, you died in the fire."

"I did," replied the youth.

"Huh! So now you're going to tell me I've been talking with a ghost."

"Why not? We all exist in many different forms. The children heard my playing after the fire had been thought to destroy me," said the youth. "And even you heard it earlier today."

"Huh!" the old man grunted again. But the memory of the

music haunted him persistently. "So how are you so young? You said it was an *old* hermit who lived here."

"True. In the beginning I was. And that is why I could never show myself after I had discovered the secret of the music. Yes, I played and played, and I knew that someone would come one day who would realise the beneficial effects of my song. Then, sure enough, it happened. My music, the manifestation of my mystical dream, cured the sick. But the more I played, the healthier I too became. I was in constant communion with my music and so I lost every ailment and weakness. And old age is only the accumulation of these – thus you see me young and always at the peak of my physical potential."

The tramp eyed the youth suspiciously.

"The villagers had seen me as an old man," the youth continued. "They were superstitious enough without my trying to explain to them my new appearance. So I always had to remain out of their sight. But the great hollow tower was my voice and without ever having to leave it, I could be heard as my music resounded across the fields." He looked down at the tramp and smiled warmly.

"And what about the Bishop? He must have been surprised by your appearance."

"Oh, the Bishop!" the youth recalled with amusement. "If I'd been only half as old as I was when I first came here, he'd have hauled me out by the scruff of my neck. How else do you think I ejected him so easily? Yes, the Bishop's surprise at seeing me so young, having been told that it was an old man he had to deal with, must have more than convinced him of my alleged pact with the Devil. Not that it mattered. He had only to observe my few books and writings relating to anything other than official dogma in order to decide what to do with me. My fate was probably sealed long before they made their visit."

The old man continued to look at him with a strange and confused expression.

"I have only told you what happened," said the youth, resignedly. "I did discover how to use music as a way of healing – but it is a special music. Anyone can discover it in time. You are a kindred spirit. When you leave this place, you will do so feeling physically replenished and with a deep serenity of mind. But before you go, follow that path and visit me in my hermitage. There are many myths in our cosmos and I seldom have the chance to meet such a passer-by. Is what I have related to you really so extraordinary in the light of your own wealth of experience?"

The old man stood up. "You want me to go to the tower?"

"It would please me if you did," the youth smiled.

"I intended to look at it anyway. It's beautiful."

Again the old man looked towards the top of the hill where now the sinking sun cast its golden light over the cascading flowers. But still he hesitated.

"It's still possible that you made up this entire story," he said to the youth.

"Yes, it's possible. But I didn't," the young man smiled back.

"You still expect me to believe you're a ghost?"

"I don't expect it, I simply ask it," the youth answered.

"Well, if you're a ghost, prove it. Disappear before my eyes."

And he did.

The old tramp looked around him in every direction. For a moment, everything was utterly still. He neither saw nor heard anything to indicate which way the youth had gone. The story he had been told hung in his mind and he was haunted even more by the memory of the music he had heard before encountering his companion. Now he wished that he hadn't asked him to prove that he was a ghost, for he felt acutely the sudden absence of his young friend. He wished he had been more open and less suspicious and would have welcomed more time in his company. But he had also known that they were about to part – his many years of travel and encounter had taught him that.

A rustling of foliage drew his attention to the tower on the hilltop as the abundant bushes and long grasses swayed in the breeze on the neglected path that led to it. Recalling the young man's entreaty to visit the tower, he moved towards the path. For a moment he thought he heard footsteps walking ahead of him and the long grasses seemed to swing back before him just as he reached them. Slowly he followed the path, which curved away in front of him. Bathed in the golden evening light, the wall of richly fragrant blossoms stretched high above him as he stood beneath the tower. He walked around it and found a gaping black hole where once a door had been. As he stepped inside, a dank smell assailed him, mingled with the faint memory of charred wood. Looking up, he saw blackened stone walls and crumbling steps spiralling up to the remnants of a solitary room that was eerily lit by the evening light. Massive shadows reached down from the high walls around him. As he walked towards the centre of the lonely tower and turned to look about, a low sound arose, as if from the building itself. It undulated around him and with each successive slow and gentle note, he recognised, unfolding before him, the same enchanted music he had heard before. As he stood there listening, a deep serenity enfolded and possessed him, just as the youth had promised.

Then the immortal music from the tower faded gradually away and with strange reluctance he turned to go. Reaching the arched doorway, he caught sight of some words, half-obscured, engraved on the stone interior. He peered closely, brushing away the layers of grime that had almost concealed them. Two lines, inscribed many years before by a sensitive hand, revealed themselves to his gaze:

Harken to the sound of the mystic flute,
When mind and soul would all their ills and age refute.

STRANGE TALES IN FACT ~
AN AUTOBIOGRAPHICAL NOTE

A brief sketch of the background against which many strange experiences took place

I seem to have had more than my fair share of odd and unexplained experiences. They began as early as pre-school and have continued over the years. My parents were Spiritualists and so I was familiar with the concept of an afterlife and the existence of another world from quite an early age. As a child, I recall my mother telling me that I had a "guardian angel" who looked over me in this life and to whom I could appeal in times of trial or crisis. I was also taught to pray and to appreciate the efficacy of the Lord's Prayer, not least because it is an ancient prayer used by millions of people over two thousand years and is therefore imbued, like a magic formula, with the psychic power that such a focus of attention and weight of devotion would create in it. Later my father developed an interest in reincarnation. In a nutshell, his belief was that this life experience, or incarnation, is a way for each of us to develop our spiritual strengths, which we do by dealing with the challenges with which life presents us. I came to share this view because it seemed to make sense to me and because my earliest strange experience seemed to suggest it so strongly.

In the next few paragraphs I will relate some incidents from my early years which are relevant to the stories that follow. I am largely self-taught. I went to a private grammar school where the standards of teaching were eccentric and erratic and many of the teachers rather odd. In junior school I enjoyed music above everything else and consequently excelled at it at that level but then our music teacher left and we had no more music lessons. Music has been very important to me from very early in my life and the seed for some of my strange experiences as well as a constant source of sustenance and strength. Although my mother had taught music before she married, for some reason she never taught me. My school reports usually showed me in the bottom third of my class and often one of the bottom two or three out of 20-24 pupils. I was always deeply distracted and found it difficult to pay attention to so many things that held so little interest and made so little sense to me.

As a child I was profoundly insecure and frightened of everything and everyone. This might have been something I brought with me into the world from a previous life or it might have been because I was born in 1943 in the middle of the Second World War amid much fear and uncertainty. Undoubtedly it was connected to the fact that my father had an unpredictable temper that frequently manifested in physical violence. I remember there always seemed to be tension and rows between my parents that led to terrible atmospheres in the house and I seldom looked forward to my father coming home from work. I was terrified of him because his violence could be completely gratuitous. He would hit me for no apparent reason and I would cry, and the next hit would be *because* I was crying. This then became his reason for continuing the hitting and he carried on until I stopped crying, which created a terrible double-bind from which I could not escape. For several years I could only get to sleep at night if I had both arms covering my face and head. These extreme circumstances seemed to be the trigger for the first of my own odd experiences. In later life, my mother told me she had never witnessed my father's temper prior to their marriage. I asked her why she hadn't left him there and then and she explained that in those times women were not allowed to have jobs and be independent if they were married and the ignominy of divorce or separation would have put an intolerable strain on her family, which was quite well-known in the local town.

I believe my mother made her marriage bearable by focussing her attention on her children. Their first child lived only eight hours, after the doctor who attended my mother put the forceps through his skull while trying to deliver him. My mother was, by all accounts, "demented" by this devastating experience and the doctor advised my father that she should have another child as quickly as possible! Eighteen months later my older brother was born and three and a half years after that I was born. My eldest brother, who of course I never knew, was to play an apparently decisive part in another of my earliest strange experiences. Despite the difficulties in her marriage, my mother was always gentle and kind and did everything she could to make our lives as children happier.

My father had an avid interest in books and the occult. He also dominated every conversation and seemed to believe that "age equals wisdom", which meant that he always knew everything while his children could never possibly know anything. His idea of humour was always at someone else's expense and usually involved the ridicule or humiliation of one of us. He drove away my mother's friends with his domineering presence and there were always audible sighs with sidelong glances if ever he began holding forth on his favourite subject of "the supernatural" at extended family gatherings. But I learned much about his ideas and beliefs for which ultimately I'm grateful – and he certainly taught me how *not* to behave in the world. He also made me aware of nature, birdsong, trees and the countryside, for which I now have a great love not unlike his own, and the beauty of nature has always remained a source of stimulation to me on long solitary walks when I'm pondering life, art, people or new ideas for stories.

As a qualified professional in engineering and draughtsmanship, he always had a job and was exempt from military service during the war. We were never a wealthy family and my mother worked part-time to help make ends meet. Life was hard for both my parents but my father's one delight was to take us on a fortnight's caravan holiday each summer to Challaborough in Devonshire. On fine days, if we weren't on the beach, we would walk along the country lanes to the nearby villages of Ringmore and Bigbury, observing the hedgerows, as my father told us ghost stories to the accompaniment of the wind whistling gently in the telegraph wires. These stories both frightened and excited me and the eerie sound of the wind in the wires was the perfect background to the tales he told us, which were not invented but were mostly from books he'd read about ghosts in stately homes or fictional tales from the paperback collections that lined his bookshelves. The idea of ghosts was perfectly normal to him. They were the spirits of people who were "dead", who were "earthbound", or caught in the astral plane of existence, unable to move on into the next world, either through ignorance of what had happened to them, undue attachment to the trappings of this life, or because of unsavoury deeds which, we were told, consigned them to some aimless wandering, cut off from the powers of light. He was appalled by the idea of "ghost hunters" who spent nights in haunted houses hoping to see some ghostly manifestation, rather than praying for these unfortunates in order to help them.

Like so much in life, he was full of contradictions and even now it is hard to reconcile how he can have had that concern for discarnate beings while beating his own wife and children. But Hitler was a vegetarian and was concerned about humane ways to kill animals! Much later in life, when my mother had been dead for several years, my father mellowed considerably but he never really seemed to come to terms with his loss and talked nostalgically of his "wife and two smashing kids" as though that was the one fact that made his life rewarding and gave it meaning – that and his belief in what life was for and what happens when we die.

Incidents that happened to my parents

My father and mother both had odd experiences of the super-normal before my brother and I were born. Once, before they were married, when they were on holiday staying in an old farm-house at Barnstaple in Devonshire, my mother was sleeping in a separate room and woke terrified and screaming as the bedclothes were lifted off her, "as though someone were looking to see who was sleeping there", and then dropped onto her again – but there was no one else in the room.

Then my father often told the tale that first engaged his interest in such matters. At home when he was a boy, his parents had a lodger living in their house. The lady in question, Mrs Rix, became pregnant and ill and died in childbirth in hospital. At home, my father [then a teenage boy] and his mother, brother and sister were sitting at the meal table and heard a grief-stricken sobbing throughout the house as though Mrs Rix had returned in her state of loss and distress, not knowing what to do or where to go. The sobbing continued until, at the instigation of his mother, they all prayed for her to be "led into the light", after which there was no further disturbance. This experience made a lasting impression on my father and led him to explore the subject of Spiritualism. As a fan of Arthur Conan Doyle's Sherlock Holmes stories, it was only a small step before he discovered the same author's book about Spiritualism, entitled *The Land of Mists,* which instantly engaged him.

My own first strange experience

By the time I was a small boy of pre-school age, my own first experience manifested. At the time it took place I was not aware that there was anything odd about it. What I remember is that there were times when I was deeply distressed and in tears after my father had hit me and I would run away into an empty corner of the house, beside myself with fear and rage. In those moments I had a "magic" word that I used to say to myself which gave me strength to resist and endure my predicament. I don't know where the word came from. It was as if I simply knew it or had invented it. The word I repeated to myself was "Rome". It was my private word that I never mentioned to anyone else. These events happened before I'd ever set foot in a school and I was later quite indignant when I learned that there was a place called Rome. It bothered me that other people knew my secret word but it didn't lessen its power for me. I became fascinated by ancient Rome as depicted in our Latin text books and pored over pictures of Roman soldiers in sandals and tunics and senators in togas. I became completely absorbed in the subject and, despite my general lack of academic ability, found myself reading and re-reading *The Twelve Caesars* by Suetonius, a book that became a great favourite at a relatively early age, sitting on my bookshelf alongside *Alice in Wonderland* and *The Secret Seven*.

This Roman theme stretched a long way into my life. By the age of 17 I was not unfamiliar with the idea of consulting a medium for a private "sitting", or "reading", as we preferred to call it. A woman in our home town had a good reputation and I took to visiting her twice a year. She would go into trances and I would, purportedly, speak to my "guides". At such moments I would not only speak with and hear the voices of a Chinese or North American Indian but would see these figures in a compelling transformation of the medium's face.

I had a considerable conflict raging inside me at this time. With my father's aggressive behaviour and his constant undermining and belittling of any attempt I made to "be my own person" or express my own interests, I grew to loathe him all the more. And so it didn't sit well with me that I was showing such an interest in a subject about which he talked interminably. I wanted to be as different from him as possible. Even so, I couldn't help but be interested in something with such far-reaching implications. Out of this inner conflict, one day at the end of a reading, I said to the medium: "I wish there was something you could tell me that would convince me of what you believe in". She immediately replied: "Does Rome mean anything to you?" I was startled by this and confirmed that it did. She then told me that I had lived in the time of Julius Caesar, that I had been very rich, powerful, handsome and sadistic and had abused my power, as a result of which I had subsequently incarnated as a slave in Persia. Then she said: "One day another medium will confirm this." Twenty-one years later I went to see a well-known medium of her day, Ursula Roberts. By the time this event took place, I'd actually lost my intense interest in matters Roman. But I had barely sat down when she said: "Does Rome mean anything to you?" In fact, she did not repeat every detail I'd previously been told but she did confirm that I'd lived in those times. There was something about the way she had asked her opening question, the fact that she used the phrase exactly as I'd remembered it and in the same tone of voice as the first medium, that made me accept it as confirmation. But I was then taken aback as she went on to tell me about another matter so deeply personal to me that I'd never uttered a word of it to anyone in my life. In fact I was profoundly shocked that she was able to tell me about something that went to the very core of my being, and her ability to do so only emphasised the remarkable nature of her powers.

A case of unaccountable good fortune?

Another early experience was when I was a reluctant boy scout. I'd been cajoled into joining the scouts by my father, my brother and the scoutmaster who had come to our house specifically for this purpose. As a result, one evening some months later, I was aboard an underground train with my brother and another friend, having been to a scout "Gang Show" [an annual event where scouts take part in a variety show that they also stage and direct] at Golders Green. The Northern Line underground train was heading for Waterloo where we would catch a Southern Region overground train to Strawberry Hill. Suddenly my brother said that we had to get off the underground train. I didn't see why and argued the point, reluctant to be told what to do by my big brother in front of our friend! But my brother was insistent and the matter became urgent for him, whereupon he more or less took me by the collar and made me get off the train as our friend followed. As we stood on the platform waiting for the next train, I recall continuing to argue that all we had done was delay our journey. By the time we arrived at Waterloo we were late and had to race up the escalator to where our connecting train was waiting. But just as we arrived at the platform, a porter pulled the gate across and refused to let us on. We stood there trying to persuade her to let us through while the train sat at the platform for some time before it eventually departed. Our parents had always told us to get in trains at the end nearest the exit of the station to which we were travelling. Had we done so on this occasion we would have been in the first coach of the train we missed. That train crashed at Barnes with fatalities in the first coach. Unaware of what had happened, all subsequent trains were delayed and we eventually arrived home well after midnight. Next morning, the newspapers carried the story of the train crash and we realised how my brother's intuition had saved us from possible catastrophe.

There is a footnote to this story. While we were out that evening, our parents had decided to go for a walk by the river at Teddington Lock. Ever since the tragedy of my mother's first child she had felt from time to time that his discarnate spirit came to her. My brother, like many children, had had an imaginary friend with whom he played when he was very young and my mother believed this to be her lost first child. On the night of the rail accident, while walking by the river, my mother had apparently said to my father that she had heard a voice saying: "Don't worry. They will be all right". She felt it was our older brother. She didn't know what it meant at the time and only began to realise when we were so late arriving home. As we talked and compared notes the next day, we realised that she had heard this voice at the same time that we were getting off the underground train.

Two very different houses

The house we lived in was also the setting for some odd occurrences. I always think of it as a cold, dark, uninviting place. But perhaps this really reflects more the feeling I had about my entire childhood rather than just the house in which it unfolded. The truly "sunny" patches in my memories of childhood all are to do with my maternal grandparents and their Georgian house at Twickenham Green. The house my parents occupied, where I grew up, was a late Victorian semi-detached in Walpole Road, Twickenham, less than ten minutes' walk from my grandparents. My mother's father was a local estate agent and he put up some capital to allow my impecunious father to buy the house that he and my mother occupied shortly after I was born. Apparently my mother had said when they moved in how much she disliked the house – but she spent the rest of her life there.

Not long after they moved in, my brother and I were playing on the floor of the front room. It was war time and I would have been only about a year old. Suddenly my mother had an impulse to come and get us and take us to the kitchen at the back of the house. Within moments of reaching the kitchen, a bomb exploded in the next street and all the windows of our front room were blown in and the entire floor was strewn with broken glass.

After the war, when my brother and I were still small, my mother would wash us both in the bath and then leave us to play with some wooden boats before coming back to dry us. On several occasions, one or other of us would ask our mother when she came back, why she had gone into a room that was never normally used, at the end of a short corridor beyond the bathroom. In order not to frighten us, she would always make up an excuse for having gone into the room, which was usually kept locked. But in fact, she told us years later, she had never been into that room at the times when we both believed she had. This is not an experience I consciously remember, though my brother does, but I was told of it when I was older.

It's always a bonus to have an experience that involves and is verified by another person. I've had two such experiences both, as it happens, concerning animals. One was at my grandparents house at Twickenham Green and the other was in the house at Walpole Road. I will relate the latter first.

For some years my parents used to hold a "circle" once a week, consisting of a group of interested people who gathered to sit together and tune in to the spirit world, to pray and possibly receive "messages" via the impressions that any member of the group might have. They were aiming to develop their psychic faculties, which my mother did over time. When they could afford it they paid a professional medium to join them, to bring additional energy into the group and to teach them how to develop their powers. One such medium told my parents that a long time ago, the upper part of the house had been lived in by an elderly couple with a dog. The main room they occupied was at the end of the corridor beyond the bathroom, where my brother and I had been sure our mother went when she'd left us to play in the bath. The medium said these people were harmless but were still present in the house. I mention this because it makes more sense of one of the two animal-related experiences I had and which my father and mother both experienced as well.

We had agreed to accommodate my uncle's two rather boisterous dogs for a week while he went on holiday one summer. They were quite a handful and much to my mother's annoyance, enjoyed gaining access to the main hallway to slide up and down the polished linoleum floor, which was left in a terrible state and covered in scratches. It was therefore quickly established that under no circumstances were the dogs to be let into the hall. One Sunday afternoon just after lunch, I was coming down the stairs to the hall and heard the dogs scratching frantically on the other side of the kitchen door, trying to get into the hallway. As I reached the door to go into the kitchen, I inched it open very carefully to stop the dogs getting out. But to my surprise there were no dogs behind the door at all. At the same time, as I entered the kitchen, my parents who were both sitting there reading newspapers, said to me: "How did the dogs get into the hall?" They had both also heard the frantic scratching at the kitchen-to-hall door and naturally assumed it was coming from the other side. In fact, we discovered that the two visiting dogs were not in the house at all but were in the back garden with my brother. We concluded from this odd occurrence that maybe the presence of two very lively dogs in the house had in some way aroused the dog that lived there with the elderly couple, referred to by the medium, and caused it to manifest in some way. Whatever the explanation, all three of us distinctly heard the scratching at the door.

These were not the only sounds that we all heard at different times in the house in Walpole Road. While alone there, I more than once heard footsteps in the room above the kitchen – the same room at the end of the corridor beyond the bathroom. My mother frequently heard them too. Yet these footsteps were not frightening. They were just a familiar sound that, at some level of consciousness, we were all used to hearing and so we thought little more about them.

The other animal-related event happened one bright Saturday morning in the kitchen at my grandparents' house at Twickenham Green. It involved their tabby and white cat which had strayed in many years before and been adopted. For several months recently the cat had been missing and was presumed dead. Apparently a neighbour had threatened to poison it because it dug up her vegetables. I don't know if that was true. All we knew was that it had not been seen for several months. My father, mother and I had arrived at my grandparents' house after shopping in Twickenham. It was something of a ritual every Saturday morning that we called in on our way home to have tea and buns. I walked into the kitchen and sat down in my favourite wooden armchair in one corner. My father sat in another corner by the window and while my mother, grandmother and aunt were all talking in the kitchen doorway, I happened to look at the floor and was surprised to see the cat sitting in the middle of the room washing itself. I knew it had long been missing and no one had said anything about its return, so I was very surprised to see it and was on the verge of exclaiming: "There's the cat!" But before I could get the words out, my father pointed to exactly where I could see it and made exactly the same exclamation. We were both astonished and looked at each other. When we looked back at the floor the cat was gone and was never seen again. I was, of course, delighted that my father had been quicker than me with his own exclamation because it proved to me that I wasn't imagining it, especially as he was also pointing to the very spot where I had seen it.

My Grandfather

As I've mentioned, the "sunny" patch in my childhood terrain was the house at Twickenham Green where my maternal grandparents lived and where we were frequent visitors. It was a place where I could let go of my fear. There was always a warm welcome, with buns and cakes and pocket money, and we found every foothold to climb the large fig tree in a back garden that afforded us many adventures with places to hide and opportunities to lose ourselves. They were the archetypal grandparents, always welcoming, generous and kind. As a child, I was blissfully unaware of the undercurrents of unhappiness that I later discovered were present in their lives too. While my grandmother, who was the one most in evidence, epitomised gentle loving kindness, it was my grandfather who made an abiding impression on me. He was always well turned out, with his gold pocket watch in his waistcoat, his big white moustache, and often with a freshly cut rose in his buttonhole. Though I didn't know it at the time, the figure he cut looked rather like Sir Edward Elgar. We were always delighted to see him and he always gave the impression that it was entirely mutual. He smelt of a mixture of ginger, peppermints, medicine and cigars, and he invariably pressed half a crown or five shillings into my hand to "buy some sweets". I always remember how fond he was of his rose garden, which lay between two trellised arches separating one lawn with its pond from another lawn, beyond which were the vegetable garden, two greenhouses, the chicken run and an old shed full of cobwebs, old cricket bats and curious smells. In the summer, he would walk to the rose garden and cut a bloom for his buttonhole before driving to his office.

Inside the house the carpets were thick and everything was old and polished and welcoming. Each Christmas, we helped to move the high mirrored sideboard to one side of the dining room so that the double doors connecting to the drawing room could be opened. On the sideboard was a tantalus, which always fascinated me, in which three cut glass decanters were visible but inaccessible. And in the drawing room was the out-of-tune upright piano with two candle-holders on it, where I often sat for hours absorbed in the sounds of its lowest notes. I loved that room, with its elaborate porcelain ornaments, the enormous comfy sofa and the French windows that led directly into the conservatory. When the sideboard had been moved, we put an extra leaf into the big mahogany dining table in readiness for the Christmas family gathering. Beside the marble mantelpiece in the dining room was my grandfather's small glass-fronted cigar cabinet, which attracted me because of its most appealing and pungent odour. On the mantelpiece itself sat the dining room clock which always chimed on the hour. I loved being in that house and I loved my grandparents. When my grandfather died, aged 84, the dining room clock stopped and never chimed again. Such accounts of clocks stopping and pictures falling from walls are not uncommon but this was one I knew to be true.

The father of a friend of mine collapsed one evening and was taken to hospital where he died at 5.05 the following morning. A few weeks later my friend's mother asked him if he would like to have his father's watch. As she gave it to him, they both noticed that it had stopped at exactly 5.05. Many years later, I met a remarkable painter, some of whose works I purchased, who told me that when he was born, a clock in the family that had apparently not worked for years suddenly came to life and continued working thereafter. I have no reason to doubt either of these stories.

After my grandfather's death, he was often in my thoughts. By this time I was living in a large bedsit in St Margaret's and one particular day I suddenly felt his presence in the room quite overwhelmingly. It felt as though he was standing behind me and at the same time there was a strong scent of roses. There were no flowers in the room at all and when I looked behind me there was no one to be seen – but the sense of his presence was unmistakeable and the perfume of roses persisted.

Premonitions

One Christmas, long after both my grandparents had died, my mother, father, brother and I spent Boxing Day evening at my aunt's flat in Strawberry Hill. My aunt was my mother's sister and she had looked after my grandparents at the end of their lives. As my mother and father got up to leave at the end of the evening and bade their farewells to the rest of us, I suddenly "knew" that we had just spent our last Christmas together. It was such a strong feeling and after my mother and father had gone, I found myself saying: "Mum won't see another Christmas". My aunt was startled – but my mother died the following August, aged 73, which was not so old in a family where everyone else lived well into their eighties.

On another occasion many years before, I was at a concert at the Royal Festival Hall. As the conductor walked up to the podium I was struck by the ashen pallor that seemed to surround him. I turned to the friend I was with and said: "That man is going to die soon". A week later his death was announced in the press.

I saw the same ashen pallor on my grandfather during his last illness and knew what it meant. Just before he died he said to my aunt, who was looking after him: "My mother came to see me."

My aunt contradicted: "No, you mean your wife." His wife was still living at the time. But my grandfather was adamant. "No, it was my mother," he said. He died that night.

Accounts of people in the last stages of life seeing departed loved ones who come to visit or meet them are quite frequent. In a recent and reliable account, I was told of a friend's sister who was close to death. She had been very ill but the moment before she died she suddenly sat up in bed with an enormous smile and stretched out her arms to someone who was plainly familiar to her. So strong and animated a reaction is, I think, quite unusual and the nurse who was sitting with her was taken aback by the energy her patient displayed in her dying moments.

Omens

All my life I'd heard my father talk of finding dead birds whenever there was a significant death. On the days that each of his parents died, as well as various other relatives, this phenomenon had coincidentally presented itself and he had found a dead bird lying in his path. It struck him by its consistency and had taken on a meaning for him. Whenever he saw a dead bird thereafter he began to wonder whether he would hear of the death of someone close to him.

My mother died in hospital from what I really believe was a lack of the will to live. She had a number of ailments, none of which in itself was life-threatening, and not least of which were rapidly failing sight [after years of taking drugs for glaucoma her sight had virtually gone] and kyphosis, which left her constantly slumped forward. She had little pleasure left in life and was admitted to hospital with a minor gastric ailment. My brother and I both arrived to visit her in the same hour and we sat with her, each holding a hand, until the nurses came to rearrange her bed so that she could sleep. My brother and I waited nearby while the nurses drew the curtain around her bed and left her for a few minutes. At that point I heard her groan and sigh and I "knew" she was dying. I also knew that she had nothing to live for and I willed her to go. It was a merciful release. My attention was drawn to the ceiling above her curtained bed and I continued willing her to go and silently said my farewell. A nurse came rushing in and they tried to start her heart but it was too late. Ten minutes later my father arrived, completely unprepared for the news that awaited him. After helping him to recover with a cup of tea, my brother and I walked with him out to the car park. On the way, we passed outside the window next to which my mother's bed was positioned in the ward where she had just died. On the ground directly under the window was a dead bird. We all saw it but, for my father, it was inevitable.

Instincts and intuitions

As life unfolded, I developed a passionate interest in "classical" music. I put the word "classical" in quotes because, strictly speaking, classical music refers to the pre-Romantic period and ends with Beethoven. But it was, and is, the Romantic and Modern aspects of "classical" music that have always interested me and by the age of 11 had first attracted my attention. I remember listening to an overseas radio station on our old wireless set, my ear pressed hard against the loud speaker, trying to savour the first symphonic sounds that came to haunt me. I learnt that the piece I was hearing was *La Mer* by Debussy and it caused me there and then to discard most of my small collection of "pop" records on 10 inch 78rpm discs and to save up my newspaper round money to buy my first LP: the Toscanini performance of Debussy's haunting master-piece. So began my lifelong exploration of "classical" music. Each LP I bought introduced me to another composer who dwelt on the other side of the disc. By the age of 13 I had discovered the music of Shostakovich, then regarded as outrageously modern, and felt I'd met a true kindred spirit. His music accompanied me through my life from that time on and his picture hung on my bedroom wall. In the same way that the word "Rome" had been my consolation in my earliest years, Shostakovich was my friend and ally through a stormy adolescence. Latterly, I've understood how this instinctive liaison made sense. While this great man lived under the brutal and unpredictable dictatorship of Stalin, he spoke to me through his music, which gave me strength in what amounted to my own unpredictable and often terrifying domestic equivalent.

It was through music that I learned much about other countries and the other arts. I was beguiled and fascinated by the names of many of the composers I discovered, especially of Russian and Eastern European origin, and felt an affinity to their world and their music. Vocal and choral works introduced me to poetry and dramatic texts while LP sleeves made me aware of the visual arts. An early musical discovery was the tone poem *The Isle of the Dead* by Rachmaninov, which in turn led me to the great Symbolist painter, Arnold Böcklin, whose painting of the same name inspired it. As my world expanded through these interests, I became aware of innate preferences and antipathies. We can't always explain why we are drawn to or repelled by the things that we are, but after my intense preoccupation with ancient Rome I found through music that it was eventually replaced by a fascination for all things mediaeval and I was drawn to Gregorian chant in particular. This, combined with pictures of Gothic cathedrals [I particularly remember one LP sleeve of Bruckner's 9th Symphony conducted by Carl Schuricht] seemed to rouse something very deep in me and for many years I was fascinated by the images and atmospheres evoked by early pictures of cathedrals, churches and monasticism. In equal measure, I was repelled at that time by anything to do with Spain or Spanish culture, although this antipathy did not extend to the Moorish influences. On the other hand, whenever I saw pictures of Prague, or even unidentified scenes of the Czech countryside, I experienced a warm sense of "recognition". These were innate, instinctive gut reactions, in no way connected with any rational process.

In my enclosed and unhappy world of constant uncertainty and domestic violence, I grew very introverted as my confidence was consistently undermined and I took refuge in my records with their pictures and literary references. These were at the centre of my world and I communed with them daily – and I couldn't help noticing the things that drew me to them and the things from which I recoiled. This polarity between Spain and Prague was always present but I never understood it. With my early instinctual belief in reincarnation, I felt that I must certainly have lived in Czechoslovakia because it seemed so familiar to me. And while I felt an attraction to the monastic life, which I became convinced I'd lived more than once in earlier times, there remained the unexplained antipathy to most things Spanish, a country steeped in a monastic tradition.

Some years later I read a book by Frances A. Yates called *The Rosicrucian Enlightenment* and everything began to make sense. Never before had I realised the close connection between such seemingly disparate cultures as the Spanish and Czech. Avidly I read that, in 1612, the Emperor Rudolph II had moved his imperial court from Vienna to Prague and created there an open and experimental culture, a melting pot of ideas, that attracted such luminaries as Giordano Bruno, John Dee and Johannes Kepler, and was tolerant to occult, alchemical and astrological studies. But when Rudolph died this renaissance paradise was immediately attacked and destroyed by Catholic forces, including Rudolph's own nephew, Philip II of Spain. As I read these revelations, I suddenly understood my deep-seated, innate feelings about these two cultures and knew exactly where my loyalties had lain. I "knew" I had been there.

My belief in reincarnation has been with me since childhood and it's how I make sense of these feelings. Some people might say that I have simply taken it on from my father, but for most of my life I have been at pains not to be like him. It is simply a very powerful feeling I have – even when, at times, I would rather have believed there is only oblivion at the end of life. It simply won't go away and, furthermore, I understand it's a belief I share with two-thirds of the world's population.

An oddity unexplained

One of the strangest things I have ever seen was from a train window just before arriving at Barnes station on my way to Waterloo one summer day. As the train glided slowly by, I looked out of the window upon a completely empty park, at one side of which was a small children's playground with a see-saw, a small roundabout and a row of three swings. There might also have been a slide but I don't recall. What I do recall most vividly is that although this scene was completely deserted, one of the three swings was gently swinging back and forth. The other swings were completely still, so it wasn't the wind. And it would have taken a strong wind to move a swing as much as this one was moving. Not that the movement was extreme – but it was gently purposeful. I have never been able explain it. This was the seed for my story, *Storm Child*.

A haunted house

In the 1960s I became acquainted with a group of people who were interested in ghosts and other psychic phenomena. One of these people was a retired man who lived alone in a 200 year old farmhouse in Essex. At bank holiday weekends he would sometimes invite a small group of us to stay in his house, where we were most generously entertained and well fed, and where we would discuss our common interests and talk of any recent accounts of ghosts or hauntings that had come to light. Our host always scanned his local newspaper for any ghostly stories that were reported, of which there seemed to be several over the years, and would make contact with those involved in the strange events, often inviting them to dinner when we were visiting, so that we could hear their accounts first hand. Alternatively, he would arrange for us to visit the person, so that we could discuss their experiences over morning coffee.

I particularly recall one visit to a local lady who lived in a cottage adjacent to an open field. She told us how she had been nursing her sick brother who had been staying with her a few years before. His condition had deteriorated over a number of weeks and the prognosis was not optimistic. Then one morning after her brother had had a very difficult and disturbed night, she stepped outside her front door and was surprised to see, standing in the adjacent field, a heron. Not only are herons notoriously shy birds [at least they were then] but they are known to frequent watery places and there was no water in the field or anywhere close to hand. She had never seen a heron in this field in all the years she had lived there and thought it very unusual.

Next morning, after another disturbed night when her brother seemed to sink hopelessly into his illness, she went outside and was surprised to see the heron again. This time the bird was much closer to the fence that separated her garden from the field. On the third morning, as her brother continued to decline, she found the heron standing in her own garden. That night the inevitable happened and her brother died. When she went to the door later that morning she found the heron actually standing on her doorstep. Thereafter she never saw the bird again. As with my father's experiences of birds, it seems that for some people they serve as portents or perhaps even as messengers.

Our host's big old farmhouse had been the scene for a number of psychic disturbances and as we retired each evening to large feather beds, I couldn't help but remember some of the stories he had told us of his own experiences while living there. For myself, I had only one experience for which I could not account and it happened within the first fifteen minutes of my very first visit. I will come to this shortly. Meanwhile, I understood that there had been a very bloody suicide in the house. A previous occupant had apparently cut his throat with an open razor. The act had taken place in a room that was now kept locked and unused, except as a repository for excess furniture and junk. Our host related some unnerving tales of his own experiences while living there alone.

He told of several occasions when he had been sitting in his large kitchen – which retained its original flagstone floor and a water pump next to the modern sink – only to be assailed by tremendous crashing sounds, as if all the crockery displayed on the dresser was being smashed on the floor. In fact, the crockery remained intact on the dresser but the noise went on interminably until, on more than one occasion, he was driven out of the house and repaired to his local inn until closing time. Upon returning home, all was quiet.

On other occasions, he would be roused in the middle of the night by violent thumping sounds as if, he said, there were half a dozen men fighting and brawling on the landing outside his bedroom door. Whenever this happened he got up from his bed and opened the door, whereupon there was instant and total silence. We always marvelled that he could live under such conditions. But, like the footsteps in the room above the kitchen at our home in Walpole Road, he simply became used to it and never felt that any harm would come to him.

The other two stories he told both involved the disappearance and reappearance of objects. After a trip to the Orient he had brought back a fine silk dressing gown that he used regularly. One day it disappeared and he couldn't find it anywhere. As he lived alone there was no one else who could have moved it. It remained a mystery for a year or more and in the meantime he had purchased another dressing gown. Eventually he had occasion to go up into one of the three enormous and rarely-used attic rooms, which were very dusty and unkempt. There, in a corner, he found his dressing gown, rolled up and moth-eaten.

The other story of an object being moved was just as simple but rather more dramatic. He had bought a new pair of secateurs for pruning in the garden. Again, he used them several times and replaced them where he always kept them. And again, one day when he went to use them, they had disappeared. Eventually he bought another pair. Then one morning about a year later, he turned the corner at the top of the stairs to come down and saw the secateurs lying in the middle of the rug on the hall floor. He identified them as the pair that had gone missing but they were now rusted, and they were wet, as if they had only just been used in the garden.

My own odd experience there was not especially disturbing but was nevertheless inexplicable. Upon arriving on my first visit I went to the bathroom to wash my hands. As I entered the bathroom I saw the wash basin just inside the door to my left. At the far end of the room was another door standing open, which led to the toilet. As I was washing my hands I glanced into the mirror above the wash basin and saw the door at the far end of the room swinging shut. Of course I'd heard a number of stories about the house before this visit and wondered whether I was witnessing something unusual. Then it occurred to me that maybe someone [I couldn't think who] was using the toilet and had pulled the door shut. But this was unlikely and there was no sound to indicate that there was any occupant. Perhaps, I then rationalised, I had stepped on a loose floor board that had somehow knocked the door at the far end of the room, causing it to swing shut. As it was an old house, this explanation seemed reasonable. I finished washing my hands and went towards the toilet door just to make sure no one was there. I opened it and the small room was indeed unoccupied. As I let go of the door it swung back against the wall, to where it had been when I first entered the room. This puzzled me and so I pulled the door to a half-open position and let it go. Again it swung open, back to the wall. I repeated the experiment a dozen times and always the door swung open. Whenever I used the bathroom on subsequent visits I couldn't resist but try the experiment again and unfailingly the door swung back to the wall. I could never explain why the door had swung shut on that first visit but I later learned that the bathroom had once been a part of the locked and unused bedroom – the haunted room, as we referred to it – and had been partitioned off to create a bathroom at a later date.

During one of our gatherings, we visited a local inn that was reputed to be haunted. With us was a dog belonging to one of our number. We had heard that no dog would walk across the middle of the bar at the inn we were heading for. When we arrived, we took the dog in with us. It refused to cross the bar and would only walk to the opposite side of the room by going around the perimeter, staying as close to the wall as it could.

There was another house in which I had a striking experience. As a result of my association with the same group that took me to the farmhouse in Essex, a number of us were due to assemble to spend a night in a residential house in Nottingham. I arrived by car with the organiser of this event at about 4.00pm. Due to various psychic disturbances, the family who lived there had moved out and we had been given a key to let ourselves in. The events that led the family to request an investigation included the appearance of a young man who had apparently committed suicide in the house. Once we were inside, the organiser said that he was going off to meet some other people at the station, and so I was left alone in the house. Naturally, I wandered slowly around all the rooms, standing silently in each one to see if I experienced any unusual sensations. Having explored the ground floor, I went upstairs and stood for a few moments on the landing. The doors to all the rooms were open and I stepped towards the main front bedroom. As I entered, I shivered with the chill that greeted me. It was markedly colder than every other room in the house and yet the sun was streaming in through the window and the room was filled with bright light. It should have been the warmest room in the house. Later I learned that this was the room in which a previous occupant had committed suicide.

Mystical states and visions

In the late 1970s I was experimenting with my time. I enjoyed living alone in rented bedsits and had no commitments and few responsibilities. I whittled my working week down to just two days and adopted a very frugal lifestyle, with the other five days to myself when I could simply "be". I sometimes wondered whether I wasn't in some way recreating the monastic lives that I was convinced I'd lived in previous incarnations. My aim was to live as much as I could to my own natural rhythm. As Thoreau said, "Let each man step to the drummer he hears". This was what I came to refer to as the "three year experiment" in my life. I ate only when I was hungry, slept when I was tired, regardless of the hour, and spent much time alone. I have never felt lonely when I'm alone and, like Thoreau, "I never found the companion that was so companionable as solitude". It occurred to me that "alone-ness" is "all-oneness". As my experiment continued, interspersed by two days of work each week, I discovered a deep contentment and peacefulness. So much so, that I began to dispose of many material possessions, rather than always adding new books and LPs to my already substantial collection. What I also discovered were states of mind, or consciousness, that seemed "super real". I remember walking by the river near Richmond Lock [within easy walking distance from my room] at about 6.30 one morning and feeling so peaceful and at one with myself. I looked at a line of trees that I'd passed by many times before and suddenly they seemed "super real", as if they occupied an extra dimension over and above the three with which we are familiar. It's impossible to put this experience into words but I've never seen trees so "present" and "real" as they were that day. It was like having an extra sense with which to appreciate them. This kind of expe-rience happened maybe three or four times during my "three year experiment". On another occasion it was a group of seagulls fighting over a piece of food. Their frenetic engagement with the fight, juxtaposed with my own sense of deep inward calm, seemed to show me something about life and gave me an insight into – if not the human condition – my own condition in relation to the world. It seemed to me that so long as we fight, we remain the same. These experiences are much harder to describe and explain than the others in this essay.

There were other strange moments arising from the "three year experiment" that are more easily described. One day, I was walking towards Twickenham Bridge along the very busy main road. Suddenly, all the traffic sounds receded and, just for a moment, I seemed to be walking across a meadow filled with wild flowers and I was wearing a monk's habit. This experience was every bit as real as walking by the road had been a moment before with cars and lorries racing by.

An even more vivid ecclesiastical "vision" occurred around the same time. I had a friend who lived in Twickenham with whom I used to listen to music fairly regularly. One summer evening I was visiting him and he played me a short piece of music that he was interested in at the time. As was often our habit, he refrained from telling me what the piece was or who it was by. We both believed in the "innocent ear" and that the best way to hear new music and avoid any preconceptions about any particular composer was to know nothing about the work at the outset. What he played was completely new to me, at least on one level. Certainly I didn't consciously know this music with its many tolling bells but what I heard had a profound effect on me.

Instantly I was somewhere else and what I saw was so vivid that my real surroundings receded completely. I was in a white room with a barred window high up in the wall. I knew it was an Italianate climate and I was standing behind a high-ranking ecclesiastical figure who sat in a chair with his back to me. As I approached him, I *became* him and found myself sitting in the chair. I could hear the bells outside the window and I knew that I had a very important decision to make. Someone had died and my decision was connected to this fact and to the bells. Then I was standing behind the seated figure again and everything faded.

It was as if I'd experienced this scene from the centre of my forehead. The musical passage ended and I came back to the room where my friend was taking off the record. Then he told me that the music was Puccini's *Tosca*, the opening of act 3, depicting a shepherd boy entering Rome early one morning. Then came the real revelation. Apparently, Puccini had meticulously notated the church bells of each Roman church and recreated some of them in the orchestra. What I'd been hearing were the accurate bell sounds that would have been heard in Rome. The vividness of what I can only think of as a "vision" must have been triggered by some far memory of these bells, with which I was much more familiar than I consciously realised. I'd never been to Rome at that point in this lifetime but I did go many years later. My associations with Rome at different times have felt very deep-rooted and my strong sense of having lived the monastic life on at least two occasions was also connected to the Roman church, as a result of which I've learned to have very deep reservations about it.

Clusters of experiences

During what I've termed the "three year experiment", I had a concentration of curious experiences. But that was not the only period when I found one odd event following hard on the heels of another. During one twenty-four hour span at another time altogether, there was a cluster of incidents that was most striking.

I was sharing a rather cramped space with a friend while waiting for a new flat to become available and during this time I wanted to concentrate on a story I was trying to write. As circumstances didn't allow me any privacy, I decided to decamp to my parents' house for a day, to commandeer one of their rooms where I could write in peace. As soon as I'd made the arrangement, I thought that it was a pity that I'd miss a phone call from a friend called Penny. She didn't telephone very often and I wasn't expecting her to call, yet this was the thought that I had. I went

to my parents' house and did a day's writing on a story I'd entitled *Sylvan Sorrow*. It wasn't an easy story to write [years later I
destroyed it] and I worked late into the evening. I became so
tired that I made up a bed on the floor and decided to stay the
night and go home in the morning. That night I had a vivid
dream in which I was in a car with Penny. She was driving and
we were travelling along a main road. Suddenly another car came
straight towards us and we swerved up onto the pavement where
we crashed head-on into a lamp post.

The next morning I recalled my vivid dream as I got up and
prepared to go back to the flat I was sharing. Upon reaching the
end of the road, I just missed a bus, so decided to walk. Along
the way I noticed a small shop full of old furniture, pictures and
curios. As I looked through the window my gaze fell upon a
most unusual pen and ink drawing, the like of which I'd never
seen before – nor since. It was a picture of some trees against a
hilly background, just like a scene I'd described in the story I'd
been writing. But one of the trees had metamorphosed into a
humanoid form and two of its upper branches had become arms
which were thrown up in the air in an attitude of wailing and
despair. It was my story personified, *Sylvan Sorrow*. It was such an
unusual and striking picture and its relevance to my story astonished me. I continued my journey, eventually walking the entire
distance to the flat. As soon as I arrived I was greeted with the
words: "Penny rang last night to say that she's been involved in
a car accident but is OK". Not only had I missed her call, as my
intuition had known I would, but the call echoed exactly the
subject of my dream. At such times I can wonder what on earth is
going on. It is as if everything is vibrant with possibility and feels
more alive and real than usual, and as if something in me, that is
usually dormant, has woken up.

Extended awareness

There have been some remarkable examples of what I think

of as "extended awareness". Almost everyone we meet can remember times when someone has come into their thoughts, perhaps someone they haven't seen or thought about for a long time, then the telephone rings and the caller is that very person. I believe this is simple telepathy. A classic case of this happened to me many years earlier when I was working at Pinewood Film Studios. There was no telephone in the room I was working in but at the other end of the corridor was an office with three phones that rang constantly all day long. Their ringing was a distant background noise that was always there and which I filtered out. Then one day, very consciously, I heard one of those phones ring and the person who immediately came into my mind was an old school friend from whom I hadn't heard for about two years. The impulse was so strong that I actually went to the door of the room where I worked and waited in the corridor for someone to tell me there was a call for me. Sure enough, it was for me and it was the school friend who had suddenly appeared in my thoughts.

A variation on this theme happened when I had a temporary part-time job doing basic office tasks. As a result of taking phone calls, I became familiar with the names and voices of several of the company's clients. When I heard a particular voice on the phone I knew who it was straight away. But on three specific occasions when there were no telephones involved, I suddenly heard in my mind's ear, and for no apparent reason, the voice of one of these clients. On each occasion, a minute or so later, someone I'd never seen before walked into the office reception area and announced himself as the very person whose voice I'd just heard in my head. It was as though, with some kind of extended awareness, I could sense the person in the vicinity.

This awareness applies in other scenarios. I was in on-going but erratic correspondence with a significant friend in America. Each morning I would get out of bed and go down to the hall to see if there was any mail for me. On some of these mornings I had the thought that there would be a letter from my American correspondent. And sure enough, there was. As I was pondering this odd intuition one day, which can often happen in a kind of mental blur, especially first thing in the morning, I decided to try to make the next occurrence more fully conscious – I wanted to make sure that I wasn't fooling myself about it. I wondered if maybe I'd been thinking "retrospectively" in some strange way, that perhaps it was only when I actually saw the letter with its distinctive handwriting that I *thought* I'd had the thought that this letter would be waiting for me. One morning as I opened my door to go down and see if there was any mail, the same thought came to me and I was alert enough to stop myself in my tracks before I came within view of the front door, the mat or the letter rack. Having stopped, I said to myself out loud that there was a letter from my American friend waiting for me just around the corner. I wanted to bring the feeling into a fully conscious focus. I stopped, spoke the words, waited a moment, and then proceeded. Sure enough, there was the letter. This "extended awareness" occurred repeatedly in relation to these letters.

Around the same time as this, I had an example of "extended awareness" that was almost out of my consciousness. I had two friends who were abroad on holiday and who I'd agreed to meet on their return in order to help carry luggage from the bus stop. They were due around 7.00pm and were going to telephone me once they arrived at the airport. But at about 2.00pm on the same day I suddenly thought that I should go and wait at the bus stop to meet them. It was raining steadily and so I took an umbrella. I didn't stop to rationalise what I was doing. I simply picked up the umbrella and walked to the bus stop where I was due to meet them. As I arrived at the bus stop, a bus was just pulling up and my two friends were on board waiting to get off. They were very surprised to see me but I'd just "known" they would be there. In fact, they had caught an earlier flight and once at the airport had decided not to telephone because they didn't think I'd be available to meet them.

Of course, there are some occasions when one will never know if an instinct like this is accurate. When I occasionally visited my parents for an evening, I would usually walk home late at night along the towing path by the river. On one occasion I had a distinct feeling not to take that route. I took note of it and walked home along the road instead. Maybe I escaped a random attack – maybe not. But it seemed foolish not to heed an instinct that had been right about so many other things.

One other incident of this "extended awareness" [or perhaps it was coincidence] happened just a year or two ago. I was about to walk to a local supermarket to buy a few things when I suddenly found myself checking that I had my wallet with me. Then I thought how frustrating it would be, not to say inconvenient, to arrive at a checkout only to find that I had no money. I'd never actually been in this predicament and I wondered why I was suddenly thinking about it now. I went to the shop, picked up the items I wanted and went to the checkout. A man in front of me unloaded a number of items onto the conveyor belt and the cashier duly rang them up on the till. Then the man reached for his money only to find that he had left it at home. Certainly everyone in the queue was inconvenienced as they scattered to find other tills but I don't believe I've ever previously known of anyone who got to this point before finding that they had no money and it was curious that it happened on the day when I'd had those thoughts about it just before leaving the house.

Coincidences

There have been so many significant "coincidences" in my life that I'm really not sure I believe in them any more. Some of them have been so remarkable that it feels almost insulting to dismiss them as "mere coincidence". There was a time during the occupation of my first bedsit that one week I didn't have the money to pay my rent, which was five pounds, twelve shillings and six pence [£5. 12s. 6d.] – it was quite expensive for the time. This was a very embarrassing situation because I'd never been behind with my rent before and it was a matter of principle for me that I should always pay on time. I was temporarily unemployed, a fact I was trying to hide from my landlady, and there was no one I could easily ask to lend me the money. On the day the rent was due I went down to see if there were any letters for me, only to find a cheque for the exact amount of the rent, which was owed to me by a friend.

In the early 1970s, I was again unemployed, funds were very scarce and my rent was £7 a week. It was a lean time but suddenly I began to find money everywhere I went – not just an occasional ten pence piece but paper money as well. What was stranger still was that these sums of money would appear right in my path. One day I got on a train and found a fifty pence coin right in the middle of a seat in an empty compartment. Another day I got off a train to find a five pound note lying on the platform right in front of the door I'd chosen to leave by. Even more strange was the day I came out of Richmond Park to walk down the hill to the town centre and passed a rubbish bin that had several pieces of paper scattered around it. As I glanced down, I saw no fewer than three one pound notes mixed in with these pieces of paper. To find one of these notes would be remarkable enough but to find three of them together seemed especially odd. Conspicuously and repeatedly I found high value coins and one pound notes wherever I went. I wasn't looking for money, it just seemed to appear in front of me. In fact, at one brief period, I *did* find myself looking out for money as I went about and I never found so much as a penny piece. But as soon as I stopped looking, it started to appear again. The number of times I picked up money from the ground during this very lean time was so remarkable that I began to keep a note of how much I'd found. By the end of the year it was £34. It is usually quite rare to find money lying in the street but when I needed it, it was there.

One day I was visiting Helen, who is now my wife, in a flat she had just rented in Balham. She came home just as I was arriving and so she checked her answerphone messages in my presence. To my surprise, I heard a voice I knew but which Helen didn't know at all. The voice was a colleague from a record company I was working for at the time who was leaving a message for "Helen". When I asked my work colleague about it the next day, it transpired that she was trying contact a different Helen, who was a singer, to arrange a date for a recording session. It turned out that the other Helen had been the previous tenant of the flat. As a result, the two Helens met, found that they had several things in common, and became friends.

When Helen and I were married, we decided we wanted a very quiet wedding, which took place at Richmond registry office, where we assembled with our two witnesses and no one else. After the ceremony, we all walked together up Richmond Hill to go back to our hotel. As we reached the terrace at the top of the hill – with its famous view overlooking Glover's Island and the bend in the River Thames – we thought how nice it would be to have a photograph of all four of us against this background. We looked around but there was not a single person in sight. A second later, a young woman walked into view heading straight in our direction. We asked her if she would be kind enough to take our photograph and learned that she was a photographer by profession. Exactly the right person and exactly on cue!

Two miscellaneous events

There are two more quite disparate events that don't seem to fit any of the categories I've mentioned. Each one made a distinct impression on me in its own strange way. One day a friend came to see me at one of my various bedsits and I happened to have on my record turntable a disc which included Sir Thomas Arne's famous *Rule Britannia*. We began talking about this piece and the jingoistic way in which certain music has been used. During the conversation I started the turntable and let the tune play at quite a high volume. My friend immediately began to mock and lampoon the music in an exaggerated Colonel Blimp voice mimicking the British Empire "stiff upper lip" attitude. We were generally fooling around in this vein and I was laughing at his performance when, quite suddenly, the pick-up lifted itself off the record and the turntable switched itself off three quarters of the way through the tune. We were both taken aback. This was a turntable I used constantly and it had never before acted with such a mind of its own – nor ever did so again. It really was as if "someone" somewhere had been offended by this tomfoolery and taken exception to our irreverent behaviour. It succeeded in stopping us in our tracks.

On another occasion I was with the same friend, visiting his parents' flat in Chalk Farm. As the time grew late it was decided that it would be easier for us to stay the night in the spare room where there were two single beds. At some point in the middle of the night I found myself suddenly wide awake with my attention drawn to the foot of the bed where my friend was still asleep. I peered into the darkness, all my senses alert and sharpened, with a distinct sensation that something sinister and menacing was standing there. A moment later my friend grew extremely agitated and woke in panic from a nightmare in which he had felt threatened by something extremely malevolent. We never understood why we had both woken at almost the same time with such disturbing feelings of menace.

Two stories from other sources

There are two more stories which are worthy of inclusion here, neither of which happened to me but both of which are most striking and have been told to me by people I trust implicitly. My wife's aunt, Mary, had died very unexpectedly. She was a cheerful and generous person and, in some ways, something of an innocent. A few days after Mary's demise, my niece, [Mary's great niece], then aged 8 or 9, announced to her mother that she had been climbing a tree and had fallen from it. Her mother asked her if she was all right, to which her daughter replied: "Yes, I'm fine. Auntie Mary caught me." She said this in the most matter of fact way and appeared completely unscathed.

This last story was told to me by the man who ran the record company that I worked for. He, in turn, had heard it from the pianist Albert Ferber, to whom this astonishing event happened. Albert Ferber was alone in his Paris flat practicing some piano pieces by the French composer Gabriel Fauré for a recital he was about to give. He found some of the pieces quite challenging and had to work hard to master them. Then the telephone rang. It was one of Ferber's students ringing to postpone an appointment. But just as Ferber picked up the telephone, he heard a distinct voice in the room behind him say: "I am Gabriel Fauré. I wrote these pieces in 18??." Ferber was startled. But he was even more startled when his student on the telephone said: "I'm sorry, Albert, I didn't realise you had someone with you."

Conclusion

Over the years, as I encountered this miscellany of odd experiences, I wrote them down so that I would remember them as they happened at the time. There have been other incidents where my memory is incomplete, many are too slight to mention, others are too similar to those I've related, and there has been a significant number of personal statements from mediums that have been most telling. What I have discovered is that most people have such tales to tell and, sitting around a dinner table, if one asks the simple question, "What is the strangest thing that has happened to you?" it frequently unleashes a torrent of stories. In this scientific and rational age we are invariably discouraged from talking about things we cannot explain and many people fear ridicule if they even mention ghosts, omens, premonitions or out of body experiences, with the result that many incidents remain untold. But almost everyone we meet has at least one such story to tell – which is a very significant amount of data that never sees the light of day or features in any equations.

What is the strangest thing that has happened to YOU?

ABOUT THE AUTHOR

Richard Howard was born in April 1943 in Twickenham, in the county of Middlesex, England. Among the strongest influences in his life has been symphonic music, which he discovered at the age of 11, especially the works of Dmitri Shostakovich, whose music, he says, helped him survive a stormy adolescence; of Gustav Mahler, whose music expanded his view of the cosmos; and of Ralph Vaughan Williams, whose music brought a deep and much-needed serenity of spirit. And later, the works of Allan Pettersson, whose Symphonies 6 to 9 he found visionary and a revelation; and Alan Hovhaness, whose music he regards as some of the most important in the world and whose many works he has catalogued. [A complete transcript of his 1983 interview with Hovhaness can be found at www.hovhaness.com where there is also a link to the catalogue of works.] Later he developed an equal passion for paintings in many different genres and is particularly enthusiastic about Symbolist and Victorian art and especially the great mystical painter, Samuel Palmer. His earliest literary interest was a fascination with the world conjured by Lewis Carroll, an interest that grew to include Edgar Allan Poe, Saki, M.R.James, A.N.L.Munby, Arthur Machen, William Samson and the shorter prose works of Oscar Wilde, as well as Henry James' novel, *The Turn of the Screw*. Much later he discovered Sarban, whose work also impressed him deeply. Among the poets, his first love is Thomas Traherne.

He is the first to admit that his education and lifestyle have been unorthodox, which has given him an "outsider's" view of the world from which he feels he has greatly benefited. After leaving school with minimal grades, he soon gained access to the film industry and worked at Pinewood Studios for six and a half years as a sound technician in the 1960s. He then worked at Twickenham

Studios for two years before leaving for Cornwall to write his first novel in 1970. This novel remained unpublished and in 1989 he destroyed it along with a number of short stories. A second novel, written in 1974, was also later discarded, a remaining fragment of which is the short story *The Prisoner*, published in the present volume. He then embarked upon several years of part-time and temporary jobs that ranged from driving, picture-framing and working in a crematorium, to sub-editing on a local newspaper and working in a well-known art bookshop in London's West End. When the bookshop was closed down, he happened to meet the owner of a small independent classical record label who offered him a job where he could fruitfully draw on his knowledge of art to select appropriate pictures for CD covers.

In 1992 he joined The Actors' Institute in London's Islington where he completed The Mastery, under the late Ray Evans, and a considerable number of intensive acting workshops. He continued this interest with Tom Radcliffe's London Group Theatre, culminating in a performance of Harold Pinter's *One for the Road*, in which he played the part of Nicholas. Subsequently he completed a three year diploma course in counselling at The Pellin Institute in South West London and has done further training in hypnotherapy.

From an early age he has been interested in anything to do with the paranormal, not least because of an unusually high incidence of first-hand experiences. He has participated in several nocturnal investigations into ghostly phenomena and is convinced that the existence we currently experience is only a fragment of an infinitely bigger picture. He began writing short stories – most of which he has destroyed or discarded – in his early 20s and has always been interested in themes that explore aspects of the paranormal and the unexplained. As well as music and paintings, his love of the English countryside is a further source of inspiration for his writing. He is married, lives in Surrey, and is currently working on his first screenplay.

ISBN 141209339-2

9 781412 093392